A COMFORTING EMBRACE

Abermont's voice surrounded her. Intruded upon her thoughts, her very being, his words loud and bold. She wondered if she'd imagined him, for he'd arrived at the moment when she needed him most.

She did not know how it happened, exactly. One moment, she was standing up right, albeit unsteadily. Her shoulders did sag, yes, but her knees were most certainly not caving—until they did, and she was falling to the ground. But then a pair of strong arms wrapped around her, keeping her standing, anchoring her. She did not feel so alone anymore. Not when he was here, not when he held her.

And she wanted to lean her head against his broad chest and pretend that it was all going to be fine. There was no mysterious man hunting her. No secrets blackening her name.

She had been wrong before. A life without feeling was not heaven.

This was heaven.

BOOKS BY ERICA MONROE

The Rookery Rogues

A Dangerous Invitation
Secrets in Scarlet
Beauty and the Rake

Covert Heiresses

I Spy a Duke

I Spy a Duke

COVERT HEIRESSES
BOOK 1

ERICA MONROE

This is a work of fiction. All of the characters, organizations, and events portrayed in this novel are either products of the author's imagination or used fictitiously.

I SPY A DUKE
Copyright © 2015 by Erica Monroe
Excerpt from *Beauty and the Rake* by Erica Monroe
Cover design by Designs by BMB

QUILLFIRE PUBLISHING

ISBN: 978-1523203499

For information, address Erica Monroe at ericamonroe.com

To Eileen R. and Emma L.
Because without you, there would be no book.

And to anyone who's ever felt like the odds are
insurmountable—
This is your fight too.

ACKNOWLEDGEMENTS

There are books that are easy to write. This book was not one of them.

I am thus eternally indebted to the kind, wonderful people who took time from their own busy lives to help me beat this manuscript into submission.

Eileen Richards, who always makes me laugh, even when I'm in the middle of a breakdown. Thanks for reading this when you were on your own crazy deadline! Emma Locke, who gives me the best line edits ever and keeps me sane. Morgan Edens, Erica Ridley, Tracey Devlyn, and Christy Carlyle all read this book on a super tight deadline, and for that I am extremely appreciative. Gaylin Walli, Kristine Wyllys, Isobel Carr, Kristen Koster, Alyssa Alexander, and Elisabeth Lane all helped me out with research.

I am also very grateful for the support of my family. My mother, for understanding when I don't call for a week that I'm not dead, I've simply flung myself into a new story. To my husband, Kevin, for picking up every last bit of the slack—and then some—while I wrote for long hours. And to my grandmother and my brother, for always saying they're proud of me.

I am blessed to have a fantastic editor in Meghan Hogue, who never flinches no matter what craziness I throw at her. All mistakes in this manuscript are of course my own.

Thank you to my Romance Writers of America chapter, Heart of Carolina, for their continued Book in a Week events, through which I wrote most of this book. Thank you also to Sarra Cannon and her online sprinting group, which often motivated me when I needed that final kick.

The original concept of this series was "Regency spies meets the *Birds of Prey* comics," so I am thankful to Chuck Dixon for creating my favorite vigilante team, and to Gail Simone for her strong writing of Huntress, Oracle, and Black Canary—the basis for the three Spencer sisters. If you're a *Birds* fan, you might notice homages throughout this series.

Thank you to Rachel Platten for the tune "Fight Song," which inspired Vivian's story arc. Also thank you to my constant music muses, Taylor Swift and Gaslight Anthem, who have been the soundtrack for every book I've written so far.

And lastly but never least, thank you to you, reader. Writing is my full-time job now and I never thought that could be possible. Thanks for helping me to live my dream.

PROLOGUE

Paris, France, 1798

Sunlight streamed in through the half-moon window in the sickroom, but the cheery brightness did nothing to improve the mood of James Spencer, Duke of Abermont. The placid weather mocked him. On the day that his sister lingered on the last edges of life, rain ought to pour from the heavens, and thunder should roll through the sky in protest of twenty-one-year-old Louisa forsaking her mortal coil.

James sighed. He sat by her bed in the sickroom. Nothing mattered anymore. Not the success of the hundred missions launched since he'd taken over from his father as the head of the Clocktower, a covert organization. Not the slice of his knife across the throat of the enemy agent who had tortured Louisa and left her for dead.

Once, he'd viewed his work as a spy for the Crown as an extension of his natural patriotism. For generations, the Spencer family had been involved with espionage. While other families prided themselves on breeding exceptional sheepdogs or on their award-winning fruit preserve recipe, James and his four sisters had been trained from childhood onward for one purpose alone: to serve as Clocktower agents.

Three sisters, from now on.

No amount of revenge would bring Louisa back. She lay stricken in that bed, propped up on five pillows. Arden, his youngest sister, had managed to clean most of the blood and bile off her pale heart-shaped face. That was nothing compared to the gore beneath the bandaged wound on her right side, or the deep imprints of a whip across her chest.

His breath came in irregular pants as he stood, forcing himself to the side of her bed. It wasn't right that she'd die here in Paris, without the rest of her family to say goodbye to her. It wasn't right that she'd die at all.

Anguish constricted his throat as he dipped a clean cloth in the basin and mopped it across her brow. For a second, her features were not contorted in pain. Then sweat pebbled her face, dripping down to the blistering burn mark on her sharp, angular chin. The bastard had used a branding iron on her when she would not answer his questions.

"I'm so sorry," he whispered, wiping the cloth across her brow again. "It should have been me they took. Not you. Never you."

Her eyelids fluttered at the sound of his voice, but did not open. The laudanum in her system left her blessedly sedated. It was better this way. Better than hearing her screams as the doctor attempted to clean her wounds. Better than how she'd looked in that darkened hovel last night, strapped to a table so that she would not move during the butcher's "interrogation."

His hand faltered. He pulled back from her, dropping the cloth into the rubbish bin with the other bloodied linens.

"I should never have let you go, Lou." He used the nickname she'd hated as a child, but had come to embrace in the last few years. "How bloody, bloody stupid am I? I should have known better. Anytime the Talons are involved, it's a bloodbath. I could have stopped this. I could have saved you."

The mission had seemed straightforward: capture the spy Nicodème, a rising star in Bonaparte's cadre of ruthless assassins, the Talons. Nicodème had a known *tendre* for tall, willowy brunette women.

Send me, Louisa had said. *I fit the profile. No one in the Talons has ever seen me. He'll never suspect my identity.*

James had acquiesced, as long as Arden accompanied her.

"As soon as we found out Nicodème wasn't alone, I should have pulled you." He'd run mission control from the Duc de Valent's old mansion, secretly acquired by the Clocktower after the duc's imprisonment and execution in the September massacres.

He dropped down in the chair again, propping his elbows on his knees, his head cradled in his hands. The same hands Louisa had once grasped with her smaller fingers to tug him along the garden path at their home estate, Abermont House.

The same hands that had sought retribution for Louisa's torture. Dragged the steel blade of his knife down in a slant across Nicodème's neck, effectively severing the artery and making him bleed internally.

Her tormentor was dead, but Louisa wouldn't last the night.

She stirred. Moaned, an indecipherable sound so unlike her usually melodic voice. Louisa was a talented high soprano—her cover in this mission had been an opera singer, another of Nicodème's weaknesses. God, how he wished she could be again like she'd been last week, practicing the song she'd planned to perform at the concert held by one of Bonaparte's generals.

Louisa lived life to the fullest—always laughing, always smiling, always finding joy in the moment.

She'd seemed invincible.

She cried out again. The sound lanced through his chest. The laudanum had begun to wear off.

Soon, she'd have no relief from the pain.

He went to the door, opening it and calling for Arden. In a minute, she appeared from the room next door where she'd been conferring with the doctor.

"Lou's waking," he said, gesturing for her to follow him inside the room. "She needs another dose."

Arden stopped him before he could reenter the room. She hesitated, something he had not seen her do in the fifteen years since his father had taken her in as his ward.

"What did the doctor say?" But he already knew the answer. Louisa's wounds were too severe for her to recover. Yet he asked anyway, as if through the power of his own desperate hopes he could surmount her fate.

Arden's shoulders slumped as she reached for the door. "We should say our goodbyes."

The control he'd struggled so hard to maintain shattered, as Louisa's brittle bones had broken under Nicodème's cruelty. He could not form words. He could not do anything but stand there in the hall in front of Louisa's makeshift sickroom, and suck in one breath after another.

"She would have gone no matter what you said," Arden murmured. So many times had Arden understood him without words.

Yet his sister could not absolve him of this responsibility. He might not have been the one to physically harm Louisa, but he had sentenced her to death the second he'd approved her part in the mission to apprehend Nicodème.

He came back inside the chamber, approaching Louisa's bedside again. "I didn't stop her. I didn't *try* to stop her. What kind of leader allows his sister to go into the fray?"

"She's always known her own mind. She wouldn't have listened, no matter what you'd done." Arden came up on the other side of the bed, taking Louisa's hands in hers. "She knew Nicodème was hurting innocent women, and she had to stop him."

Remembering the stream of Nicodème's blood down his blade gave him no comfort. "The bastard won't hurt anyone ever again."

Louisa stirred. Slowly, her eyes opened and her gaze traveled from side to side.

"I can't hold on," she whispered, her raspy voice a far cry from the confidence with which she'd always spoken. "Jim?"

He took her other hand. "I'm right here."

"Protect them."

He squeezed her hand. With that one last request, life shuddered out of Louisa. A silent, sad end to the indomitable girl who had blazed through life louder than cannon fire.

He remained by her side. Her body went cold. He held her hand until the servants came to clear out the room, and still he did not let go. Not until Arden tugged him away, forcing him to down a shot of brandy so he could speak again.

Protect them.

Louisa's last words would become his personal crusade. From this day forward, he vowed he'd protect his agents with his very life. No one else would die because of his mistakes.

It was the only way he knew how to go on.

CHAPTER 1

Maidstone, Kent, March 1799

ON THIS OF all days, James Spencer, code-named Falcon, had even less patience for social niceties than the small amount he usually possessed. Today, he'd give the great majority of his vast family fortune to be on a boat in the Atlantic Ocean, or perhaps in a little villa in the south of Switzerland. Bloody hell, at this point, he'd even accept the stifling heat of India, if it meant he was far away from the confines of Abermont House and everything familiar.

Yet he could go to the ends of the Earth and the memories of Louisa would not stop. Still, a year after her death, the recollections drowned him. Louisa, as she'd been as a child of four, her grubby hands digging through the dirt. A dozen governesses throughout the years could not curb her enthusiasm for nature. Louisa, a debutante during her first Season, wearing a pastel purple gown as she danced at her coming out ball. And lastly, Louisa's beaten and unconscious body, thrown over his shoulder as they escaped from the Talon's lair.

He curled his fist, desperate rage boiling within him as he pictured her mutilated body in the crude sickroom. Heard the pierce of her cries in his ears, then the shallow intake as she inhaled her last breath. He was useless to stop her death. Powerless. Still the fury seethed within him, a crazed, rancorous animal he could not cage.

Three hundred sixty five days had passed, and he remembered every damn detail as though it were yesterday.

In the hall outside his study, the clock chimed nine. Three more hours until this godforsaken day was over. Each minute dragged on interminably, compounded by the weight of his guilt. His blasted responsibility as head of the Clocktower. His failure.

He closed his eyes and breathed in. His office should have smelled like brandy, old papers, and soap from a fresh cleaning by the maids. Instead, his nose pulled in the pungent sweetness of dried blood, combined with the rancor of bile. His stomach lurched, brought on by the haunting smell insinuating itself on his mind once more. He was in Nicodème's dungeon again, as he was every night, but this time he did not need sleep to usher in the horror. This day had been a living nightmare all by itself, an onslaught of memories he could not fight off.

Opening his eyes, he let out a shoulder-shaking sigh. So much for the attempt at meditation. That had been a suggestion of his eldest sister, Elinor, and a part of him delighted in proving her wrong, even if it was on something as inconsequential as deep breaths not helping to relieve his stress.

As an alternative, he borrowed a tip from his second oldest sister, Korianna, and downed a third of a snifter in one gulp. The burn lit up his throat, a welcome diversion. He drank another third, and then the last. He'd conveniently placed the decanter on the edge of his desk in case of emergencies such as this one. A man had to have priorities, after all, and he now counted brandy very high on that list.

But even brandy was a temporary release. The miracles of spirits could not bring his sister back—no matter how many times he tried. They could not erase the fact that he'd allowed her to go on a suicide mission. His hand clenched around the empty snifter, wondering if the victory of shattering it in his palms would improve his mood.

Protect them.

Louisa's scratchy, pain-drenched voice resonated in his ears. The Clocktower had achieved a seventy-five percent mission success rate in the last year, and there had been no fatalities. He'd protected his fellow agents—but not his family, who should have meant more to him than anyone else.

Under James's leadership, a new era of prosperity appeared to be dawning for their organization. They'd managed to turn a key member of Fouché's secret police to their advantage, and plant the seeds of rebellion against the First Consul. William Wickham, Under Secretary of State for the Home Department, had personally commended James for his service. The Clocktower was considered a secret sect of Wickham's Alien Office.

But none of that meant anything when he'd failed Louisa. When the sound of her staggered, desperate cries filled his ears at every interval.

His hand tightened around the snifter. Squeezed the glass for all its worth. Suddenly, a crack resonated through the quiet office.

The crystal fractured.

He was left holding the sharpest piece, slit through his palm. For a second, he simply stared at the new wound, watching the blood drip down onto his desk, too numb to register it.

Pain pierced through him, drawing out a loud groan. With his good hand, he tugged the shard of glass from his palm, his breath hissing out as the fragment clinked onto the top of the desk. So much for being a hardened spy, used to bullet holes and stab wounds. His pain tolerance had gone to the devil with him not being in the field these past four years.

Blood splashed his desk, flowing freely from the open laceration. First things first, then. Pressure on the wound. He fished in his pocket, drawing out his handkerchief. He pressed the handkerchief to the cut, attempting to staunch the flow of blood.

Footsteps sounded down the hall, coming toward him. Blast it all. Most likely, it would be one of his sisters. He'd have to face their nagging questions, adding insult to injury. He steeled himself for the oncoming assault.

Yet the petite, blonde woman in the brown dress who rushed into his study was most certainly *not* one of his sisters. He didn't know if he should consider himself lucky that his brother's governess had found him, instead. After all, he barely knew her, outside of a few conversations they'd had since her hire six months prior.

Miss Vivian Loren's large blue eyes rounded as she caught sight of his hand wrapped in the blood-soaked cloth and the shattered crystal. "Your Grace, I heard you cry out and came running. You're hurt."

He shrugged. "It's nothing."

She arched her brows at him, unconvinced.

"You may go, Miss Loren." He adopted his most autocratic tone, the one usually reserved for when he wanted to remind members of the *ton* that he was a duke, and their opinion mattered little.

She stood her ground, her eyebrows still arched, and her nose crinkled. Her nose intrigued him—thin and narrow. Crooked, except somehow that made her more alluring. As if she could be as flawed as he was.

He decided he liked that she didn't leave. It had been a damnably long time since anyone had stood up to him. He did not count his sisters—they'd argue with the king himself, if given the chance.

"Enough of that," she ordered in a no-nonsense tone. "Your wound needs attention. I am quite used to blood. If you're concerned about my fragile female mind, you needn't be. I shall not faint."

"That's the furthest thing from my thoughts." Growing up as he had with a fierce mother and even fiercer sisters, the "fragile female mind" myth had long ago been proved false.

"Good," she said. "Then you needn't be so strong around me. Let's look at your wound."

God, how he wished that was true, on today of all days. But it was his job to be strong. To hide his pain beneath a veneer of proficiency. "Really, this is not the first time I've been cut."

She ignored him, coming to his side of the desk. Pushing up her sleeves, she leaned down to inspect his hand. He expected her to wince at the sight of so much blood—but again she surprised him. She pursed her lips, reaching for the edge of the handkerchief. No fainting, no histrionics, just pure efficiency.

"There might be a spot of bleeding again without the pressure, but I need to see how deep the cut is," she explained to him in that same factual tone, as though he were a child like his brother.

He ought to bristle at this. He was a grown man fully capable of taking care of his own wounds—he'd done so many times before. Yet there was something comforting about her competence.

She tilted her head to the side, bringing the scent of roses from her soap to his nose. He clung to that smell, allowed it to fill every crevice of his lungs, for it blocked out the cloying tang of blood and memory.

"The cut is not too deep," she determined with a swift nod. "It should heal nicely, provided we clean it now."

Her azure gaze dashed around the office, evaluating every object. She settled on the brandy decanter, uncorking it without asking for permission.

She balanced it in one hand, her other hand sliding underneath his palm, raising him up off the soiled handkerchief.

"This might sting a bit," she cautioned.

The brush of her hand against his warmed him in ways he neither anticipated nor understood. His hand *tingled*. What in the devil? He never reacted this way when a woman touched him. He forgot the pain, focusing in on the comfortable heat of her flesh against his. This soft, supple woman was at best two heads shorter than he was, yet she seemed unconquerable in her self-possession and surety.

Belatedly, he realized she was waiting for a response—he could not leave her forever supporting his hand, the bottle of brandy poised and ready. "I'm no stranger to pain."

That made her brow quirk once more. He didn't know why that pleased him.

She slanted the decanter, splashing brandy on his cut. The air rushed out of his lungs, as the sting of the alcohol cut through his fog.

Bloody, bloody hell. No matter how many times he was injured, he'd never become at ease with this part of healing. The quick stab of pain was worse than a dull, constant ache.

"My apologies, Your Grace," she murmured. "If it helps with the pain, the sting means it's working."

She set the decanter back down on the desk, but she did not release his hand. His bloody, oozing hand, which if he was any sort of gentleman he'd pull from her immediately, whether or not he derived some inexplicable relief from her touch.

His eyes fell to her face. He saw fortitude in the lock of her jaw, concern in the wrinkle of her forehead. But there was no sign that their proximity affected her in any other way.

He should not have been disappointed by that.

Eying his wound, she reached for her own wipe,

but then decided better of it. "Might you have another handkerchief?"

He nodded. "In the top left drawer." All the files pertaining to the Clocktower were kept in a secret room located behind the main library. There was nothing in his desk that she couldn't see.

She opened the drawer, drawing out two handkerchiefs. The first she used to clean his hand with gentle strokes, until the red disappeared and there was only tanned flesh with a cut across the middle of his palm. Pushing the stained handkerchief off to the side, she spread out the second clean linen and then rested his hand on top of it.

"I'll bandage you up now," she said.

He was quite able to handle his own wound, but curiosity took hold of him. He wanted to see if she'd complete this task as proficiently as she had the rest.

As she began to wrap his hand, he reviewed what he knew about her. All servants employed by Abermont House were subject to a thorough investigation, given the nature of their business. Elinor had interviewed her after the last governess left to tend to her ill mother, but James had verified the dossier and made the final judgment.

After the death of her parents at a young age, Miss Loren's aging uncle, the Viscount Trayborne, had raised her and her brother. When Trayborne died, the title passed to his eldest son, who wanted nothing to do with his father's poor wards. In consequence, Vivian and her brother, Evan, had moved into a small cottage in Devon. Later, they'd relocated to London. A fatal move, for Evan was murdered in a robbery gone wrong. Left with no family to support her, Vivian was forced to enter service.

From a purely selfish standpoint, Society's loss was his gain. She was the best governess his family ever employed. His brother, Thomas, adored her.

A fact he needed to remember, because when she

leaned down to bandage his hand, her bodice gaped the tiniest bit—presenting him with an all too tempting view of the tops of her lush, creamy breasts.

Reluctantly, he averted his eyes. She might be beautiful, but she was not for him.

"All done," she pronounced, bringing him back to the present.

He glanced down. His jaw fell in surprise at the sight of his hand all bound up in a secure, but not too tight, bandage. She'd not just completed the field dressing quickly—she'd done it *correctly.*

"Where did you learn to wrap wounds like that?"

Her lips curled into a small, almost enigmatic smile. "My brother and I were quite rambunctious as children. We grew up on my uncle's estate in Devon with few other children to play with. I liked to fence, and my brother was convinced he could beat me. He was wrong, of course, but those battles usually resulted in one of us becoming injured."

He had no problem imagining this headstrong woman running wild through the countryside. "Your uncle couldn't have been pleased by that."

Her smile grew. God, she had a glorious smile. "Which is why we learned to truss ourselves up before the servants could tattle on us."

Oddly, she exhibited no chagrin at the change from having servants to *being* one. He marked that for future examination, for it did not align with what he'd expected.

But as much she amused him, he couldn't have her regaling his brother with tales of her reckless youth. Thomas had enough bad influences already. Christ, last month he'd caught the boy down in the abandoned quarry with Korianna, watching as she lit the fuse on a black powder bomb.

"I don't want my brother engaging in any sort of dangerous activity," he said, a bit more authoritatively than he should have.

Thomas would have a normal childhood. His younger brother wouldn't know of the Clocktower until he was old enough to make his own decisions.

"Of course not, Your Grace." Her tone became more formal, respectful.

While it was his own fault for reprimanding her, he missed the officiousness from before. It had been nice for a few minutes to have someone else tell *him* what to do.

She crossed to the other side of the desk. He felt a momentary ping, not of pain, but of sadness that she'd leave so soon. For a few minutes at least, he'd been able to breathe normally. He'd not thought that possible today.

Decisively, she pulled out the chair in front of his desk and sat in it. He'd not asked her to stay—her audacity should have been offensive. Instead, relief trickled through him. He dared not examine it further, simply grateful for the distraction.

"How exactly did you hurt your hand?"

"The glass slipped." Not the full truth, but even she couldn't be so bold as to call a duke a liar.

Her eyes narrowed. "Is that so?"

Usually, when someone beneath him dared question his assertion, he'd strike back with a cut so brutal they would never again doubt his power.

Usually, when someone dared question him, he did not feel the urge to smile and chuckle at her forwardness.

Yet with Miss Loren, he sensed she did not mean to gainsay him. Her queries were driven by concern for his well-being. In his days as a field agent, he'd been most adept at reading people—deriving their motivations and goals from a glance or a particularly pithy remark. That talent carried over into his leadership role, as he had to identify the strengths of each of his agents and match them to the proper missions.

Except for that one horrible, agonizing time, he had never been wrong.

"It has been a long, terrible day," he said. "Perhaps I gripped the snifter too hard."

"Perhaps you did," she agreed, the twinkle in her eye telling him she approved of his honesty. "If by some chance, you wish to talk about this long, terrible day..."

She let the offer trail off, incomplete but enticing. It wasn't appropriate for her to engage him in conversation, nor should he have been drawn to accept. Talking about the past had never solved anything before. But it was the way she'd worded it; giving him the option of discussing it with her or not. As if it was quite normal for a duke to speak to a governess about his private life.

Evidently, she had not become accustomed to her new place in the social order, and he'd be damned if he'd remind her of it after her kindness to him. Her unexpected forwardness was exactly the distraction he'd wanted. Who was this woman?

She'd allowed him the opportunity of a sympathetic listener, which left him wondering if maybe he'd find solace in talking to someone who wasn't connected to the spy game. Correction: not just talking to *someone*.

Talking to her in particular.

He leaned forward. Watched her as though he was seeing her for the first time—in a way, he was, for he'd never really noticed Miss Loren before. Oh, he'd known of her existence, and acknowledged her presence when they passed each other in the house. He'd appreciated her dedication to his brother.

She shifted in her chair, but she matched his inquisitive stare. He liked that too, almost as much as he liked the intelligence in her sparkling eyes. Her fine features were all sharpness and angles. A long heart-shaped face, high cheekbones, pointed chin, and a swan-like neck that immediately conjured images of pressing his lips to the juncture of her collarbone and neck.

He had not reckoned the skeptical swoop of her sandy brown brows, nor the slight blush across her arched cheekbones at his scrutiny. And he certainly had not realized how her pink lips, parted a little to reveal white teeth, would appear so kissable. Or how though she was delicate-boned, she'd have curves in all the right places—a body better suited for the risqué costumes of a Cyprian, not the drab dress she currently wore.

He carded a hand through his hair and tried to refocus his thoughts, repeating silently that she was his employee. Not the kind of woman he should be lusting over.

She looked at him expectantly, waiting for him to talk about what had caused him to cut himself on the crystal. Fine. If it would direct his mind elsewhere, he'd indulge her desire for conversation.

"The difficult thing about loss," he began, hunting in the second drawer from the bottom of his desk for another glass, "is that you never quite escape it. A year goes by, a year in which you think you've made some sort of progress in moving on, and then you're thrown back in time again."

"I know exactly what you mean."

He supposed she did, given what he had read in her file about the death of her brother. He placed the glass on the desk and reached for the decanter with his good hand.

"The anniversaries are the worst," she murmured, her voice so soft he suspected she spoke more to herself than him. "My brother died only a year and a half ago. I spent the first anniversary of his death curled up in a ball in bed, sobbing. *Everything* reminded me of Evan, even the breakfast porridge."

For a second, he could not collect himself. His

hand paused before he lifted the decanter toward his glass. He was not used to hearing people speak so freely about their grief. The Spencer family motto alternated between "Bottle It All Up" and "Keep a Stern Upper Lip."

He matched her soft tone, for these were words to be spoken in the darkness, not in the harshness of day. "Then you know precisely what I am going through today." One turn of honesty deserved another, did it not? In the morning, he could return to a properly British decorum.

The flicker of the Argand lamp was the only light in the room, and it cast a gloriously golden glow on her, making her look almost angelic with her pretty flaxen locks.

"I am so sorry." There was no sign of the grating condolence of the *ton*, uttered more to make one feel superior than to convey actual sympathy. Only compassion.

He liked that most of all.

She leaned forward in her seat, her hands starting to slide toward him. His body was tense with anticipation of her touch. Then, as if she remembered exactly whom she was speaking to, she stopped. He wanted to give her permission to run her fingers across his uninjured hand—to make him feel something other than sorrow.

But there was only so much propriety he could afford to dispense with and maintain his reputation, so he did not.

"Who was she? Or he?" she asked tentatively. "Or if that is too much, you don't have to tell me."

She'd been in the house long enough to know of his sister's death. He saw her ploy—she hoped that through feigning ignorance, she might persuade him to talk.

And for the first time in a long time, he *wanted* to talk about Louisa.

"My sister." He raised the decanter, sloshing brandy into the glass. This gave him something to do, for he could not risk seeing her expression transmute into one of pity. He needed her to be different. "It happened while she was on holiday in France with Miss Spencer. There was a terrible accident. Someone was hunting in the same woods. There was no chance to save her."

Repetition did not make the faux story of Louisa's death any easier. He could not summon up the actual feeling that should have accompanied such a story — not when he knew it was all a lie. A lie that hid *his* responsibility.

"Sweet Mary," Miss Loren murmured. "Your Grace, that is terrible. Your poor sister. Poor *you*."

"I do not deserve your sympathy." He couldn't stop himself, for the words came too fast, and with them the darker edge to his tone. His head screamed that it was his fault, all his fault. Louisa was dead because of him.

At his harsh tone, Miss Loren sat up straighter. He ought to tell her to flee from here, away from him. Away from what he could do to her, for if she was not careful, he'd hurt her too. He hurt those who trusted him.

Yet it would take more than a few sharp words to cow Miss Loren. She folded her hands in her lap. She met his gaze, a rolling tempest in her eyes. "Everyone always feels bad for the person who has died. But they are dead, and they can't come back, no matter how much sympathy you have for them. No matter how much you wish you could bring them back. No matter how quickly you'd trade places with them."

Her voice had become hollow. He was the worst of blackguards. Of all people, of course she'd understand. Of course she'd have felt his pain — at least she did not have the guilt of knowing it had been all her fault. Her brother's death had been a random act of violence.

Unavoidable, for there was no real reason behind it, other than Evan Loren having been in the wrong place at the wrong time.

He should say something. Help her deal with her pain, too. But he could not think of a single word that would give her comfort. He was too broken, too lost, too dark. He could not bring her light.

"Rarely does anyone ever speak of the survivors," she continued. "I think that is a mistake. It is left to us to fight for justice for the departed. To seek revenge against those who took them from us." She drew herself up to her full seated height, and her chin lifted.

This diminutive beauty became quite intimidating when she turned her cold, unwavering gaze upon him. He knew the haunted look in her eyes too well—the same look he'd worn when tracking Nicodème that fateful night.

So her next question did not surprise him, though he wished so badly that she did not have to share this kind of ache.

"Did you catch the blackguard who killed her?"

His hand shook as he reached for the glass of brandy. He remembered the last breath escaping from Nicodème's throat, a winter wind roaring in the relative quiet. "Yes. I made sure he could never hurt anyone again."

She gave a perfunctory nod, signaling her approval. "Then you have done your duty to your sister."

It was on the tip of his tongue to tell her she had no idea what she'd said. She was a gently bred lady who should have no acquaintance with such brutal bloodshed. But he stopped; reminding himself that in her eyes, 'revenge' probably meant arresting the man seemingly responsible for his sister's death. It did not mean a righteous execution. Or a heinous, grisly death.

He reached into his desk drawer, bringing out two more glasses. Pouring brandy into it, he passed the snifter to her.

She did not take it, staring at him as though he'd lost his mind.

Perhaps he had. In the last year, he'd existed in halves, never complete. But he could not shake the feeling that tonight was a new beginning.

"To us." He motioned for her to lift the glass, raising his own. "For we have survived when we wish we had not. We are too strong for our own good, but we cannot change."

"I appreciate your sentiment, Your Grace, but you cannot expect me to drink that." She eyed the glass, then him, seemingly tempted but unwilling to chance such scandalous behavior.

"I can and I do." He kept his glass level, again indicating she should lift hers. "Tonight, honor the dead. You are not just a governess. You're a sister who lost her brother."

She hesitated for a second more. He watched her make up her mind, a definite shift passing over her face. Swiftly, she grabbed her glass and clinked it against his. "To Evan."

"To Louisa."

She knocked back a quarter of the glass in one gulp. He blinked, startled by her alacrity.

And then, slowly, surely, she winked at him. "I did not say it was the first time I have honored the dead. Only that I was not sure it was proper, given my station."

As he drained his snifter, he was left wondering just how improper Miss Loren could be.

CHAPTER 2

SHE WAS A terrible person.

She had to be. Because only a truly terrible person would sit there for an hour with the Duke of Abermont, listening to him pour his heart out, and still lie to him.

Vivian could almost still taste the brandy on her tongue from the finger they'd taken together last night. *To survivors*, he'd said, but she didn't feel like a survivor. The life she'd known—the stability she'd once prided herself on—had disappeared the night she'd had to identify his mangled body in the coroner's office.

Smoothing a hand down her walking dress, she took a seat on a bench in the rambling garden of the Abermont estate. A few paces in front of her, her young charge Thomas Spencer squatted down on the ground, picking up various small pebbles that made up the rocky path. Every now and then, he looked back at her, as if needing confirmation that she was still there. As if somehow, even at the tender age of five, he still could sense that her time here was limited. That she was poised to flee at any moment.

This was all a ruse, and she had no right to dream

about it becoming permanent.

She didn't deserve the easy affection of a young child, who now expected her to guide him through life. How could she help instill good morals in him when she belonged in gaol for what she'd done, was trying to do, to his family?

Six months of spying on them. Six months of reporting anything they said, did, or even *thought* about doing to a mysterious benefactor she knew only as Sauveterre. The French term for "safe haven" had given her hope—perhaps finally, after a year of wondering and grieving, she'd find respite. But the information Sauveterre had promised to reveal about her brother's death had not been forthcoming. After half a year of following the shadowy *éminence grise*'s every direction, all she knew was that her suspicions had been right: Evan had been murdered. When he'd been stabbed in a fetid rookery alley, it hadn't simply been a botched robbery. He'd been specifically marked for an untimely death.

No matter how many letters she'd written to Sauveterre, begging for more information, he hadn't revealed the identity of Evan's killer. She'd begun to doubt if he even knew the truth. Had she given up everything she knew, lied to the very people who had shown her kindness, all on a false promise? The appalling likelihood of this made her stomach churn.

The Bow Street Runners claimed it had been a robbery gone wrong. Evan had been on the wrong side of Westminster, in the heart of the Seven Dials rookery. Supposedly, he'd resisted when the footpads had stolen his purse. He'd been found on Monmouth Street, his body so badly beaten he was almost unrecognizable. Only the label Vivian had sewn into his coat kept him from being listed by the coroner as a vagrant. "Made for Evan Loren with love," she'd embroidered; never thinking it would someday become the key clue to his identity.

She still couldn't look at her embroidery basket without thinking about that gruesome coat.

"Look, Miss Loren," Thomas called, gesturing to the tower he'd made out of the pebbles and a few twigs.

"Quite impressive," she praised, glad he'd found something to occupy him. Her head was far too muddled today for clear instruction. She'd suggested this jaunt in the garden for that exact reason. Here, Thomas could run and play free, as long as she was close by to supervise.

Thomas grinned at her, and went back to his building. He placed another rock on top, adding in an alternative layer of leaves and twigs. The gardener would deplore the clutter he'd made, but for now, she'd let him enjoy his game.

With one hand holding her straw hat upon her head, she leaned her head back, staring up into the brilliantly blue, cloudless sky as though it might provide her with all the answers. But even the beauty of the blooming Kent countryside in spring could not lessen her dread, her guilt. She'd accepted this governess position under false pretenses, and she continued to tread on the trust of the very people who'd offered her shelter.

A home.

Because no matter how many times she told herself this was all going to fade away, she could not deny the pull Abermont House had on her. Not only were the grounds gorgeous, but the family had surprised her with their generosity. The sisters were always kind to her.

And then there was the duke himself. Sauveterre had claimed that James Spencer must have ties to British intelligence. Given Sauveterre's last missives had asked for financial information, she gathered he suspected that Abermont was funneling money to Bonaparte's supporters. Vivian had seen no indication of that, and certainly nothing to support the idea that Abermont was an active spy. She'd always assumed spies were closed-off creatures, with a hundred different aliases and no steady home. James Spencer was simply too entrenched in his life here for that to be true.

The duke disconcerted her, but not because she felt endangered by him. Rather, the easy comfort his presence offered her was the cause for her concern. When she'd originally sat down in his study last night she'd had two goals: tend to his self-injured hands, and solicit his confidence in hopes he'd reveal something she could send to Sauveterre. But the longer they'd talked, the less she'd thought of Sauveterre. She'd lost herself in the weight of his gaze, the pain in his voice.

His soul was as wounded as hers was.

Thomas scampered by, his pockets bulging with stones he'd collected. She might not be able to solve her own problems, but at least she knew what to do with Thomas. Vivian flipped open the guidebook she carried to the tabbed page. She pointed toward the Grecian bust on their right. "Tell me what that statue is constructed of, Master Spencer."

"Lime, of course," Thomas stated in the condescending way only an erudite five-year-old with far too much fortune could manage.

She consulted the guidebook, more out of routine than any doubt that he was correct. Thomas loved geology. "Very good."

Thomas grinned. "That was too easy, Miss Loren."

Vivian mock-sighed. "Pert boys do not get rewarded. Perhaps we should return inside? You haven't finished your arithmetic lesson. Don't think that I haven't noticed."

Thomas was quick to protest, shaking his head vigorously. "But it's so nice outside."

There was a light breeze wafting through the air, while the sun had finally managed to peek through the clouds after several days of rain. It was beautiful, but none of it belonged to her.

"I suppose we could stay out a bit longer," she proposed. "If you promise to finish your arithmetic tonight."

"I swear," Thomas vowed, making a cross over his heart with two fingers.

He looked so solemn she couldn't help but laugh. "Lord Thomas, I will know if you are bamming me. Besides, your tutor won't be very happy with me otherwise, so we must be sure you are caught up on your schooling."

Thomas stopped in the middle of the path, giving her a disbelieving look. "Mr. Martin likes you. Everyone likes you. You are much better than nasty old Mrs. Garring, who always smelled like stinky cheese."

Everyone likes you.

Little comfort, as no one would after they discovered her spying.

"That's not a very nice description," she said.

"It's true," Thomas retorted. "She does smell like cheese, and you always tell me not to lie."

She was saved from a response by the sight of Abermont coming up the path. Suddenly, it was as if a hundred butterflies had set upon her stomach, flapping their tiny wings. Oh, no, this could not continue. She would not harbor feelings of an intimate nature for her *employer*. The man she'd been hired to spy on, for heaven's sake.

But she could not deny how powerful, how utterly masculine he appeared. He was tall, long and lean. His jet-black hair was kept close-cropped. His brows were thick, his chin more rounded than sharp, and his nose had a deliberate hook to it that made him appear quite imposing. There was a sternness to his face that almost overshadowed his attractiveness.

Yet it was his eyes that arrested her every time she saw him. Gray-blue, reminding her of waves rushing against the shores of Deal. She could lose herself in his eyes.

No, that wasn't quite right. Last night, for the first time since Evan's death, she'd felt *found*.

"Jim!" Thomas cried, running to his brother.

Abermont caught the boy in his arms, lifting him up effortlessly as though he weighed as much as a newborn, not a strapping youth. He whirled Thomas in a circle, and the boy's laughter echoed through the garden until Abermont put him back on the ground. Thomas leaned against his brother's side as they both waited for Vivian to approach.

"Miss Loren." Abermont greeted her with a nod, the same polite incline of his head he always did, that indicated he saw her but did not feel her presence honored him in any way.

She'd glimpsed a different man last night, one of deep feeling, but perhaps that man only appeared once a year.

"Your Grace." She curtsied.

He nodded. "Miss Loren. Tom, why don't you go inside?" Abermont stared at her still, his eyes never once leaving hers, as he spoke to his brother.

"But Miss Loren said I could play for a while," Thomas protested. "Didn't you, Miss Loren?"

"Ah," Vivian began, struggling to find the proper words. "I did say that, Lord Thomas, but I should think your brother—"

Abermont gave a swift nod, this time one meant to silence her. Gracious, the man could say more with the tilt of his head than she could with five hundred words. He gave his brother a little push forward. "Lord Haley's in the schoolroom with a new game he thinks you will like to play," he said.

That was all Thomas needed. "Richard!" He took off at a gallop toward the house, his little feet kicking up gravel.

She made the mistake of meeting Abermont's gaze

after the lad's swift departure. All rational thought departed. Instead, she wanted to run her hand up the smooth superfine of his coat to ascertain if his arms were truly as muscular as they looked.

"Miss Loren," he said again, and in that moment she simply wanted to hear him say her name, over and over again.

She took another deep breath and regretted it. The air around them became charged, somehow thick with the very scent of him, pine and leather. He stepped toward her. Then again. He was so close to her now she could see the individual flecks of gray in his eyes. His buckskin breeches and black coat complemented his strong, athletic physique, and she could not help but remember all the times she'd watched him play tennis from the window in the nursery. Heavens, his broad shoulders filled out his coat far too well.

She swallowed. If she reached out her hand, her palm would rest easily on his chest. How she wanted to know if his muscles underneath the silk of his waistcoat would feel as hard as she'd always imagined.

"I was just—" No, that wasn't right. Nothing was right when he stood here like this. It was all highly improper.

She stepped back from him, willing her capricious heart to stop pounding so swiftly. She should say something. Break the tension. Last night, she'd had a clear objective. Bandage his hand. Get information. He'd seemed to respond to the woman who knew how to take charge of a situation. The same woman she'd been when Evan was alive. Competent. Capable. Fierce.

Blast it all, she could be that woman again.

"Good afternoon, Your Grace." There. She'd managed to keep her voice level. That was something, at least.

"I saw you outside from the window in my office. I wanted to thank you for bandaging my hand last night." He held up his hand, showing her that the wound was but a scratch now.

"It was no trouble at all." Her brows wrinkled as she examined his hand. "Just as I thought. The cut wasn't deep, so it should heal up nicely."

"Thanks to your expert bandaging. Shall we take a walk?" He extended his arm to her, motioning to the path in front of them.

Her uncle had always said not to refuse dukes, but Uncle Timothy had spent a large part of his adult life thoroughly foxed, so Vivian didn't trust his opinion. How could she possibly focus when she was touching Abermont? When he stared at her so, as though his attention was completely upon her—as though they were the only two people in this garden, in this house, in this world.

But it was not as if they were truly alone. The estate buzzed with activity. A few paces to the right, a gardener tended to the rose bushes, while another pruned the trees. Everywhere she turned, someone else was near. Those were fears for nonsensical gels, not ape leaders like her.

She accepted his arm, her gloved fingertips barely brushing against the sleeve of his coat. A minimal touch that should not have resonated through her body as it did. Dash him and his infuriatingly good looks, the likes of which could make a woman on the cusp of spinsterhood believe in flights of fancy again.

Abermont slowed his ground-devouring strides to match hers. "I trust you are well today, Miss Loren?"

The duke had asked her this very same question at least twenty times in the past, whenever she saw him in the nursery. Before, she'd wondered if he really cared about her response.

This time, however, was different. His head tilted toward hers. His tone lacked distance; he spoke to her as though she were his peer. Maybe last night had begun a new bond between them, one forged in the sad kinship of mutual grief. Fitting, when the loss of Evan was one of the few things she'd been honest about in the last six months.

"I am well enough," she said. Though the emotional quality of her life left something to be desired, she had ample shelter and food. She lived.

He caught her distinction, arching a brow at her. "Just *enough*?"

"As you said, sometimes the days are long and terrible. It becomes hard to see past the memories." She focused on the path ahead, one foot in front of the other in a defined route. Certainty, when the rest of her life mired in shadows. "But sometimes, I remember what it was like before his passing, and I pretend that I feel like myself again. It's easier on days like this, when the sun is bright and the heat leaves no room for the cold hand of death."

She didn't know why she spoke so freely around him, when she never talked about what had happened with anyone else. He, of all people, was the last person she should have confided in—yet the words spilled out before she could stop them.

He nodded, this time in solemn understanding. "On most days, I consider well enough an accomplishment."

She bit her bottom lip, frowning. "I must believe that it will someday get easier." When she finally looked Evan's killer in the eye and exacted sweet vengeance, she'd begin again, her duty fulfilled.

Revenge was the most important thing. Perhaps the *only* important thing.

They'd reached a fork in the path. Would Abermont choose the sunny road to the left ending at the gazebo, or the more secluded stroll through the orchard? When he hesitated, Vivian took the decision from him. She started down the path most traveled. The safest path. Because this pull to him was dangerous, and she had enough danger in her life.

What she needed was stability. Answers. Neither were things the Duke of Abermont could provide for her.

Something new flickered across his face as he registered her choice. Perhaps disappointment that she'd chosen a path less secluded; perhaps her eyes deceived her entirely. She could not be sure, and she did not want to examine it. She'd made her decision.

She walked with purpose, quickening her stride. He fell into step with her, never missing a beat, in tune to every change.

"Perhaps all we can hope is for a new normal," he ventured. "It's never going to be the same as it was. But I think, eventually, you'll achieve peace of mind. You've much to accomplish still."

She managed a small smile. How she wanted him to be right, but she doubted it. "Your optimism is reassuring."

"It ought to be, as I am right about nearly everything," he teased.

She grinned for real now. "Is that so?"

"I'm afraid it's a family trait," he pronounced, as they strolled down the rhododendron-lined path. "While I am right a solid eighty-five percent of the time, my sister is right an absolute ninety-five percent of the time. If you find me an officious bore, I challenge you to engage in conversation with Elinor for more than two hours and not wish to club her over the head with the nearest vase."

She laughed. "'Officious bore' is the last phrase I'd use to describe you."

He led her through a section filled with poppies, roses, and lupins, the juxtaposition of the colors reminding her of one of Thomas's kaleidoscope toys. "Oh, really? I'll admit, the scandal sheets have described me as 'infuriatingly handsome' and 'deliberately standoffish.' Which one is closest to your thoughts?"

She did not confess that the former was the most apt description she'd ever heard of him. Nor did she tell him how much walking with him made her forget the chasm between them. Her father had been the second son of a viscount—even before she'd accepted Sauveterre's mission and became a governess, they wouldn't have been on equal footing.

"Neither," she replied, careful to keep her voice as light as his. Lying had apparently become second nature. "I would say that while the Duke of Abermont thinks a bit too highly of himself, he is startlingly easy to talk to, and he has excellent taste in brandy."

He stopped in the middle of the path. "Ah, you reveal too much, miss. It's my brandy you want, not my company." His grin never faltered as he started walking again.

She swallowed the sigh of relief before it escaped her throat. Of course, the brandy. The drink that had seemed so scandalous last night had barely crossed her mind today.

"You've caught me, I fear." She tilted her head toward his, lowering her voice conspiratorially. "I might as well tell you now, but at night I sneak into your office and filch half a shot from that brandy decanter. Just a little nip, mind you, never enough that you'd notice it."

He tipped his hat to her. "You clever little thief. 'Tis a brilliant plan, were it in any way factual."

Her heart jumped into her throat. She spun around to face him. He couldn't suspect her, could he? No, she'd been careful. She'd never mailed a report to Sauveterre from the house; she'd always gone down to the village. She kept his letters in the bottom tray of her jewelry box, which she wore the key to around her neck.

"That is the art of a good crime, is it not?" The merriment in her words did not reach her insides. She could not lie to herself, yet. She was a thief, not of physical objects but of information. She knew more about his family than any servant should. "It must be perpetuated in a way that no one ever suspects it's occurred in the first place."

"Why, little governess, I do think you are much more cunning than I'd originally suspected." The amusement twinkling in his eyes, so different from the grief the night before, made her heart squeeze perilously.

She'd made him laugh.

And she'd be the one to rip that joy from him and stomp upon it because she needed whatever dirty secret he hid so that she could convince Sauveterre to give up the name of Evan's killer. Faced with the choice between revenge for her brother and guarding Abermont's feelings, she'd choose Evan. Every time.

But she could at least make it hurt less. No more pretending they could be friends, no matter how easily her past sorrows spilled out when she was around him.

She drew to a stop in front of a thriving patch of narcissi, removing her hand from his arm. "Would you excuse me, Your Grace? I've just remembered that I promised Lord Thomas I'd help him with his arithmetic before dinner. He wants to impress his tutor, you see. Mr. Martin wagered one night free of lesson work if he solved every problem right on his exam tomorrow."

Abermont's eyes widened. He was likely surprised by her abrupt exit. She dropped a quick curtsy before scurrying away from him.

She was an explosion waiting to happen, and she needn't make him be the one to trigger the tripwire.

CHAPTER 3

THE NEXT DAY after dinner, James sat in the parlor with his best friend, Richard Denton, the Earl of Haley. The Haley estate bordered Abermont House, and the two boys had grown up together. James could not remember a single day of his childhood where Richard and their other neighbor, Deacon Drake, weren't present.

Both Richard and Deacon now worked as agents for the Clocktower. In fact, Deacon was currently in London, overseeing operations while James was with his family.

"When you return to London this Season, your cover will need to be intact," Richard declared between puffs on his cheroot, crossing one long leg over the other. "Sitting out one Season was acceptable when you were grieving your sister, but missing two is unconscionable. The *ton* is clamoring for the return of the new Duke of Abermont."

"Tell me something I don't know," James grumbled. "Elinor has already counted six mentions of our family in the scandal sheets."

The upcoming Season would be an unmitigated disaster, as every old dragon with a marriageable age chit would corner him at balls and routs, as intent on making her daughter a duchess as Bonaparte was on reshaping the world in his vision.

Devil take him, he didn't have *time* for distraction, and he certainly didn't want to take a wife. England's national security depended on him—even when all he wanted to do was run in the opposite direction.

"At least Korianna has already left for London." Smoke wafted from Richard's cheroot as he nodded. "With her in Town, it'll give you time to plan ahead. The gossipmongers will be so focused on what Korianna's doing that they won't have time to look closely at you."

James stifled a groan. He dreaded what the papers would write about his middle sister's latest exploits. Korianna was too brash, too reckless. So far, she'd never come up across a situation she couldn't lie or fight her way through, but every time she was in the field he worried.

She refused to take his direction. Just like Louisa had.

James ran a hand through his hair. "Let's just hope she doesn't blow something up again."

"*Again?*" Richard stopped mid-puff, the cheroot dangling limply from his fingers.

He raised his eyes meaningfully at his friend. "Hanover Square." He'd had a devil of a time explaining that one to Wickham. His heart constricted. Of course, Louisa had thought it hilarious. That had been the end of Korianna and Louisa partnering on missions. They were too similar, spontaneous and forceful. They needed a tempering influence on them, like Arden or Richard.

But even that had not been enough to save Louisa.

"You're quizzing me," Richard said. "She blew up Hanover Square?"

"Swear to the Virgin Mary."

"Only in your family." Richard threw his head

back, his throaty laugh echoing through the parlor.

"I'm glad *somebody* is amused by that giant blaze," James remarked dryly. "The three enemy agents who were injured weren't particularly thrilled."

Richard sniggered. "The French are never happy when we're winning."

"Her *orders* were to cause a distraction so that Louisa could drug the agents," James said. "Apparently the bomb was her first choice."

That only made Richard laugh harder, for as a field agent, he certainly didn't have to handle Korianna, or her aftermath. Her exploits were simply amusing. Richard did not feel the gut-twisting dread every time one of the agents was on a mission.

James rose from the settee, going to the liquor cabinet in the far corner of the room. Pouring the brandy into a crystal glass, he eyed the amber liquid for a moment, remembering how a captivating blonde had downed a quarter of the glass in one gulp. He'd never seen a woman shoot liquor like that before.

And he'd never known how damn arousing such a sight could be.

He shoved that inconvenient thought to the back of his mind, where all the memories of his jaunt with her around the garden yesterday currently resided. A spy needed to be focused and committed to the mission. In no way, shape, or form did that include "inappropriate thoughts about his brother's governess."

Richard slapped his thigh, ashes from the cheroot drifting onto the plush Oriental rug. "I always knew Korianna was fiery, but I never imagined such a pronouncement would be literal."

"The carpet, Richard." Narrowing his eyes, James pointed to the cheroot. "I know you take no care with your things, but could you please exercise some diligence in my house?"

The words felt false on his tongue, tasting of lead

and grime. It wasn't *his* house. Ninth Duke of Abermont or not, this countryseat didn't belong to him, and it never would. On paper, of course, he owned the furniture, and the land was entailed to his title. But he could never live up to his father's legacy. Known as the Lion to his associates, the old man had been one of England's top spymasters, second only to the Under-Secretary himself.

James's gaze skimmed from one end of the room to the next. Everywhere, he saw traces of the old duke. The heavy oak furniture of the study, chosen because the duke had believed it would hold up nicely to bullets if they were ever attacked at home. The crimson accents, for the duke's favorite color was red. And the tapestry above the mantel, an African jungle scene with two zebras and a majestic lion to rule over them, in homage to the duke's code-name.

Louisa had loved that damn tapestry. James thought it was hideous. But still he kept it, a tangible token of an intangible girl.

"I take every care," Richard protested, as he moved his foot to cover up the ash. "Just because I like to carouse does not mean I don't understand responsibility."

"How many times have you made that speech to Elinor?" The smallest hint of a grin slid across James's lips. "Careful, old boy, for you know she could tell me exactly how often she beseeches you to be serious."

"Curse Ellie and her blasted brilliant memory," Richard muttered. "Ever since we were tots."

"How I know your pain." James chuckled, allowing himself to feel the happiness of old memories, just for a moment.

When they were children, it had always been him, Richard, and Deacon—with Korianna running after them, constantly trying to prove that she was just as strong, as fast, as the boys. Louisa had followed in Korianna's footsteps. And when his parents had taken in Arden as their ward, she'd toddled along too; content to play whatever game they liked as long as she could spend time with them.

But not Elinor. He remembered Elinor watching them from the library window, a book spread across her lap and a pensive expression on her angular face. Rarely had she felt well enough to join them.

As if summoned by their discussion, Elinor poked her head into the open doorway. "I thought I heard your voice, Richard."

James hadn't heard her approach. But then, he never did, for Elinor was as fleet of foot as she was of mind. In a household of spies, footsteps rarely sounded.

Richard sat up straighter as she entered the room, his posture no longer so relaxed. "Good day, Ellie." He snuffled out his cheroot in the ashtray and stood, sketching a quick bow to her.

Elinor nodded in return. Sitting on the settee Richard had vacated, she smoothed out her skirts—he hadn't seen her in anything other than lavender or gray for the past six months, for the family was still in half-mourning for Louisa. Elinor reached up, patting at her titian chignon.

She did not ask for permission to join their discussion; she simply assumed she was invited. James took another sip of brandy, swallowing down his irritation. Elinor always had a way of taking over a conversation; he ought to be used to it by now.

"We were discussing James's cover," Richard supplied, pouring out another cup of tea. It was his fourth in the last quarter of an hour—James swore that the tea merchants in England remained afloat mostly on Richard's habits. "Would you like some tea, Elinor?"

Elinor nodded, clearly grateful not to have to move. Her pain must be bad today. How did Richard always pick up on those things? She accepted the cup of tea he offered her, delicately wrapping her hand around the china. Tall and slim, everything about Elinor appeared delicate, as though she might tumble to the ground at the next gust of wind.

Until she turned her eagle-eyed glance upon someone, and then immediately, one realized she was an unconquerable force. No matter how much pain she was in, her mind remained fierce.

"I think you should marry," Elinor said to James, with the same flatness as though she'd just informed him he should take clotted cream with his scones from now on.

He'd been mid-gulp of brandy, which promptly went down the wrong way. He sputtered and coughed as his throat burned.

"You want me to *what?*" He finally managed to squeeze the question out, though it was a fruitless endeavor. From Elinor's staid expression and Richard's quirked brow and failed attempt not to laugh, he was certain he'd heard her right.

And then Richard and Elinor exchanged a conspiratorial look, and he knew he was outnumbered. This was no casual afternoon. This was a trap.

When the two of them planned something together, they were unstoppable.

"You two talked about this before dinner so could you ambush me, didn't you?"

Richard grinned, while Elinor shrugged as if it was his fault for not seeing this coming.

"It is a perfectly logical step. We have to move on sometime, and Society will expect us to do so soon." Elinor laid one hand on the arm of the couch, while her other hand balanced the teacup and saucer. "This Season, you are out of full mourning. You'll be expected to settle down."

He didn't want to move on, and he didn't want to settle down. He wanted to cling to his bleeding memories, every last one of them, and throw himself into the Clocktower. If he gave the organization his full attention, then the chance of someone else dying on his watch would be reduced. Sometimes that was the only thing that helped him through the day.

"If I'm the bloody duke, then the rest of the *ton* can simply wait another year," he said.

Elinor's eyes widened. "You are a duke, Jim, not the king. You cannot just wave your hand and say it will be so."

"But it would be quite fantastic if he could," Richard interjected.

Elinor scoffed, and Richard winked at her. She rolled her eyes, and he grinned more. They continued like this for a minute, giving James an opportunity to puzzle over the situation.

Customs had to be followed, if they were to blend seamlessly into London's Upper Ten Thousand. The *ton* could think of them as eccentric, yes, but they did not have *carte blanche* to act with complete disregard for the rules. No one could know their true occupations.

The rules dictated that a single duke would be in want of a wife, whether or not James actually was. Swallowing, he tugged at the stiff points of his cravat.

Elinor's cool gaze followed his movements. She leaned forward, reminding him of a tiger about to pounce on an unsuspecting antelope. "What if you could avoid the Marriage Mart entirely?"

Richard watched them both silently, a smirk toying with his lips. Somehow, no matter how dark or treacherous their double lives became, Richard managed to find the humor.

"You mean marry before the Season starts?" James eyed his sister suspiciously. At Elinor's nod, he frowned. "Impossible. We're due to arrive in London in less than two months. How am I supposed to find a suitable bride in such short time? There's courting rituals, banns to be announced, not to mention developing feelings for her..."

"I never knew you were such a sentimentalist," Elinor said. "No one marries for love, Jim. Especially not people in our family's line of work."

Was it his imagination, or did Richard flinch at Elinor's cold declaration? James turned his head to look at his friend directly, but Richard's expression had smoothed.

"It would take at least three weeks to verify your possible duchess's background," Richard added, supporting his argument. "Wickham will want to check her personally."

Elinor nodded. "The bride in question must not only be of a solidly English line of no reproach, but she must hold no unconventional political opinions."

"Wollstonecraft devotees are out of the question," Richard agreed. "Kori will be so disappointed."

"One woman causing scandal for this family is more than enough." Elinor set her teacup down on the table and reached into her reticule, drawing out a crisply folded square of foolscap. "I've made a list of six potential candidates. I'm sure you shall find one of them agreeable enough."

He'd been raised to inherit the dukedom, yes, but he'd always hoped that when he finally married it would be to a woman who actually liked and wanted to be with *him*. But perhaps Elinor's list wouldn't be so bad.

James came toward her, taking the paper she offered him. He grimaced as he read the names.

No, it wasn't bad. It was worse.

He recognized the women as the *ton's* diamonds of the first water. Each woman was a sweet, timid debutante, who probably sang beautifully, painted reasonably pretty landscapes, and was well versed in the latest fashion trends. Perfect for the rest of the bachelors in the *ton*, but he led a dangerous life. He couldn't see subjecting a milquetoast woman to the perils and uncertainties of his existence.

A woman like Miss Loren might know how to handle his complex life. She certainly already had the field dressing skills. And she'd made him laugh.

God, he hadn't truly laughed in months.

He thought of her alabaster skin, her inquisitive blue eyes; that spirited smile she had when she teased him. The sharpness of her chin, her perfectly straight nose, and her high cheekbones dotted with pink when he'd touched her.

If he had to take a bloody wife, then why couldn't it be Miss Loren? He suppressed a sigh. Because the *ton* would expect him to marry someone of similar standing. A daughter of a duke, or at the least, of a marquis. Miss Loren's lineage traced back to a viscountcy, which wasn't high enough. Her position as his governess made the match even more ill advised. While his family certainly wasn't normal by most standards, he couldn't see bringing on such societal stigma unless he had a damn good reason.

Sadly, his comfort around her—and the physical attraction she sparked within him—did not warrant enough of a reason.

Still, she'd given him a small morsel of hope. If talking to her came so easily, perhaps, someday, he'd be able to speak to his future wife about the past too. Perhaps he was not completely jaded.

He refolded the list, handing it back to Elinor. "No."

Elinor's forehead creased. "No?"

"No," he repeated, ignoring the archness of her tone. "I don't want any of these women."

"But they're all suitable in disposition and dowry," Elinor protested. "What reason could you possibly have to refuse them?"

"How about, I've never once spoken to any of them on a topic of substance? Or that I have nothing in common with them but our collective fortunes?" He paced the area in front of her settee, pivoting with each suggestion. "Or, and I cannot possibly stress this enough, the fact that I don't need my sister to choose my betrothed?"

"Well, you needn't be so piqued about it," Elinor admonished, annoyance flashing in her eyes. "It is a sound plan, and if you were smart, you'd recognize that we cannot have the scrutiny your being unmarried brings us."

"If I were *smart*?" James repeated, spinning on his heel. "Elinor, do you hear yourself? You admonish me for my authoritarianism, but people are not chess pieces you can move around as you see fit. The world is not yours to control."

"You think I don't know that? I need only look at the bloody Clocktower," she shot back, a scowl darkening her pale features.

Instantly, he regretted his harsh words. He'd never met anyone who could predict the outcome of an event, or find patterns in random occurrences, better than Elinor could. Details of every agent and every mission of the Clocktower were all stored in her encyclopedic memory.

But Elinor would never be allowed be to be an active field agent because of her sickness. She'd be forever stuck on the edge of the action.

And he'd thrown it back in her face. What an arse he was.

"I shouldn't have said that, Ellie," he murmured. "I didn't mean it."

Elinor's eyes narrowed. "Of course you did."

"Ellie—" Richard started, closing his mouth when Elinor glared at him. Instead, he stood up and ambled across the room to her, plopping down on the settee next to her.

Elinor's rigid posture relaxed, ever so slightly, at his presence. Somehow, Richard had always been able to break through her icy reserves, even when her own siblings couldn't.

James dropped into the chair Richard had vacated, sloshing the remaining brandy around in his glass. The amber liquid remained enigmatic as always; while liquor made many men spill secrets, it did not offer up any answers to his quandaries.

"Wickham values you, you know that," James said. But it wasn't enough—it would never be enough.

She was absolutely devoted to the Clocktower, but she'd never get to reach her full potential.

"Whatever that matters," Elinor groused.

"I strive to make sure your opinion holds weight in the organization," James said. "You know I always will, don't you? We're Spencers, damn it, you, Kori, Arden, Thomas, and me. We're a unit."

And Louisa.

"And me," Richard piped up with a grin.

James nodded. "And you, Richard Denton, honorary Spencer family member."

"As well as whomever *you* shall choose for your duchess," Elinor added pointedly. "You can be reluctant and sentimental all you want, but it won't change anything. You need to marry. And quickly."

He looked to Richard for assistance, but the other man simply shrugged. Some help Richard was—the lucky bastard would be a bachelor for the rest of his life, most likely.

"Miserable fate for you, chap, but she's right," Richard stated. "You take a bride and the *ton* talks about it for a few weeks at most, and then they move on to the next scandal. You don't marry, we spend the next four months besieged by curious ninnies, and suddenly the French know who we are."

"It's a risk we can't afford to take." Elinor's eyes shone triumphantly, for she knew she had him now.

With Bonaparte's ongoing invasion of Egypt, the organization couldn't risk any impediments to their operations. The Navy needed the intelligence that their missions provided. The Clocktower relied on a system of hand-offs at societal functions, hiding in plain sight amongst the aristocracy. James, and his sisters, had to be able to attend the Season's most popular routs without drawing too much attention.

Damnation. As usual, he couldn't argue with Elinor's logic. A love match wasn't in the cards for him.

Our lives are meant for more, my boy. So many times, he'd heard his father say that. His entire childhood had been about learning to become a spy. At first, he and his siblings had thought they were simply playing games—but as they'd entered adolescence, they'd learned what their family legacy *really* was: not the Abermont title, but espionage.

He drained the last sip of brandy from his glass, and considered his options. His own mother and father had not been besotted with each other, but they'd achieved a companionable enough arrangement to sire four children. The Lion's second wife had been much younger than he was, but they had shared a friendly bond too. Perhaps James could achieve the same dynamic, if he chose wisely.

"I'll do it," he declared. "I'll marry quickly and with little fanfare. But I will choose my own bride."

CHAPTER 4

TWO DAYS AFTER she'd strolled through the garden with Abermont as if she belonged in this house, Vivian was reminded once again that her life was not her own. How she both loathed and eagerly anticipated the first and third Mondays of every month, when Sauveterre's next orders would arrive. She'd trek down to the post office on the other side of the village, and pick up missives from her supposed old aunt Aline Stuart, Sauveterre's alias when writing to her.

This time, there was more than a single letter waiting for her. The postmaster handed her a parcel wrapped in brown paper, not much wider than the width of her two hands pressed together, but about as tall as a shot glass in height. When she shook the box, she heard a slight shifting sound.

The knot in her stomach that always formed upon receipt of Sauveterre's missives tightened, until she had to lean against the post office window to catch her breath. She fought the urge to rip the package open here, out in the open, daring anyone who watched to judge her. Maybe, if the right person saw her, they could help her out of this ordeal.

Foolish girl, she chided herself. *No one will help you.*

They'll throw you in gaol for what you've done, and then how you will find out who killed Evan?

No, she must soldier on. She pushed off of the post office window and began the long walk back to Abermont House.

More lies. More secrets. With each passing day, the web she spun grew more complex, until the simple act of remembering what she'd *said* she was doing versus what she was actually doing required a herculean mental effort.

Yet the sole chance for release was when she completed this mission to Sauveterre's liking. The police had no new information. She doubted they were even still investigating Evan's death, a year and a half later. They'd been so quick to claim it was a robbery that had escalated into murder. If she went to the authorities now, she'd lose any opportunity to identify Evan's murderer.

She was alone in this, just as she'd been alone in everything else since her brother's death. It had always been the two of them against the world. When her cousin, the new Viscount Trayborne, had thrown them out of the home they'd grown up in, Evan had found a small cottage for them in Devon by the next day. It did not compare to the sprawling estate of the viscountcy, but she hadn't cared. Everything would be fine, as long as they had each other.

If she hadn't asked him to move to London, maybe he'd still be alive. If only she'd known how dangerous London could be.

A half hour later, she'd returned to Abermont House. Taking the servants' entrance upstairs, she passed by the nursery, entering her own room next door. She waited until she'd locked the door and taken a seat on her bed before opening the packet. As she sliced through the seal with a penknife, her hands shook. What would Sauveterre ask her to do this time? Each missive from him had brought increased demands. He wanted additional information, and not just odd details about the family's whereabouts. He wanted the kind of information she could only get by listening in on private conversations, her ear pressed against the door, risking exposure. She'd even sent him notes on the duke's investments, obtained by snooping through the drawers in his office.

The very office in which she'd shared a drink with Abermont.

She was a survivor, yes, but she was also a traitor.

And nothing seemed to satisfy Sauveterre. He always wanted *more.*

Her knife bit through the last speck of sealant. Vivian tore into the package, dropping the contents onto her lap. A letter in Sauveterre's handwriting, written on the same thick, stiff paper he always used. Whoever he was, he was rich enough to afford high-quality stationery.

The letter was not surprising. But the second item in the package concerned her. An emerald velvet bag no wider than her hand, held closed by a black-corded drawstring. She picked it up by the string, examining it. There was no insignia anywhere on the bag, and the velvet was uniform, giving no indication of where it had been made. It was neither extravagant in make, nor low enough in caliber to be conspicuous.

It, like the blasted Spencer family, was blatantly *normal.* Not a hint of covertness anywhere.

Yet for all its typical appearance, there was something insidious about it. She couldn't put her finger on what unsettled her, only that the second she had touched the bag, she'd felt troubled, as though the contents would change her life in a way she wasn't prepared for yet.

Nonsense, Vivian. It's probably quite innocuous.

But she couldn't think of a single thing a man such as Sauveterre would send her that wasn't in some way damning. She glanced from the bag to the letter and back again.

Holding the bag between her pursed thumb and index finger, she raised it to eye level and gave it a shake. An ominous muffled rattling emitted from inside, not tinny enough to be coins, nor as tinkling as glass. Her palms began to sweat. The beat of her heart was now akin to the repeated slam of a door. In one swift motion, she upended the bag, dumping the contents in her hand.

Teeth. Sauveterre had sent her yellowed teeth. Seven jagged, broken teeth.

Oh, God.

The world crashed around her. She didn't scream. She couldn't. Her mouth opened, but no sound came out. Panic clogged her mind, until all she could do was keep breathing, one breath after the other, faster and faster. No amount of air seemed to help her. Her chest contracted, but she didn't move. It was impossible to tear her eyes from her outstretched hand.

Each tooth was no bigger than her fingernail. The buds were a dingy white, but the roots were stained with long-dried blood, as though the teeth had been forcibly ripped from someone's mouth.

This can't be happening.

That one phrase kept repeating in her mind, over the din of her pounding heart, and the roaring in her ears. She could not be here, with *teeth* in her palm.

The room spun around her. Her head felt so light. For a minute, she could not focus on anything. Her hand dropped, falling to her side. The teeth scattered onto the bed, contaminating everything they touched. Her sheets. Her skin. Her mind. She'd never be clean again.

She burst from the bed, seizing the basin of water and the soap she kept on the bedside table. She scrubbed her hands until they were red and raw, but still she could feel the grime on her. The rose scent of her soap wafted to her nostrils, but it could not erase the foul odor of decay.

Whirling back around, Vivian dried her hands on a towel. A part of her had hoped that the teeth would disappear while her back was turned. That this had all been some awful nightmare. But no, the offending molars remained on the bed. She breathed in again, trying to calm her racing heart to no avail.

She needed to get the teeth out of sight, and she needed to never, ever, ever touch them again. Wrapping her hand in the towel, she lifted each tooth back into the bag and then closed the bag. Still using the towel, she picked the bag up and took it over to the window. She opened the window, tossing the bag outside. It fell to the ground with a horrid rattle.

One of Abermont's many gardeners would find it and dispose of it. She'd never have to see the teeth again.

She tugged the counterpane down on her bed and then sat back down, her legs no longer able to support her. Why in God's name would Sauveterre send her this? And perhaps more importantly, whom had those teeth originally belonged to? She bit at her bottom lip, fearing the answer.

What if—what if the teeth were Evan's? Evan's face had been so badly beaten when she'd went to identify his body. She closed her eyes, the image of his body on a slab in the coroner's office appearing before her. Her stomach seized, and for a second, she thought she might vomit. Swallowing the bile back down, she put her hand on her stomach to quell the roil. Dash it all, she'd been too distracted by his bulging eyeball, the footprint across his cheek, to notice if his teeth were missing.

She opened her eyes. A speck of white peeking out from the edge of the quilted counterpane caught her eye. The letter.

With trembling fingers, she plucked the paper up from the bed and slit the seal. For once, Sauveterre's missive was quite short. The first line read:

You see now what I did to your brother.

Her mind reeled, as the pieces of the puzzle smashed into place. No, no, no, no. How had she missed this? She was so stupid! Fury boiled within her, threatening to take hold when she needed logic the most.

Sauveterre had killed Evan. She'd wasted six months of her life obeying his every bloody order. Six months of being led around like a pony with a carrot in front of its nose, when the man she'd wanted all along had been right in front of her.

Except she didn't know a damn thing about Sauveterre, other than the fact that he could afford expensive paper and his letters were postmarked from a coaching inn in Chatham, Kent. Five months ago, she'd written to the proprietor of that coaching inn for information on Sauveterre—but the proprietor had claimed they never received, or sent out, any letters for such a man.

She reached in the top drawer of her bedside table for a map, spreading it out on the bed. Chatham was approximately eight hours away from Maidstone, or a day's ride in a carriage. She had enough blunt saved up for at least the trip there. But once she arrived at Chatham, what would she do? She could go to the coaching inn and demand an explanation, but there was little chance their answer would be any different. As someone in service, she simply wasn't important enough to warrant the truth.

And if by some slight chance they *did* tell her where Sauveterre was, what was her play? Yes, she was a skilled fencer, but she'd never handled a gun before. The blade of her sword triumphed in close combat, but her ability to defend herself from a distance was minimal at best. Evan's body had been badly brutalized, and he was a much better fighter than she'd ever been—not to mention he'd had five stone on her. The ludicrousness of her plan was now startlingly clear. If the police hadn't believed he'd been a targeted murder when the crime scene was still current, why would they believe her now when she had only shadowy evidence? She couldn't fight Sauveterre on her own.

Any hope she'd cherished in the last six months ripped from her. Her head hung down, her chin in her hands. Tears rolled down her face, slow at first, but then faster, as sobs shook her shoulders. She cried until her throat ached. Until she had no tears left, and all that came forth was silent, dry bawling.

But wait. There was more to the message.

Find me confirmation that James Spencer is in British intelligence. If you disappoint me again, I'll send you to hell in the same manner I did your brother.

A keening whimper escaped from her throat. She'd refused to think of her own life in the last few months, so focused was she on getting revenge for Evan. Her existence had seemed immaterial if she couldn't accomplish that goal. But now, faced with the immediate threat, she could only think one thing: she did not want to die.

We have survived when we wish we had not. We are too strong for our own good, but we cannot change.

Abermont's words resonated in her mind. He'd called her a survivor. He believed in her strength. His confidence in her bolstered her more than it should. More than she wanted to admit. She grasped at his support, letting it shape her mind. If it would take a day for her to get to Chatham, the opposite was true. Sauveterre could be on his way here. Or, Chatham could simply be a forwarding address, and he was already in Maidstone. Watching her.

When she'd seen the duke's hand bleeding, she had not hesitated. She'd done what she had to so that the bleeding stopped. This could be no different. She had to act with determination and purpose. Remain alert, for at any moment Sauveterre could come for her. In order to stay alive, she must develop a plan.

She set the letter down on the bed and exhaled. If she could get the information Sauveterre wanted, then the threat would disappear, for the moment at least. Tonight, she'd search the duke's library one last time.

And if she still couldn't find anything, then she'd have to go to the duke himself. Even gaol was a better alternative than waiting for a madman to kill her.

At least in gaol, she'd be safe from Sauveterre.

VIVIAN STOOD IN the center of Abermont's personal library. Behind her, filing cabinets lined one-half of the back wall, while floor-to-ceiling bookshelves covered the rest of the wall. To her right, the red draperies were pulled across the big bay windows, blocking out her movements from the outside. She breathed a sigh of relief at that, for at least here, she felt somewhat protected—as long as no one found her.

She directed a glance over at the door. No one was in the hall. For now, she was alone. The duke had gone to the local public house, while Lady Elinor and Miss Arden Spencer retired to their rooms early. Thomas was already asleep. The other staff took advantage of their master's absence to natter on in the servant's hall.

Sucking in a deep breath, she went to the door and gave it a push. Almost shut. A little space so that she'd hear if anyone approached, but closed enough to hide her actions. Her stupid, fruitless actions—for she'd searched this library before and turned up nothing, as she no doubt would now. How was she supposed to prove the Duke of Abermont was a spy, when he clearly had nothing to do with anything out of the ordinary?

One last try to forestall Sauveterre. One last fool's

errand.

She rubbed her palm across her skirt, her fingers digging into the fabric. The muslin was light and soft against her skin, yet the hairs on the back of her neck prickled as though she'd brushed up against the smooth slickness of bone again.

She dropped her grip on her skirt. Summoned the little bit of courage she still had left. Stepping to her left, she rifled through the popular novels stacked on the low table. Fanny Burney's *Camilia. Lyrical Ballads,* which had her favorite poem, *Rime of the Ancient Mariner.* Her hand wavered as she flipped through the pages of the book, looking for...something. What in particular, she didn't know. Messages in the margin, perhaps, or papers folded inside.

But it was simply a book, with no hidden answers. She stacked the books back in order. Had they been facing straight ahead or off to a jaunty angle? She couldn't remember, so she left them centered on the table.

She paced to the cabinets against the wall, slowly opening the top flat drawer. Architectural plans for some sort of quarry, if the first few sheets were any indication. Nothing there, either.

Oh, God, she was going to bleed out in the street like Evan. Alone. No one would stop to help her. No one would care.

An image of Abermont as he had been that night in his office, the fresh bandage tied on his hand, sprang before her. She'd felt comfortable around him. Almost normal. As if somehow her mind knew she could trust him, despite the fact that prior to this week they'd only ever exchanged a few pleasantries. As if he'd mourn her death, no matter how much she'd betrayed *his* trust.

Yet feeling sorry she'd died was a different emotion entirely from wanting to help her stay alive. She couldn't guarantee he'd help her if she were forced to confess what she'd done.

Vivian moved to the next drawer. More plans, this time for improvements to the farmer's cottages in the villages. The next drawer was deeper and taller, housing a big bound volume. She pulled it out, staggering under the weight. She rested it on top of the cabinet, flipping through the pages. Lists and lists of tenant rents, costs of the quarry, expenses pertaining to the upkeep of the house.

The same type of information she'd already sent, to no avail. Sauveterre claimed that Abermont was financing some sort of revolution in France, but she hadn't been able to locate any indication of that in the duke's financial records.

She slipped her hand into her pocket, her fingers brushing against the note written by her brother's murderer. He'd shaped his quill, dipped it in ink, and formed threats to her with the same hands he'd used to thrash Evan. He'd walked the letter down to the post with the same booted feet he'd stomped onto Evan's face.

And he'd kill her with the same hands he'd used to squeeze out the life from her brother.

Not if she had anything to say about it.

Vivian yanked her hand from her pocket. Thrusting her chin out, she crossed to the window seat and pulled off the cushions. She had too much to accomplish to let Sauveterre win. The bastard would pay for what he'd done to Evan. A life for a life, and she certainly wouldn't be trading hers.

She opened up the wooden bench. The cavity inside was stuffed with extra pillows and a few blankets. Again, nothing useful. But she did not break down. She did not cry.

She was stronger than that.

She crept to the escritoire pushed up against the wall near the door. As she pulled open the center drawer, the slides stuck, letting out a tremendous groan. Vivian halted immediately, directing an apprehensive glance at the door. Still no one. But if anyone had heard the squeak, her time was limited.

She moved quicker, shifting through a pile of recent mail. Invitations to house parties, invitations to routs, invitations to the musicale...Good Lord, how did one man know so many people, let alone have that many friends? While she fought for her life, Abermont went to musicales! The absurdity of their opposite situations struck her, snapping her head back up. Stuffing the invitations back in the proper space, Vivian yanked open the next small drawer, all cautiousness forgotten in the wake of her ire. Writing quills. The remaining tiny cubbies were for sand, a blotter, and an inkpot.

Nothing. *No, no, no.* It was becoming glaringly obvious that she'd have no choice but to throw herself at the mercy of Abermont. But first, one last check...

She kept searching through the desk, but all she could find were half-written notes to his secretary about the village, and blank stationery for future purposes. She knew he kept his seal locked in the left top drawer, but she hadn't been able to lift the key off of him when he'd visited the schoolroom.

"Blast," she murmured. "Blast, blast, blast."

Footsteps sounded outside the library, approaching swiftly. Closing the drawer, she crept to the left, pressing herself up against the back of the door. Within a minute, the interloper appeared in the hall—the housekeeper, heading toward the servant's stairs in the back of the house. Her breath stilled in her lungs until the housekeeper passed by.

Finally, as the door to the stairs clicked shut, Vivian let out the breath she'd been holding. That had been close. Too close. If the housekeeper was out and about, the rest of the servants might be too. With one last fleeting look around the room, Vivian fled the library, slipping into the murky darkness of the hall.

Tomorrow, once she'd completed her morning responsibilities, she'd go to Abermont and tell him everything. Tomorrow, she'd beg him to not to throw her in gaol. Tomorrow, she'd put her life in the hands of another man, all based on a *feeling* she had when she was around him.

Tomorrow, she'd cease to be a free woman.

CHAPTER 5

JAMES STALKED DOWN the hall, intent on completing another hour's worth of work before bed. After he'd finished going over the mission assignments, he'd headed down to the tavern to meet Richard. That had been a mistake, for Richard was brimming with "suggestions" on who James's new bride should be. After an hour of listening to his friend's running commentary on every available chit—and some who weren't—in the Beau Monde, James craved the solitariness of the secret room behind his library. Nothing but two desks and a wall of filing cabinets in there. No one to tell him who to be, or how to conduct himself. Or more importantly, who to marry.

It had been easier around Miss Loren. He'd sought her out in the garden because talking to her had made him feel...functional. Like finally, someone else understood—someone who hadn't known Louisa. Someone he could talk to without feeling as if he had to apologize for her death.

Someone he could simply be himself around.

Whoever that person was now.

His Hessians made almost no noise as he stole

silently through the dark hall. He had not bothered to have to the servants light the sconces, for after years of night missions, his eyes adjusted quickly to the black. Welcomed it.

He stopped dead in his tracks halfway to his library, the hairs on the back of his neck raising.

The door was ajar.

The door should never be ajar at this hour, so long past when the maids were due for their cleaning rounds.

Pressing himself up against the wall, he drew a knife from the slit in the inner lining of his boots, wrapping his hand firmly around the handle. With the blade in his hand, he immediately felt more in control, far more than he'd have been with the pistol in his waist holster. The pistol might misfire, but the knife was always accurate. Deadly. He could slit a man's throat as easily as he could count to a hundred. The motions had become routine. Training and a decade of experience had solidified him into a killing machine, built for blood and pain and not much else.

Creeping forward, he kept his back to the wall. Light peeked through the crack. The Argand lamp had been lit inside. Damnation. That would limit the nearness, and the angle, of his approach.

He edged closer, thanking God for Elinor's strange desire to stick foliage in every open space. The tall, capacious potted plant was next to the entrance to the library, and offered him cover while he looked through the small opening in the door.

There was a woman. She stood with her back to him, but that made no difference. He recognized her instantly, from the flaxen curls contained atop her head in a prim coiffure, to the subtle curves hidden by a dreary gray dress just a smidgen too big. His mind rebelled at the very idea, even as his body answered with the same fervor that began whenever she was around.

Miss Vivian Loren.

His Miss Loren.

Possessiveness flooded him. He wanted to storm into that room, take her by the shoulders, and demand an explanation. God, he'd thought she was different. Untouched by the cruel spy game that had already taken too much from him.

He should have known better. He'd been made into a hardened spy. That life was all he'd ever have. Everyone, even his own bloody governess, would eventually hide an ulterior motive.

He pressed back against the wall, careful to keep out of sight. There was nothing to gain by acting now. He'd let her keep hunting. The more information he had, the better equipped he'd be to deal with the peril she now presented.

He forced the rage down. He needed to remain calm. Gather all the details, *then* make a decision. Through the sliver of open door, he could make out her movements. Her posture was rigid, her movements tentative as she flipped through the blueprints.

She was nervous.

Good.

That gave him a perverse flicker of pleasure. A trained agent would never exhibit such hesitance. A trained agent would move with efficiency, and a trained agent would not make the mistake of lighting the lamp. He'd bet a monkey that Miss Loren either had not been involved in covert activity for long, or more likely, she was a common thief.

Either way, she'd be no match for him.

She leaned over the cabinet where he stowed his plans for improvements on the village. Nothing incriminating there. Since her back was to him, he leaned a bit further into the room, scanning for further signs of upset. She'd moved the books on the low table. That was no issue either.

He held back a sigh of relief, for she bypassed the

bookshelves on the back wall. If she'd pulled out a *certain* book on the wall and then pressed the far right volume on the third shelf, the back panel would be activated and the entire shelf would recede, revealing the secret room where he kept the records for the Clocktower.

Instead, she stepped to the right. As he watched, she tugged his ledger from the bottom drawer. His eyes narrowed as she flipped through the pages, finally getting to his financial records. All this searching, yet she hadn't removed a single thing from his office. Her being a thief was becoming more and more unlikely.

As she turned, he was forced to retreat from the doorway back to the shadows of the potted plant. He dare not risk being seen through the crack in the door when she faced him. Though he couldn't ascertain exactly where she was, the creak of wood moving against wood told him she'd found the window seat. In a minute, she'd closed it again.

She hadn't found what she was looking for.

He heard her approach, then stop. From the length of her strides, he guessed she'd paused in front of his desk. He remained in the shadows, not daring to emerge, for her position would bring her directly in front of him. A loud squeak broke the relative quiet. She'd opened the top drawer of his desk, and she wouldn't find anything there but writing supplies. For a few minutes, the room echoed with opening and shutting drawers, shuffling paper, and finally a muffled curse.

That sealed it—she was no thief. A thief would have seized the gold paperweight on his desk; the ancient Chinese vase on the low table, worth more than four times her annual salary; or the small red chalk study known as the "Three Graces" by the Italian painter Raphael, framed above the filing cabinets. The gilded gold frame alone was worth a mint, even if she did not recognize the value of the sketch.

Not to mention the fact that she was a bloody bad sneak. In all his years with Clocktower, he'd never seen anyone conduct such an inefficient, noisy search. Her strengths laid clearly in handling his rambunctious brother, not in stealth. So why in the devil was she searching his library? Had someone sent her here? Wickham had checked her background, but something must have been missed.

None of this made a damn bit of sense.

All he knew was that she'd betrayed his trust. If she didn't have a damn good explanation, he'd make sure she paid for that mistake.

A shaky light appeared at the end of the winding hall, coming toward him. His fingers tightened against the handle of the knife. The beat of his heart quickened as his other senses sharpened, readying for attack.

But as the figure advanced, he discerned the hazy features of Mrs. Engle, his housekeeper. She held a candle in her hand, accounting for the moving flicker. His heartbeat returned to a steady rhythm. Though he did not fear Mrs. Engle, he tucked further between the wall and plant, taking refuge in the darkness. He couldn't chance that the housekeeper would acknowledge him, thus alerting Miss Loren to his presence.

The housekeeper headed toward the stairs. When the door clicked shut, Miss Loren sighed in what he imagined to be relief. To her knowledge, no one had seen her. James held his breath as she came out from the library, willing her to pass by without noticing him.

As Miss Loren strode in the opposite direction, James inched after her. When the hall forked off, she took the right turn, heading toward the nursery. Her room was located beside the nursery, so that she could tend to her charge at all hours, if need be. Stopping at the entrance, she glanced over her shoulder. He ducked behind another potted plant. Never again would he question Elinor's purchases of more plants.

She went inside the room, shutting the door behind her. Yet it did not close all the way, as Abermont House had heavy oak doors, and hence an extra tug was needed to seal the lock. James nudged the door with the tip of his boot, enlarging the gap enough so that he could watch her.

The oil lamp sputtered to life as she lit the wick, casting a shadow away from the candle's flame. She faced him as she sat down on the bed, sliding off her slippers and lining them up neatly at the foot of the bed. In the lamplight, her hair looked even more golden than normal, reminding him of the softest satin. God, how could he still want to run his fingers through her hair when he didn't know if she was an enemy or not? His body refused to listen to reason, ruled instead by primal urges.

She stood, facing him. For a second, he wondered if she could see him. But her nimble fingers plucked at her fichu, untucking the cloth from the neckline of her gown. His mouth went dry at the revealed expanse of porcelain flesh, the swell of her breasts. His cock hardened as she tilted her head back, rubbing her hand in a circular motion against her neck.

Bollocks.

If only he'd known how traitorous she could be when she'd offered to bandage his wound. *Demanded* to bandage his wound was more like it. He would have told her just what he did to people who betrayed him...or so he wanted to think. Because even now, watching as she strode to her jewelry box, a small voice in his voice sounded. Claimed this was not who she really was, that she'd been forced to spy on him. The woman who had listened to him talk about Louisa without pity could not be an enemy agent.

Please, Lord, not her.

He couldn't explain how in such a short time this woman had come to mean so much to him. It lacked logic, and it certainly was dangerous. He couldn't afford to be distracted by what he *thought* he knew of her.

She pulled open her jewelry box, dropping in her earrings. His eyes zeroed in on that jewelry box—there was a piece of parchment inside the bottom drawer. A letter, from how it was folded. Had there been more papers in that drawer? He'd have to investigate it further.

Closing her jewelry box, Miss Loren proceeded to the wardrobe in the far corner of the room. He could not track her movements in his small window of light, but he marked the swish and sway of fabric. She emerged from the wardrobe, and made her way to the bed, pushing the sheets down. Selecting a book from the bedside table, she crawled into bed.

He wouldn't risk trying to find answers tonight. He'd wait until tomorrow when she was in the schoolroom and complete a thorough sweep of her room, starting with that note. He'd planned on staying in Kent for a few days, as the Clocktower was headquartered in London, but he'd write Deacon in the morning that he was extending his stay.

Miss Loren might have secrets, but she was about to find out that in a house of spies nothing remained unknown for long.

THE FOLLOWING MORNING, James reviewed the notes he'd received from the housekeeper on Miss Loren's schedule. Mrs. Engle was one of the few servants who knew the family's secret—she'd grown up in service at Abermont House, as her mother had been their cook until her death. James had not given Mrs. Engle a reason for his enquiry, and the housekeeper had not asked.

James appreciated that about her. Mrs. Engle

understood the importance of "need to know" far more than his sisters ever had.

He reviewed the note one last time as he stood in the hall outside of the nursery. From down the hall, he heard the clock chime eight times. Miss Loren awoke with the sun. At six, she would prepare herself for the day ahead. From the hours of seven to eight in the morning, she breakfasted with Thomas in the nursery. From eight until teatime, she was in the schoolroom with him as well. Then she'd go on a walk with Thomas, and eat dinner with him.

Outside of Thomas, he doubted Miss Loren had regular communication with anyone. Mrs. Engle had informed him the servants did not like her, for they considered her too highbred to be one of them.

What a lonely existence. Here in Kent, she had no family, no friends, no one who would understand her grief.

He understood her pain. Too well.

He scowled down at the paper. Damnation, he would not feel sympathy for Miss Loren, not until he knew exactly why she'd poked through his library the night prior. The knife sheathed at his side, and the other secured in his boot, reminded him that he needed to treat this like any other mission.

She was a suspect. A possible traitor.

James passed the nursery, stopping at the next door to the right. Miss Loren's room. He glanced up and down the hall—no one was coming. He pushed the door open and entered, shutting it quietly behind him. Though Miss Loren was not due back for hours, he did not want to risk that someone else would see him and ask questions. For now, he kept his suspicions to himself. He pretended that his reticence was simply because he wanted to have all the facts before he presented the case to Wickham.

He knew better.

He stood back, his gaze darting from one corner of

the room to the next. The furniture was sparse. A bed, a desk and chair, a wardrobe, and a bedside table. Abermont House's various servant quarters were considered spacious in comparison to other estates, but even with that Miss Loren's room was the size of his dressing room. One hell of a change from the viscountcy where she'd grown up.

His vision focused in on the jewelry box she'd opened last night and he stalked toward it. The lid stuck when he tried to open it; upon further investigation, a small brass lock clasped the two fasteners together. He took a seat in the chair, propping his foot up on his opposite knee. His top boots had been specially designed by the weapons expert at the Clocktower. A small repository was in the sole of each shoe, just wide enough for a pick and a tension wrench. He selected both, closed the receptacle, and stood.

Surveying the lock, he let out a derisive snort. The most inept of child thieves could pick this. If Miss Loren thought this tiny trinket would keep him out of that box, she was even more inexperienced than he'd thought. He selected the thin tension wrench, sliding it into the bottom of the lock and applying pressure. He heard the click as the lock opened. Gathering up his tools, he slid the case back in his pocket and removed the lock from the box.

"Let's see what you have hidden." He popped up the lid.

Four broaches, two necklaces, and three pairs of earrings lined the upper tray. All were clearly paste. The lock had not been to protect their monetary value. He'd encountered enough seemingly innocuous objects to know not to immediately discount them. He picked up each one, checking for secret caches in the metalwork, or defining marks that did not fit with the rest of the piece. Nothing. These pieces might have held sentimental worth to her, but that was all.

He removed the top tray and set it on the desk. The bottom cavity was not deep. A pink silk scarf folded twice covered the area, and to the casual onlooker, there appeared to be nothing else in the box. But he'd seen her place foolscap here.

"She thinks she's clever, doesn't she?" He addressed the box as he lifted up the scarf and deposited it on the desk. A handful of folded up parchment scraps littered the space. "But she's not clever enough."

Miss Loren must have affected his senses, if he was talking to a damn box as if it could deliver a response. He ran his hand through hair, frowning down at the notes. A part of him thrilled at doing something active again—though this was a far cry from the usual danger and exotic places of his old field missions—yet he could not crush the dread that welled up with him.

"Enough dillydallying," he muttered. Too much time in the office had made him soft, if the betrayal of one meager governess unhinged him.

Drawing out the chair behind the desk, he settled onto it, careful to keep his weight evenly distributed so that the wood wouldn't groan. He flipped over the first letter, glancing at the postmark. Written to her back when she'd lived in London, almost a year after her brother's death. Though he was not as good at analyzing handwriting as Elinor, he knew enough to garner a few observations. The large, spidery script ran together, as if the writer both craved attention and crowded those around him. The letters were also sharply pointed, indicating the writer was aggressive and intelligent.

Great. Just what he needed.

He unfolded the letter, reading the message.

If you ever want to learn why your brother died, you will apply to be the Spencer family's governess. When you are accepted, expect to hear from me again.

-Sauveterre

Whoever sent Vivian Loren to his door had done so by offering her with information about her brother's murder. For a minute, he forgot to focus on the mission. Whatever she'd done, the pain in her eyes over her brother's death had been real.

He clenched his fingers together in a fist, vise-gripping the note as memories besieged him. Nicodème had laughed when James encountered him. He'd gloated over Louisa's torture, up until the moment James dragged the knife across his throat, effectively silencing him for good.

When he found Sauveterre—and he *would* find him—he'd rip him apart, limb by limb. Not just for daring to threaten James, but for hurting Miss Loren.

He remembered how hollow her voice had sounded when she'd asked him if he'd sought vengeance for Louisa's death. She lived with this hole every day in her life, not just the guilt of having survived when he did not, but the inability to make it right. While Nicodème could never hurt anyone again, her brother's killer was still out there, possibly preying on innocent lives. And instead of coming forward as a good Samaritan would have, this foul creature had preyed upon her grief.

That bastard. That violent, deceitful, immoral bastard. Fury boiled up inside him, threatening to take hold. He told himself his anger was purely intellectual. This was the lowest form of cruelty, using the demise of a loved one to get information. There were certain cards one simply didn't play when controlling an asset.

He placed the note on the desk. Reminded himself that information was power, and the more he knew, the better prepared he'd be. He started with the signature. *Sauveterre.* He didn't recognize the name— though that didn't necessarily mean anything, for in his line of work people had many names.

He pressed his lips together, considering. Given

that the sender had purposefully instructed Miss Loren to instill herself at Abermont House, the most likely scenario was that the sender was an enemy agent. Perhaps one of Bonaparte's Talons—Nicodème had been one of the First Consul's favorites. James had expected Bonaparte would seek revenge—he just hadn't been prepared for it to come in the form of a pretty governess who was far too memorable for her own good.

Reaching upwards, he pinched the bridge of his nose. Her lack of experience could now be explained. He doubted she'd ever worked a spy before this. Why had Sauveterre chosen *this* woman? How had he known about her brother's death—was it through personal involvement in the murder, or through a third party?

He flipped to the second note, which congratulated her on her successful hire and requested a list of people in the house and their usual schedules. Standard, easily obtainable information, most likely meant to test her skills. Sauveterre would likely match her responses against what intelligence he'd already received, gaging her willingness to tell him the truth. It was what James would have done.

The next few were more detailed. Inquiries on what she'd sent him. The handwriting became larger, the formation of the letters more erratic. Sauveterre's tone became more brusque. He pushed her to dig further. To bring him something valuable.

James pulled in a deep breath. At least that was comforting. Whatever Miss Loren had sent him, Sauveterre wasn't pleased. This meant that the threat might be more easily minimized—if this mysterious benefactor didn't have concrete proof of James's covert activities, he'd be easier to contain.

And if there was one thing James was good at, it was eliminating threats.

Unfolding another note, he spread it out on the

desk beside the rest. In the final missive, he could almost feel Sauveterre's frustration ebbing off the page. There was another demand for more information, and then this line:

I think you've become too comfortable in your position there. Don't forget that easily as you obtained that job, I can take it away. Find me something useful.

James's brows furrowed. Elinor had hired Miss Loren because of her education and social class. Had her past been forged as part of Sauveterre's plan? He discounted that idea. Wickham had performed a stringent background investigation, which involved talking to many of her relatives and acquaintances. But he still had many questions about her that needed answers. What exactly had she told Sauveterre? What exactly did Sauveterre suspect him of? The fact that he'd sent Vivian Loren in, instead of attempting a frontal assault on Abermont House, was intriguing.

Abermont House was well fortified, with seven guards who patrolled the grounds at all times. Any unusual activity was immediately reported back to him, or in his absence, Elinor. Had Sauveterre attempted entry into the home himself, and been refused? James skimmed over the staff in the last year. No one else new—there was little turn over at the estate, for he made damn sure that their salaries were well above average. Well-paid servants were loyal servants.

The only position they'd had available in the last four years was governess, and that was only because Mrs. Garring's mother had taken ill. Damnation, if he were going to instill an operative in the staff, he would have chosen the governess too.

He gathered up all the notes, and placed them back in Miss Loren's jewelry box, rearranging everything exactly as she'd had it. Slipping the lock back on, he closed the box. A quick search of the rest of her room revealed nothing more.

Slipping his hand down, James checked the knife at his side, then the one strapped in his boot. He had no intent of using either on Miss Loren—unless absolutely necessary—yet their presence made him feel prepared for whatever was ahead. He wouldn't wait for Miss Loren to finish her school day. He'd confront her now.

CHAPTER 6

THIS MUST BE what hell felt like.

Not the stab of sudden pain, nor the squeeze of one's lungs gasping for air, but instead the slow tick of a clock toward doom. It was the waiting that would undo her. The agony of not knowing when her demise would come, yet all the while being fully aware that destruction was imminent. Unavoidable. She waited as the sun rose, stripping away the darkness of the previous night. Waited as she took in breakfast. Waited as she taught Thomas an hour's worth of French, then assisted his tutor with the history lesson.

By the time the hour struck three and she was finally able to extricate herself from Thomas's side, Vivian considered a quick death a humane alternative to the torment of her present situation. She'd never been so glad to see Miss Spencer, who had come by the schoolroom to take Thomas out for an afternoon ride. Finally, finally, she could cease waiting and *act*.

If she could only find the dashed duke.

She'd checked the dining room, the parlor, the billiards room, the gymnasium, the ballroom, and a seemingly endless supply of other rooms, for Abermont House was nothing if not spacious. He was not there. Nor was he in the library she'd raided, or the office where she'd drank with him and been considered—for a few minutes anyhow—his equal. She did not know if she should feel relieved by that; perhaps Fate paid her some small gift in forcing her to speak to him somewhere not already clogged by memories.

She stood now under the archway of the exit door out into the garden. One half-boot on the tiled floor of the conservatory, the other on the grass of the lawn. The symbolism was not lost on her, even as she debated going outside. She'd be exposed in that long swatch of green. Nowhere to hide, not until she reached the maze deep in the garden, and that was far away from here. While some shrubbery lined the paths and trees were interspersed amongst the flowerbeds and statuary, the garden had been created for visibility and atmosphere. It was a garden of the indolent rich, those with so few problems they had hours in the day to while away in the tranquility of the outdoors. It had not been created for women with threats against their lives.

Stepping back, she worried her bottom lip between her front teeth. Sauveterre could be watching her right now, plotting her demise, as she waited at the threshold. In the house, she had some level of protection. Guards patrolled at all hours, for the Spencers liked their privacy. At first, she'd found this fact odd, but she'd attributed it to the habits of the highly wealthy. When one estate harbored so many priceless objects, it was bound to attract thieves.

And deceitful spies like her.

She laid her head against the cool wood of the door. Pretended that it steadied her, when in truth her heart beat so fast she feared it might burst free of her chest. Wouldn't it be better, to live without a heart? That fanciful thought took hold of her, and she sucked in another breath, wishing for a life where she did not hurt so. Her heart had brought her nothing but pain and suffering. A life without passion, without the bitter thrust of a knife to her gut every time she remembered Evan: now that would be heaven.

But she could not close her eyes without seeing him on the coroner's table. His skin bloated. His abdomen discolored and green, while his legs appeared marbled as if violet-black spider webs interwove across his body. Sauveterre had done this to her brother, and now he was coming for her.

A sob tore from her throat before she could stop it. Her frayed nerves were splitting at the seams and she had nothing left to patch them back together. For a year and a half she had waited to find Evan's killer, and now that she had a name, she was even more powerless.

"Miss Loren?"

Abermont's voice surrounded her. Intruded upon her thoughts, her very being, his words loud and bold. She wondered if she'd imagined him, for he'd arrived at the moment when she needed him most. When she was so frail the act of turning around to face him nearly made her drop. She'd fought for so long, lied for so many months, all for nothing.

She did not know how it happened, exactly. One moment, she was standing up right, albeit unsteadily. Her shoulders did sag, yes, but her knees were most certainly not caving—until they did, and she was falling to the ground. But then a pair of strong arms wrapped around her, keeping her standing, anchoring her. She did not feel so alone anymore. Not when he was here, not when he held her.

For a second—a blissful, fleeting second—she allowed herself to breathe in his woodsy scent, pine and leather. It wove through her senses, mingling in her mind, until everything was him and he was everything. His hands burned through the gossamer sleeves of her sienna day dress, catching her body aflame.

And she wanted to lean her head against his broad chest and pretend that it was all going to be fine. There was no mysterious man hunting her. No secrets blackening her name.

She had been wrong before. A life without feeling was not heaven.

This was heaven.

Too soon, he pulled back from her. It had not been more than a minute passed, yet she felt the inexplicable change echo through her. She stood again, on her own two feet, her stance firm. She remembered exactly who she was. At nine, she'd learned to ride astride, despite the objections of her uncle. At fourteen, she'd bested her brother in a fencing match, and when he'd claimed it was a lucky riposte, she'd done it again. And again.

She was a survivor, blast it, and she'd make it through this battle as she had all the rest.

Her chin notched higher, she met the duke's inquiring gaze. Perhaps a flush slipped across her cheeks, for his eyes were so intense, twin whirlwinds reaching for her. But she ignored their pull. Ignored his appeal. In recalling her sense of self, she was again aware of the chasm between them.

Abermont gave another of his nods, as if he was assured she wouldn't faint again.

"I need to speak with you," she said.

Just as he said, "I need to speak with you."

She blinked. What would he need to talk to her about? Her weekly report on Thomas's progress wasn't due for another few days. He'd already thanked her for bandaging his hand. There was little else between them.

Unless he already knew she'd been spying upon him. Wouldn't that make life easier, if he already knew? But she'd have no chance to turn the story to her benefit if he'd already made up his mind. Her gaze flitted to his face, yet his gray eyes were unreadable, a calm sea when she longed for a storm to indicate his intent. His lips flattened into a thin line as he peered down the bridge of his hawkish nose at her.

He did not speak. When her own words died in her throat unspoken, he gestured for her to follow him deeper into the conservatory. Wall to wall glass window panes ensconced in white window frames faced the garden, allowing the onlooker to enjoy the beauty of the outdoors without exposure to the elements. Allowing Sauveterre to see inside. Was he looking now, as she trailed after Abermont? As she handed over her life's fate to *another* powerful man whose moves she could not anticipate?

The sound of her steps seemed akin to the coronach played at Evan's funeral. Onward they walked, until they reached the center of the room. Several whitewashed iron benches grouped around a marble fountain featuring three women, each with a hand extended to the giant basin atop their heads. She'd loved this spot. The tree ferns placed strategically all around the little alcove had made this spot secluded, cut off from outside problems. Here, she'd felt free.

She did not feel free now.

But the alcove in the conservatory was private. The ferns surrounding them were tall enough that no one outside in the garden would be able to see them. A few short years ago, she would have been expected to have a chaperone any time she was alone with a man such as the duke. Now, she would gladly embrace that scandal, if it meant her true misdeeds would never see the light of day.

How quickly the tides of her life had changed. From a viscount's ward to a governess to a criminal in a few small jumps.

Abermont sat down on a bench, looking expectantly at the spot next to him. She gulped. Too close to him. Instead, she sat on the opposite edge of the bench, as far as she could get from him without disobeying his order.

Abermont turned on the bench so that he faced her. "You said you needed to speak to me. Was there a particular matter that concerns you? Is my brother not doing well in his schooling?"

He did not know, then. For if he knew, his voice wouldn't sound so bloody emotionless, whilst every breath she took in was a fight against panic. He must suspect *something*, but not the real truth.

"Thomas is fine." An automatic response, born out of rote. When he relaxed against the bench, she remained stiff, her shoulders back, her chin forward. An imitation of strength, when she felt none. "I have not been honest with you."

His brows knit. "I'm not sure I understand. What, precisely, have you lied about?"

"Everything." She could not meet his gaze. Instead, she looked at the potted fern farthest from him, beginning to count the number of branches. One. Two. Three. Twelve.

Abermont's tone was still unbearably even. "Everything is a very broad term."

"I suppose *everything* is not correct," she granted. "My name is truly Vivian Loren, and the family history I gave your sister when applying is quite true. Even the references from my uncle's friends were genuine, all born out of their sympathy from seeing me reduced to service."

She chanced a look over at him and instantly regretted it, for he was nodding along with her words. Not pity, but the factual acknowledgment that she'd been reduced in circumstances. She didn't want him to think of her like that, a fraction of what she'd once been.

"The story you told me of your brother's death." The smallest hint of emotion lined his voice, belying his imperturbable mien. "Was that true?"

"Yes, though I wish it wasn't." If only that had been a lie. If only she could bring Evan back with the power of her words.

Was it her imagination, or did Abermont seem relieved by the fact that their shared pain was not fabricated? She did not know how to perceive that. She ran her hand down her skirt, smoothing out a nonexistent wrinkle. Once, twice, thrice, until the gesture was more about keeping her hands busy than the semblance of normalcy.

"My brother's death was not a random act of violence. He was murdered." She forced the words out, for it was so much harder to say this to him than it had been to anyone else. Her fate lay in his hands—but there was something else she did not want to acknowledge, yet she felt it all the same. The fear that he might not believe her. The shock that his opinion mattered.

He waited for her to continue, his reactions not fitting at all with what she'd predicted. Where were the questions? The fury? She'd anticipated following his prompting. But in this as in all other things, she was alone.

"I came here because I wanted to find out who killed him." Damn the tremble of her voice, that fragile weakness when she wanted so badly to be fierce.

Abermont's intense eyes fastened on her face, his complete attention upon her. "And did you?"

"Yes." She opened her hand, half-expecting to see yellowed teeth upon her glove. Their absence did not make her stomach seize less.

Abermont tracked her motion, a spark of concern lighting upon his face. "I believe you'd better start at the beginning, Miss Loren."

So she did. She let her mind fly back to the very beginning, the night of Evan's death. It did not take much coaxing to bring back all the details. The overwhelming odor of chemicals could not hide the nauseating stench of decomposition from the various corpses in the coroner's office. She'd had to cover her nose with her lilac-perfumed handkerchief just to be able to breathe without choking. And when the coroner drew back the sheet from Evan's body, the rank pungency made her gag. It reminded her of the pig they'd once found on uncle's estate, mauled by wild animals and left to rot.

"A Runner came to our townhouse in Clerkenwell. It was a Thursday. I remember that because Evan always left early for work on Thursdays, so that he'd be able to leave the bank before three and take me to the circulating library." She reached for her handkerchief, her fingers fisting in the scented fabric, just as they had that day after she'd identified his body. "I hadn't seen him since the night before. If I'd known it would be the last time I'd ever see him, I would have held onto him and never let him go. I would have told him I loved him."

"I am certain he knew that," Abermont murmured. So many people before him had tried to tell her that—but when Abermont said it, she believed him, because he too had experienced the regret of a last day. She wondered what he wished he'd said to his sister.

"The Runner asked me to come with him to the coroner's office. He said they'd found my brother dead in an alley in Seven Dials. The damage..." Her nails sank into the fabric of that handkerchief, but she could not stop her voice from breaking. "The damage done to his body was so extensive that had I not sewn a label with his name in it into his coat, they would have just thought he was another dead drunk in the stews."

Abermont brushed his hand over hers. His soft touch anchored her in the present. "That was clever of you. I shall have to tell my valet to sew labels into all my coats." He released her hand, catching her eye.

A short, biting laugh escaped. His attempt at

gallows' humor had broken some of the tension within her.

"It is always good to plan ahead," she rejoined, with some steadiness to her voice. "Were you to check the collar of my dress now, you'd find my name stitched into the muslin." She tried to play that fact off as a light—albeit morbid—joke.

Abermont sat up straighter, his eyes narrowing. "Do you fear for your life, Miss Loren?"

His directness caught her off-guard. She'd grown used to his not asking questions, yet she couldn't shake the notion that he'd been waiting for her to reach a certain point in her narrative. As if he'd ferreted out the *reason* behind her coming to him, and all the rest before it had been inconsequential.

He saw a problem, and he was going to fix it.

She nodded, releasing her hold on the handkerchief and spreading it across her lap. Digging into her pocket, she dropped Sauveterre's notes into it, and lifted up the handkerchief by the ends so that it formed a small purse. A half hour ago, after her initial search for him had been fruitless, she'd gone back to her room to collect the notes. At least then she'd have evidence of her claims.

Abermont watched her, his hand out to receive the makeshift bag, but she did not give it to him. Not yet.

"My brother was beaten to death in an alley in Seven Dials. When I asked the Runners why he'd been in Seven Dials, they couldn't give me a reason." She clenched her teeth, her grip on the bag like iron. "You told me you'd avenged Louisa's death. So you must understand; you must be able to imagine, how it feels not to have answers. To not be able to get revenge for your loved one."

Abermont nodded again. Such a simple gesture, yet it conveyed more anguish than any of the pithy sayings repeated to her in the last year and a half. That nod, combined with the sorrow in his eyes, was enough to get her through the next few sentences.

"I lived without answers for almost a year. A horrible, exhausting year, in which I did nothing but search for *something* that would tell me why my brother died." For a second, she closed her eyes, letting the darkness soothe her. She'd always felt better in the blackness, for it was what she deserved. "Evan had enough money saved that after the townhouse was sold, I was able to let a small flat in Clerkenwell too. But everything reminded me of him, and then the money ran out."

"Did you think of going home?" Abermont asked. "Not *home*, per say, but to your other relatives."

She shook her head. "My cousin, Viscount Trayborne, wants nothing to do with me. My grandfather has never met me. Grandfather stopped recognizing Papa as kin as soon as he married Mama. Supposedly, Grandfather didn't agree with the match."

"Still, maybe..."

She raised her chin higher, meeting Abermont's inquiries with fire. "I would rather work myself to the bone than rely on the charity of others."

"I admire that." The tiniest smile creased the duke's lips. "So you became a governess. But I still don't see how this has anything to do with lying."

She held up the bag. "For six months, I have been receiving instructions from a man named Sauveterre. He wrote to me, and I didn't question it. I should have, I know. A missive arrives on your doorstep with no return address, signed by an obvious pseudonym. Usually, people want to know where it's from."

"But you didn't."

"I think I was scared to question it," she said. "Every attempt I'd made in investigating Evan's death met with failure. Here was this person who promised me the keys to everything I wanted—answers and employment. I didn't want to look deeper and find out it was a ruse. I just wanted to believe for a little while, I had a chance at revenge."

Her grip on the handkerchief shook as she breathed in. Nothing would ever be right again, and she'd done nothing to stop it. "But I failed. I failed my brother, and I failed you, because the very man who killed my brother is the same one who claimed he'd help me."

Abermont did not focus on that detail. "What did he want in exchange?"

"Information on you."

There it was, the marked change in Abermont's countenance. The suddenly autocratic tilt to his neck, as he looked *above* her, no longer keeping her gaze. The way he swept back in his chair, putting distance between them.

"Who could you possibly fear more than me, Miss Loren? You must know what I could do to you as duke. Yet you confess your treachery to me..." He paused, dragging his hand through his hair, an expression she'd come to mark as him being lost in thought. "You come to me as if you think I can *help* you."

Her resolution lagged. She'd made a terrible mistake coming to him. What would he want with a governess who had hurt his family? She'd be better off running, for then at least she'd be independent. But then what would she do? She couldn't get another position without references from this one, and the duke would surely tell all his friends not to hire her. She couldn't go far on what she had saved.

So she had no choice. Convincing him to help her became her only salvation. For herself, and for Evan—for the Runners worked on a reward system, and they'd be much more willing to look into Evan's murder again if they thought they'd get a hefty sum from Abermont.

"I can explain, Your Grace." She handed him the makeshift bag. "That is every letter I ever received from the man who calls him Sauveterre. I have carried the last letter on me since I received it yesterday, as a reminder of the true nature of this blackguard."

He took the folded handkerchief, emptying the contents on his lap. She had numbered the margins on each note, so that he could follow the story.

With each note, the impassiveness of his features contorted, until the raggedness of his emotion washed it away entirely. The fury that had shone in his eyes spread to his cheeks, even to the tip of his crooked nose. She saw it in the death grip he had on the notes, in the way his shoulders hunched over the paper. When he deposited the notes into his coat pocket and turned to her, she expected to be blasted with his ire for what she'd done to him.

Yet something had changed. She would have bet an entire year's salary on that. His eyes were so bright and full of fire that her breath stilled in her throat.

"A man who threatens a woman is the worst sort of man," he said finally, his voice so gravelly, so raw that it sent a shiver up her spine.

Never had she heard him sound so...candid.

So dangerous.

He'd thrown his arm around her before she could react. God's above, he should be furious with her. Instead, he'd taken compassion on her. She leaned into him, resting her head against his shoulder, the superfine of his coat smooth against her flaming cheeks. Yes, his body was as hard as she'd imagined. Yes, he was as strong as she'd always thought. His body was rough and toned, reminding her of a warrior.

And though she knew it was the pinnacle of insanity, she wished he'd be *her* warrior.

But she'd betrayed him. She'd broken his trust. She'd hurt him and his sisters, all for some false promises made by a man she did not know and could not find.

"He's going to kill me." Droplets of water streamed down her cheeks. She'd dreamed of being wild and free, but this was something differently entirely. Giving in to the knowledge that she was doomed, no matter what she did. "He sent me my brother's *teeth*."

Abermont shuddered. That such a robust man as him was repulsed by Sauveterre's actions did not comfort her.

"He's going to kill me like he did my brother and I'm never, ever going to get revenge for Evan. Everything I have done for the last six months has been for *nothing*."

He pulled her closer, his big hand heavy against her arm.

"No. Nothing is going to happen to you, Miss Loren." His rich, clear voice rang out in the conservatory, his unshakable determination making her believe him, even though she knew the odds were against them. "I'm going to protect you."

CHAPTER 7

IN THE SPACE of five minutes, Vivian Loren had transformed from a traitorous enemy to the asset he needed to keep safe.

During, his time in the field, he'd learned to judge when a person was lying. Her voice did not lower; she did not slant her head to the side before responding; she did not stare at him without blinking. Miss Loren was as real, as broken as Louisa had been that day when she'd begged him to send her after Nicodème. *He's hurting innocent women by forcing them into prostitution,* she'd pleaded. *We have to stop him.*

He'd thought that since he'd grown up with four sisters, and worked countless missions where he was required to turn women against their own traitorous husbands, that he was prepared for crying women.

He'd thought wrong.

As tears splashed down Miss Loren's face, his grip on impartiality did not just loosen. It released completely. Her frail body trembled so badly. He couldn't help it—he'd thrown his arm around her before sense took hold. Before he knew what was happening, he was promising her he'd keep her safe. He'd left a trail of bodies in his wake. Justified countless morally deficient decisions with his duty to the nation.

And once the words were said, he couldn't take them back. That vow became like a brand upon his soul. He had not saved Louisa, but by God, he would save Miss Loren.

All thoughts of turning her into Wickham fled his mind. The spymaster would interrogate her for hours upon end, and even after he'd discovered that she knew relatively nothing about Sauveterre or their true occupations, she'd still be kept in gaol on the very slight chance she might present more of a threat down the line.

Under his watch, no one would ever hurt her again.

He tugged her closer to him, snug against his body. They did not speak; no words were needed now. She leaned into him, resting her head against his shoulder. He wanted to tunnel his fingers through her flaxen hair, see if it was as silky as it appeared.

He ought to release her. Yet he slid his hand down her arm, relishing the satin of her bare skin. Her walking dress had cap sleeves, leaving a tiny space between her elbow-length gloves and the edge of her sleeve.

Already, the stirrings of arousal slid through him, hardening his cock. Never had the touch of a woman undone him so, yet the mere act of holding her to his chest affected him more than the nakedness of any of the women he'd seduced for the Crown. She was too warm, too soft in his arms. And oh God, she smelled delicious. Roses, sweet but with an under-layer of spice. He breathed in deeply, thinking the scent of her soap most apt—that hint of something more beneath the surface, a minx disguised in the prim trappings of a spinster.

She was far too tempting. She made him forget who he was. Who he'd been. He did not deserve to forget.

He pulled back from her, settling back on his side of the bench. The distance did not make him less aware of her presence. Her eyes, reddened from crying, focused on him as if he'd provide her with all the answers to her questions. As if he was the only one who could solve her problems.

He handed her his handkerchief, and she took it gratefully, dabbing at her running nose.

"Tell me everything you told Sauveterre." He'd be calm, rational. The Clocktower had faced worse before than this threat to his cover. Once he had all the details, he could manage the situation.

"He asked about your schedules," she said. "He wanted to know your hobbies, and that of your sisters. Any gossip or strange occurrences around the house. So I would listen outside the door, and tell him what I heard."

Though he was careful to exhibit no outward signs of panic, his stomach dived. He *thought* they'd been fastidious about where they conducted their business, but he'd spent most of the last year in London—he couldn't be sure what happened at the estate when he was not home.

"What did you hear?"

She inhaled deeply, closing her eyes. Leaning back against the bench, she began to recite monotonously from memory. "Lady Korianna abhors a man named Simon Travers, but Lady Elinor thinks he's a smart man and Korianna would do best to forget about her feud. Miss Spencer did not want to go to the ball Lord Haley has to commemorate the end of winter, until Mr. Drake told her that he'd be sure to save a dance for her. You think that Mr. Drake is far too rakish, and should exercise more care when it comes to the ladies. Lord Haley agreed with you, but he thinks that's simply because Mr. Drake is twenty-two and has not learned the finer points of..."

On and on the list went, for a total of fifteen minutes. He tracked her movements as she spoke, and found no signs that she was telling anything other than the truth. While she'd overheard enough *on-dits* to keep the *ton* stewing for months, nothing she revealed was covert. The most "secret" thing she'd uncovered was the state of his investments.

But her memory was damnably good. He could use that in the future.

Miss Loren opened her eyes. "And that's it. Everything I told him. When Sauveterre used to write to me, he'd post his letters as Aline Stuart. I told the postmaster Mrs. Stuart was my aunt."

He nodded. "Your recall is impressive. So much so that I think even Lady Elinor would admire your skills."

She looked pleased at that. "Lady Elinor's memory is frightfully acute."

"Oh, my dear, you have no idea." He smiled wryly. "But what I don't understand is *why* Sauveterre sent you here. What does he want from me?"

"He is convinced you are financing a revolution in France. No matter how many times I told him his theory didn't have any evidence to support it, he kept *insisting*." Miss Loren's brows furrowed. "You aren't, right?"

James smothered a smile. "No, absolutely not. If I were ever to get involved in revolution, I'd prefer to be actively involved, not just the moneybags."

Technically, that was true. The Clocktower had its own budget, funded through the Alien Office. And his years in the field had certainly been *active*, to say the least.

She let out a sigh of relief, shifting on the bench to face him. "I thought so. You don't even take your seat in the House of Lords. What interest would you have in the politics of France? It doesn't apply to you."

He nodded, though he hated to agree with that

description of him. He sounded so shallow—if only she knew that he didn't take his seat because there simply was no time. He was committed to serving in England in a much more direct way.

She'd already moved on. "How can you want to protect me, after all of this?"

A pithy lie about duty and the obligations of honorable men was on the tip of his tongue, ready to be used. But with her, it didn't feel right to outright lie. When was the last time he'd felt something genuine? Pleasure or pain that didn't contain artifice? He couldn't remember.

And in that moment, sitting on this bench with her, he wanted *one* thing that was real.

"I want to protect you because I believe in you." More truth than he'd meant to reveal, but for one moment, he didn't want to hide. She was smart and vivacious, and he found that bloody attractive.

"Oh." A flush spread over her high cheekbones. "Well, thank you."

She reached for him, curling her fingers around the back of his hand. He made the mistake of looking down, and all he could think of was how her hand would look wrapped around far more erotic parts of his anatomy.

Christ. Releasing her hand, he gulped down his rising desire and tried to pretend he wasn't aroused at all by her. That she was an asset, and nothing more.

"It won't be easy," he warned her, his voice coming out gruffer than he'd wanted. "The man who killed your brother clearly won't hesitate to use extreme measures to get what he wants. If I'm going to keep you safe, you'll need to follow my instructions. No questions asked."

Her eyes narrowed. "I want to know what's going on. It's my fate we're discussing. And I won't stop until I personally have Evan's killer brought to rights."

He recognized the flash of fire in her eyes, for he'd

seen it in every one of his sisters when they'd argued with him over mission objectives. Lord save him from stubborn women. His job of protecting them would be so much easier if they simply *listened* to him.

He opened his mouth to tell her he knew the best way to handle this, but then she set her jaw. Head held high, sapphire eyes shining, Miss Loren definitely wasn't a shrinking wallflower. And she was already involved in this.

Right now, she thought the problem was limited to simply her brother's murder. Keeping her out of the loop might actually endanger her more—he had a sinking feeling she'd burst into the middle of a meticulously planned mission and blow all their covers if she wasn't aware of the stakes. She'd need training. *Lots* of training, if her sneaking in his library was any indication. Yet she had a quick mind, and she refused to drop a matter until she'd ferreted out the answers she wanted. He'd refine those skills. Harness her raw energy into something with purpose and direction.

Given Sauveterre's knowledge of her existence, he couldn't risk that whomever the man worked for would try to recruit Vivian too. Nor did he want Wickham to get his hands on Vivian. She deserved more than years of missions that would corrupt her soul. If he took her under his wing, he could watch her, make sure she wasn't harmed. Assign her to missions that wouldn't put her in great danger.

"If I keep you informed, you must do the same for me," he said. "If Sauveterre contacts you again, I need to know. Every detail counts. If there's anything you're leaving out..."

She nodded. "I've told you everything I know."

"Meet me in my office tomorrow night after dinner. We can discuss where to go from here." He stood up from the bench, extending his hand to help her up too.

She took his extended hand, but she held on after

she stood. "Partners?"

He shook her hand. "Partners."

Whether she knew it or not, Vivian Loren had become the Clocktower's newest agent.

EARLY THE NEXT morning, James sat at the small Cuban mahogany desk in the secret room attached to his library. He had always hated this desk. It was overly ornate with gilt mounts and tapered, fluted legs. He drummed his fingers on the black marbled top of the desk, pounding out the same beat his father had always hummed. But that didn't help his concentration, and neither did sitting behind this damnably French desk. He tugged on the gold-enameled circular handle and wished for answers.

It was in times like these, when he had a difficult decision to make, that he missed his father the most. The Lion made choices swiftly, and it was the right course of action. Always. Though James inherited his father's name, title, and responsibilities, he had not gained his infallibility; nor his ability to remain impartial, even when the ramifications would affect their own family.

He'd allowed his emotions to cloud his logic the day he'd sent Louisa out on that fatal mission. Now he had Miss Loren depending on him—what if he made the wrong decision? When it came to assigning missions to the seasoned agents of the Clocktower, he tried to remember that they knew the consequences of their covert work. They'd made an informed choice about their fate.

Vivian Loren hadn't made that choice. She'd been used by a brutal killer to get to him. Her actions had been the by-product of her grief, not a deliberate desire to enter the world of espionage. Hell, after six months, she *still* believed that Sauveterre had the wrong idea about him.

He pushed the chair back from the mahogany desk and stood. No amount of old relics from successful missions would help him channel the Lion's wisdom. After he'd left the conservatory yesterday, he'd immediately informed the guards that patrols around the estate needed to be increased. Then he'd spent all evening in this little room, for here he thought the best.

James turned on his heel, facing the wall of cabinets holding data on the Clocktower agents. The files were a small percentage of information compared to that kept in the organization's headquarters in London, yet Elinor had lovingly cataloged each record as though this were the lost library of Alexandria. James paused in front of the drawer labeled L-M, pulling out Miss Loren's file. He already knew the contents, yet the act of browsing through the paper always soothed him. As he set the file down on his desk, the panel clicked and the wall receded. James's hand slid down reflexively to his knife, but he didn't need to draw out the blade.

Richard took the seat he'd vacated behind the Lion's desk. "Hundreds of missions and this place still makes me feel like I'm in the *Mysteries of Udolpho*. I like that. No matter what Ellie says, I'll always have a soft spot for disguises and secret identities."

"For the sake of everyone in the Clocktower and most importantly, my sanity, I beg you not to bring back Malcolm Mustachio," he said, remembering Richard's favorite costume from when they were children.

Richard placed his hand over his heart, feigning a wound. "You said you loved that mustache. You asked me to borrow it!"

James chuckled. "I was eight. Cooler heads have prevailed."

Richard muttered something that sounded vaguely like "grumpy old badger." It was their usual routine—Richard would tease his solemnity, and James would claim Richard needed to take life more seriously.

Their friendship had stretched from childhood to their schooling at Eton and now, as agents of the Clocktower, they relied on each other to stay alive.

That thought sobered James. He and his siblings had grown up so entrenched in spycraft that he'd never known anything different. Not until he left home did he realize how strange their upbringing truly was. This life had already taken so much from the people he loved.

But if he didn't bring Miss Loren into the fold, she wouldn't be prepared for the danger ahead. How could he keep her safe? Not just from this threat, but also from any other peril she might face? He couldn't explain why he felt so protective of her—how she'd dug so deep under his skin.

Richard took a seat at the desk, crossing one leg over the other. "Why'd you call me here, Jim?"

James passed the folder to him and leaned against his own writing table. Solid oak, square-legged, and sturdy. Now *that* was how a desk should be.

Richard's brows shot up as he flipped through the file. "Your governess? Hardly a cause for such secrecy, unless..." He paused, grinning wolfishly. "Did you bed the governess? I've noticed her too, you know. Quite a beauty. Wish she wouldn't hide underneath those out-of-fashion garments. If she wasn't in your staff, hell, *I'd* tup her."

"Must you be so bloody crass?" James clenched his fists at his sides. He'd never minded his friend's sordid comments before, as long as Richard didn't attempt to flirt with his sisters. But now, when the subject was Miss Loren, his blood boiled.

A sly smile slid onto Richard's lips. "From your

growls, I'm guessing you have a personal interest in Miss Loren, but I still don't know why you called me here."

He handed the notes to Richard and explained what Miss Loren had told him about her brother's death and Sauveterre's reason for sending her to Abermont House. When Richard finished reading, concern washed over his normally jovial features. "So this man thinks you're financing a revolution. That's a damnably fancy way of saying he suspects you're a spy. Well, this certainly complicates things."

James snorted. "Understatement of the year, mate."

Richard gave him back the letters. "But when are our lives not complicated? You'd think by now we'd be used to it."

"There are many things I will never get used to." He did not need to specify, for Richard could tell the dark turn his thoughts had taken. Though his friend had not been on the mission that claimed Louisa's life, he'd tracked the Talons before.

Richard sighed. "I'm not going to tell you it wasn't your fault, because you wouldn't listen to me anyhow. Just know that I would have made the same call. She was a damn good spy, Jim, and she died doing her duty to the country."

He frowned. There was that word again: duty. From the time he'd been old enough to form coherent sentences, the Lion had drilled into him that it was his duty to serve the nation. It was never up for debate. Spencers fought for the Crown. Death, destruction, and diabolical plots were all perpetuated under the name of the empire.

Before Louisa's death, he'd never questioned their missions. He'd accepted, without any further thought, that what they did was for the good of the people. The needs of many outweighed the life of one. As they faced their hardest fight ever against Bonaparte and his assassins, James still did not doubt their *cause*. Bonaparte was an egotistical blackguard who wanted to remake the world in his own image. He needed to be stopped. Now that James was no longer in the field, Korianna and Arden were the best agents the Clocktower had.

But that did not mean that he had to like it. Every time his sisters were on a mission, his stomach twisted. He did not sleep until they came home. Hell, he did not sleep in general, usually.

And now he contemplated dragging Vivian Loren further into this muddle.

He pushed back his chair and stood. He needed to move, to be active, to feel the ground shift beneath his feet and know that he was in control. His Hessians pounded the carpet, back and forth, back and forth. He felt like he hadn't stopped moving since the day he'd taken over the Clocktower.

Richard watched him pace, his hazel eyes following James's every step. "You want to bring her in."

James was again reminded why he and Richard had been so successful in their missions together: they understood each other, even without talking. He made another circle of the room before responding. "I fear what she'll do if she doesn't have all the information. She wants revenge on Sauveterre for killing her brother. If we don't train her, she'll get herself killed. But if we *do* take her in, we'll not only protect her, but hopefully catch Sauveterre before he gets definite evidence against me."

Richard shook his head. "Of course you'd manage to employ the lone governess who's out for blood. It never ceases to amaze me how stubborn women just flock to you. Do you remember the Countess of Marcondeux?"

He blanched. "All too well." The Countess had requested he visit her bedside—while her husband was right next to her. Needless to say, he hadn't taken her up on that, ahem, generous offer.

Richard laughed. "I found her delightfully bawdy."

James grimaced. "I prize loyalty far more highly than nice bosoms."

"Your loss." Richard shrugged. "You think Miss Loren can be trusted with our secret? After lying to you for six months?"

He remembered the tears raining down her face, the agony of her cries. It would take the theater district's finest to fake that much emotion. Besides, she'd fought for a year and a half for answers to her brother's murder. Long after most of people would have given into despondency and accepted the Runners' party line. He admired her diligence. A woman that dedicated to her brother's memory was a woman he wanted on his team, for hopefully he'd earn that same loyalty from her too.

"She lied to get answers on her brother. I do not classify that on the same level as a selfish lie told to gain fame or fortune." Pulling out the red-cushioned chair next to Richard, James sat down in it, finally content to stop moving about the room. "Besides, the nature of what we do is deception. We all play parts to obtain information. I have lost count of the number of aliases I've had over the years."

Richard grinned impishly. "That's because yours aren't as memorable as Malcolm Mustachio." Before James could retort, Richard continued, "Yes, I know. Spies aren't supposed to be memorable. We're supposed to fade into the background, so no one ever remembers we've been there in the first place. I swear, if it weren't for the Beau Monde, I'd begin to think no one remembered me at all. I'm counting the days until the Season starts."

Therein lay the difference between the two men. While Richard thrived on attention, James was content to remain in the shadows.

James let out a groan. "The bloody Season. For a moment, I almost forgot Elinor's dreadful plan."

Richard waggled a brow at him. "Which of my suggestions was the most promising? You're thinking of Lady Penelope Smythe, aren't you? It's her arse. Worthy of smacking, I tell you."

James scowled. Lady Penelope could go rot. "Considering that last year at the Travers' ball I caught Lady Penelope giving the cut direct to Arden, I'd sooner marry the Countess of Marcondeux." Nobody insulted Arden and maintained his favor. Several cavalier members of the *ton* who'd decided to treat Arden as lesser because she was the old duke's ward and hence not a true blue-blood aristocrat had found this out the hard way, for they no longer received invitations to any Spencer family routs.

"Ouch." Richard winced. "Fantastic arse or not, that strikes Lady Penelope off my list too."

That made James smile. "I appreciate your support."

"Arden's like a sister, you know that. I'd do anything for her." Richard cuffed James's arm. "What about Lady Melisandre Andrews then? A wallflower like her surely won't go about insulting your family, no matter how wonderfully unconventional they are."

"Lady Melisandre would last two minutes in this house. The first time Korianna starts experimenting with black powder again, she'll be running for the hills." And that wasn't even mentioning Korianna's habit of "pruning" the potted plants as target practice for her pistol, despite Elinor's protests.

"Fair enough," Richard agreed. He leaned back in the chair, clasping his hands behind his head, elbows out. "I believe we'd arrive at an easier conclusion if you told me who *you* think is worth considering."

James let out a frustrated sigh. "How am I supposed to protect Miss Loren, catch Sauveterre, *and* find a suitable bride by the beginning of the Season? There's simply no time."

Unless...

This was either the best idea he'd ever had, or the maddest.

"What if I marry Miss Loren?"

Richard startled, losing his balance. The chair slammed against the desk, almost toppling him off of it. He barely managed to right himself. "This is the same Miss Loren we've been discussing, yes? You did not just magically produce one of her relatives out of thin air, did you? Because otherwise there's no way under the sun that Ellie's going to go for this."

"She'll be *my* wife. Elinor's opinion is inconsequential." He pursed his lips together, pausing for a moment to think. Before he'd known of the threat to Miss Loren's life, he'd dismissed her as unsuitable— even though being around her had been the best few days he'd experienced since Louisa's death. It had seemed selfish before to ask his family to undergo social scrutiny simply because he wanted to continue spending time with her.

But now she was in danger, and she depended on him to protect her. It didn't matter what the *ton* thought when compared with saving a woman's life.

"I need a way to keep watch on her, even when I'm forced to attend these God-awful parties," James said. "My marrying her ensures she'll be protected. Wickham won't touch her when she's my wife, and the Runners will afford her the same privileges of a peer. Even this Sauveterre, whoever he is, must know that the consequences of killing a duchess will be so much worse than a mere governess."

"Ah yes, the whole 'marriage to get a better day in court' defense," Richard quipped. "You'll make your ancestors so proud with that one. Most people marry for money or a better position in society, but not you, Jim. You'll marry only to protect a chit's life."

Richard was having far too much fun at his expense.

"Is this a ludicrous idea?"

Richard shrugged. "Unexpected, yes. Ludicrous, not entirely. You're the bloody Duke of Abermont. I'd imagine you could marry a guttersnipe and eventually even the gossip-mongers would accept it."

"It's the *eventually* that concerns me." He didn't want to take Miss Loren from one fire and drop her into a conflagration. In Society, the time passed like sand in a broken hourglass; every minute an eternity. "But God, how I dread more months of balls. I'd avoid the whole bloody Season if I could."

For decades, the Clocktower had used the shroud of high society events. Vauxhall had plenty of secluded avenues perfect for hand-offs, while a night at Covent Garden provided sufficient distraction for him to slip away to the cloakroom and meet with an informant.

Richard snorted. "Your invitations will decrease if you marry your governess, so you might actually escape that torture."

"A definite point in Miss Loren's favor," James mused. The large number of parties he'd be expected to attend would diminish if he were no longer considered eligible marriage material. "You know, while I don't agree with Elinor's original principles for choosing my future wife, I do have to admit her logic is sound. I could maintain my cover *and* devote more time to the Clocktower."

Richard smirked. "I suspect your future wife will want you to spend time with her."

"Yes, of course," James muttered, trying to play it off as though he'd thought this notion through, instead of concocting it in the wee hours of the morning.

Eying him suspiciously, Richard pulled his chair closer to him. "Please tell me you didn't conceive this idea as a tactical strategy, without any thought to the woman you'd actually be pledging your troth too."

"I've thought about her." He'd thought about Miss Loren a little too much. He ached to run his fingers down her tantalizingly soft skin, kiss her luscious lips.

"If you're willing to take the societal risk, and you trust her, then I say to do it." Richard stood up, going to the tiny peephole in the wall and looking out. He turned back around to face James again. "Look, Jim, I believe in your judgment, even when you don't. I've never met a more skilled interrogator than you because you understand people. Their thoughts, their motivations, their actions. If you think Miss Loren is worth your time, then I will defend her to the death."

James clenched his teeth. This family had already seen too much bloodshed. "Let's hope that won't be necessary."

"One thing, though." Richard held up his hand. "Can I be there when you tell Ellie?"

"Absolutely, bloody, not," James groaned. "I'm going to have my hands full already. The last thing I need is you needling her."

"I don't needle," Richard objected. "I *banter*. There's a difference."

James narrowed his eyes. "The answer's still no."

Richard let out a loud sigh. "You're a killjoy, my friend. But congratulations, nonetheless." He skirted out of the room before James could tell him nothing was certain yet.

As James reentered the library, he prayed that Miss Loren was as loyal as he believed. Otherwise, the Clocktower's very foundations might crumble before his feet.

CHAPTER 8

AS THE CLOCK struck nine that evening, Vivian paused outside the door to the library. She ran a hand across her skirt, smoothing out the wrinkles from sitting on Thomas's bed as she read him his bedtime story. Should she have changed her dress? She'd never bothered to change after dinner before. After all, her meals were always taken with Thomas, not the rest of the family.

She did not know the etiquette for sudden partnerships with dukes to prevent one's death. Most likely, a practical appearance would be preferred, in case one had to flee suddenly.

She patted her chignon and prayed that she looked acceptable. She wouldn't wish for beautiful, for at twenty-four she was close to spinsterhood. Her mind had always been her best feature. Age hadn't dimmed her intellect; rather, she'd grown wiser.

Or at least she'd considered herself wiser until she'd scurried off to work here at the bidding of a murderer.

Vivian gulped down the lump of dread building in her throat. No point in worrying now. Her course of action had already been laid in. "Full speed ahead!" Papa had always claimed when he began a new business venture; that saying was one of her few memories of him.

She'd pretend she was ferocious. She was a Loren, and Lorens never gave up.

She pushed open the door to the library, somewhat taken aback by the sameness of the room. Somehow, she'd expected it to appear different when she entered at the duke's request, and not a snooping burglar. But no, there were the supple red leather armchairs, the mahogany low table with *Lyrical Ballads*, and the dark cherry paneled cabinet with the silver crescent moon handles pushed up against the rich coffee-colored back wall. A gray stone fireplace broke up floor-to-ceiling dark mahogany bookshelves on the far left wall, a stodgy portrait of one of Abermont's ancestors centered over the top of the mantel.

Vivian toyed with the simple locket charm she wore around her neck with a white ribbon. Evan had given it to her for her eighteenth birthday, and the ends of the ribbon frayed. She ought to change it out, but she couldn't bear losing one more thing that connected her to him.

Abermont was probably used to women who wore huge rubies and pearls. Emeralds probably, for they were expensive too. Well, she couldn't be anything more than what she was now—a governess. There was no point in trying to be anything different. Or in thinking that anything more could come from this partnership with Abermont. That was her old fanciful mind talking, from when she'd been younger, before her cousin had kicked them out of Trayborne estate.

Abermont was late. She ought to take advantage of his absence to choose her seat strategically. She could sit in one of the armchairs, thus avoiding close contact with Abermont. But would he think her closed off then? She didn't want him to think she didn't appreciate his offer of assistance, because oh, she did. For the first night in six months, she'd slept soundly, knowing that he'd manage everything in that powerful, commanding way he had.

It was just so blastedly wonderful to no longer be the only one looking for Evan's killer.

She instead chose the pair of red and beige brocade sofas drawn in front of the fireplace with the low table placed in between. If she was going to work with the man, she needed to learn how to sit next to him without her mind muddling. Vivian fidgeted, tapping her foot against the carpet. Impatience picked at her. She poured herself a cup of tea from the sterling silver pot on the low table, and sat back down on the sofa.

When Abermont entered the room, she popped up from her seat, executing a hasty—albeit highly flawed—curtsy to him. "Your Grace."

Instead of returning her greeting with his usual perfunctory nod, Abermont waved his hand dismissively. "We needn't hold to such proprieties. In truth, I've never liked being curtsied to. Makes me feel rather uncomfortable." He smiled, making her heart thump precariously. She'd shared her secret with him, and now he'd let her in on a confidence too—much smaller than hers, yes, but it was more to bond them together.

She nodded. "Very well."

Abermont poured himself a cup of tea, adding cream and a lump of sugar. "I'd far prefer brandy in the evening, but I figured you'd like tea."

She lifted her cup. "That was thoughtful of you, Your Grace."

He sat down next to her, crossing one long leg over the other. "Please, James. Your Grace was my father."

James. A perfect name for him. Somehow at once steadfast and intriguing.

"Vivian," she said, though it felt so intimate to call each other by their first names. Partners, indeed.

"Well then, Vivian, I've set the wheels in motion for investigating your brother's death. I have personally promised a substantial reward if they turn up information on Sauveterre's location. I'm also looking into *why* your brother was targeted." He spoke with the same calmness as when he received her report on Thomas's progress. As if he hadn't opened up a new avenue for her. As if this wasn't the greatest gift he could have possibly given her.

"Thank you." Though those two little words were a small outpouring of her gratitude, she couldn't make them sound less effusive. While he was nonchalant, she was a bleeding heart torn open in front of him.

"I've also increased the number of patrols by my guards, so you are sheltered here. That said, do not venture outside the gardens. While you may visit the stables, I'm sorry to say that any trail rides must be reconsidered." Abermont—James— gave her a sympathetic smile.

She nodded. While she'd miss riding, she wasn't sure she'd even feel secure in the gardens. These precautions made her feel safer, but Sauveterre could be anywhere.

"Now I have a matter to discuss with you." He leaned in, holding her gaze. "It's of a bit more intimate nature, though."

Tingles shot down her arms, flooding her fingers, when he said "intimate." She gulped for air, the room suddenly hotter than it had been a moment before. The fire in the grate had already burned out; she could not blame it. Nor could she look away from him.

She'd thought that one moment in the garden was a chance encounter, as much in her mind as the many nights spent dreaming of his touch. What it would feel like to have his muscular body atop hers, the glide of his lips along hers, the pine and leather scent of him overwhelming everything else.

Then he held her gaze, his gray eyes like the most

turbulent of waves crashing down upon her and rendering her helpless to swim back to the shore. She wondered what he saw. Her hair was not golden, but instead the color of straw. Her chin was too sharp. Her nose was crooked.

Yet this man, with his aquiline nose and strikingly black hair and that extraordinarily capable way in which he solved every problem, stared back at her with the same deep interest.

She blinked. The world around her crackled back to life. It had been just a minute or two, but in that short span of time she felt things shift.

And she did not have any idea how to proceed.

But James was, as she'd come to expect, in control of the situation. He continued as though nothing had happened. "I think I've come up with a solution that will allow me to make sure that you are kept secure, while also solving a predicament of my own. You see, the Season is about to start, which means every vulture with a daughter of marriageable age will be lined up to snare my time. The very last thing I want is to be the most sought-after bachelor in London."

"I see," she said, but she didn't see at all. What did this have to do with her problem? And not to seem ungrateful, but why were the duke's marriage woes on the same scale of importance as her *life?*

James's steady gaze never left her face. "So I believe you can help me as I'm helping you. I want you to become my duchess."

Vivian blinked. She must have heard him wrong. The Duke of Abermont could not have proposed marriage to her. She wasn't his peer. She wasn't even the peer of his steward. Men who were one step away from royalty did not enter into matrimony with governesses, and certainly not governesses who had admitted to spying upon them.

James looked at her expectantly, as if he considered his request a logical one. She'd misunderstood him, then. A rational man like him would never consider such a preposterous request.

"I'm sorry, could you repeat that?" She hated how breathy her voice sounded. How hopeful. Still she clung to the foolish illusion that the duke saw her—really saw her, as if the breadth of her soul could be conveyed in a week's worth of conversations.

"I asked if you'd marry me," he said, enunciating each word with such pristine pronunciation she knew there could be no mistake.

The drumming of her heart slowed. Every muscle in her body seemed to become tighter with this confusion. She knew now she'd heard him correctly, but how was she supposed to respond? Marshaling her wits, she closed her mouth. She couldn't think of anything to say, anyhow.

He pursed his lips. He'd expected an immediate acceptance. He was duke, after all.

"I want you to be my duchess, Vivian." Abermont made a sweeping motion with his hand to the garden. "All of this could be yours too."

While she loved Abermont House dearly, this could never be. How could she possibly belong here, as part of the family she'd betrayed with her reports to Sauveterre? In the home Sauveterre would know to search for her?

Her, a duchess! The concept was insane. Unless, of course, *he* was insane too.

"Are you mad?" The question popped out of her lips before she could stop it.

His brows furrowed. "Most assuredly not."

She swiftly jumped to the next most reasonable explanation. He was punishing her for her duplicity. "Then this must be some sort of awful joke. You're bamming me, Your Grace, and I do not find it amusing."

He directed a reproachful glance at her. "I asked you to call me James."

"And *I* never asked to be the brunt of your teasing." She launched herself up from her seat, running to the door. But there was no one listening in the hall.

"What are you doing?" He eyed her quizzically.

"I'm looking for your sisters. Or Thomas." She scowled at him. "I should have known you wouldn't help me, after what I've done to you."

"No one else is here." James stood up. He crossed the room swiftly, his strides devouring the space between them until he was right beside her.

He laid a hand on her arm, and suddenly everything was warmer around her. Softer, in a sense. How could she possibly be objective when he was so near? She was lost in the way her stomach flip-flopped, in the speed of her own beating heart.

"I'll find Sauveterre, Vivian, and I will do everything in my power to make sure you aren't harmed." He spoke with the utmost seriousness, as if he was making an earnest pledge he'd take with him to the grave. "When I agreed to work with you, I meant it. What I am suggesting is the natural extension of our partnership."

He angled her head closer to his, and her breath caught in her throat as she waited for him to say those magical words again.

I want you to be my duchess.

Her heart panged for a life she'd never dared to consider possible. A life that *shouldn't* be possible. But when James watched her like this, his eyes so kind and blastedly gentle, she found herself doubting whether social mobility was really such a catastrophic notion.

"I don't understand," she said. How little accustomed she'd been to not understanding things. She'd always been considered remarkably quick-witted, perhaps to her detriment since she'd never caught the eye of a suitor before.

But Evan's death had changed that. Now the act of

living, carrying on through grief, perplexed her.

James walked back to the sitting area, and she followed him. They sat down on the same settee, on opposite ends. "Marriage is like an equation. You and I are both variables. You need someone to protect you from Sauveterre, and I need a wife before the start of the Season."

She blinked. While she knew the rich treated matrimony more as alliances than pairings of the heart, she'd never heard it explained in such a...commercial fashion. Hardly the impassioned proposal she'd always dreamed of receiving.

She peered up at James. His handsome features might as well have been chiseled in stone, for all the emotion they conveyed. "In this equation, as you put it, why insert me? You could have an amiable partnership with any number of women. Women who haven't spent the last six months with an agenda."

"I could, perhaps." He did not sound interested in that prospect at all. "But I don't want them. I want the woman who demanded I let her bandage my hand in the study. The woman who won't take no for an answer, even when it's her own safety we're debating."

Her cheeks flushed. In that description, she sounded almost...strong. Like she'd been when Evan was still alive.

Then he continued, and the spark that had lit within her was dimmed by his practicality. "I've seen the way you are with my brother, and my sisters like you. What I want is a wife who already knows my family and can fit in seamlessly."

Significantly less flattering, yes, but given her current predicament, did it matter *why* he'd chosen her? The comfort of routine could not be overstated. He was not home often, but when he was, the entire atmosphere of the house changed. Lord Thomas adored him, and the servants were devoted to him.

That thought sobered her. The man had servants.

Sweet Mary, *she* was one of his staff! It was absurd to consider this.

Surreptitiously, she allowed her gaze to travel down the length of his frame to his starched cravat with its mail coach knot, at once dignified yet simple. To the cut of his coat, accentuating his broad shoulders. To his tan breeches showcasing his muscular legs, and his gleaming top boots with the silver tassels. All that power in one man. Could he protect her from Sauveterre? He seemed to think so.

He was the finest male specimen she'd ever laid eyes on, and he couldn't be hers. But oh, how she wanted him to be.

She forced her eyes forward. "Surely, you must be able to find those qualities in someone of your own class. I have no ways of increasing your stature in society. If anything, a bond with me would decrease your influence."

His lower lip curled when she said "influence."

"I am the Duke of Abermont," he said, as though that title contained every bit of information she'd need. When she did not show any sign of comprehension, he shrugged. ""The Spencer family is the third richest in all of the empire. Do you really think that the *ton* shall dare question my choice? If I present you as my wife, they will accept you. They are but a herd of cattle, easily rounded up and shown direction."

"How unbecomingly you speak of the people you consider friends." She could not curb her scorn, so surprised was she by his callous words.

He drew himself up, no longer appearing so at ease. "Let me make one thing clear to you," he ground out, the force of his words pelleting her as if they were stones. "Greater Society is *not* my friend. I consider few people truly my companions. Lord Haley, Mr. Drake, and a few others you are not acquainted with yet. The rest are mere acquaintances I associate with because my position demands it. Were I not duke, I would dispense with their company entirely."

"It must be a horridly lonely existence." She lifted her chin, refusing to cave. Given she'd spent six months under the scrutiny of his servants—the majority of whom refused to speak to her once they'd found out her relation to a viscount—she knew a few things about loneliness. "I repeat then, why *me*? What do you think I will add to your exclusive club?"

"Because you see me." His steely gaze sent a shiver of awareness up her back. In that look, she saw the emotions he held at bay, shimmering beneath the surface. "And I desperately need someone who will see the man behind my title."

Barely, just barely, she resisted the urge to press her palm up against his chest once more and feel the beat of his heart against her flushed skin. He was first a real, raw man before a duke.

Did she truly know him? She'd thought she'd drawn an accurate summary of his character over the last six months. With his close friends and family, he was apt to laugh and be merry. Yet in casual society, he was dour and reserved. What if underneath all this pomp and circumstance, he was as lost as she was, just waiting for someone to salve the wounds of the past?

"This...arrangement." She struggled to find the right term, finally deciding to refer to it more as a business enterprise than a true matrimonial intent. "What exactly would it entail? Say I agree to be your wife. What then?"

He seemed far more at ease when she followed his plans. "We would be married as soon as possible."

"The banns would need to be announced," she said. "That's three weeks, at least."

He shook his head. "Not if I procure a special license. I want to make sure you're protected from Sauveterre's grasp as soon as possible. Besides, once he hears of our marriage, he will act. Expediency is in our best interests."

"A special license would be a great cost to you."

"It is not as if I cannot afford it," he reminded her. "Besides, speed aside, I should personally like to be married at Abermont House, instead of in the village parish. A special license makes that possible, and thus a special license I shall purchase."

How empowering it must be to arrange things to one's liking without regard to expense. He'd promised to protect her.

Finally, after six brutal months of more questions than answers, she had the chance to bring Evan's killer to justice.

"I know it's a lot to think about," James said. "But I assure you I am absolutely serious. This is an arrangement that we will both benefit from. I think we'd suit."

We'd suit.

And even if they didn't suit, and this marriage damned her to a life of misery, how could she refuse? The alternative was to be at Sauveterre's mercy. James was her best chance now, probably her only chance.

She owed it to Evan.

His tone became softer, almost apologetic. "As tactless as it might sound, there are certain rights afforded to my class. Our laws do not take kindly to attacks on peers. When you become my duchess, you will then have an added layer of protection against Sauveterre."

Certain rights afforded to my class. She'd witnessed that first hand. How sickening to think that if Evan had been a duke, his murder would already be solved.

As if he could read her mind, James's voice became softer. "The system is highly flawed. Do not for one minute believe I don't know that. But my first concern here is *you.* Your safety. If I can use these laws in your favor, I will."

The timbre of his voice drew her to him. He had a smooth way of speaking, as though every word was the auditory equivalent of velvet. But this time, he was gritty. She liked him so much better for it. For the genuineness behind his speech. For the emotion that sank in every word and made her feel sheltered. She could believe in this version of him.

If she agreed, gone would be her old life. Her independence. Since James could give her the tools to destroy Sauveterre, she didn't care what she'd give up.

"I accept your proposal," she said. "I'll be your duchess."

"Very good." He did not reach for her hand, or pull her into an embrace, or do anything she'd imagined would be the correct response. He simply nodded—this nod was to tell her he appreciated her agreement. "You'll be a brilliant duchess."

She sincerely doubted that, but suspected he'd prefer her agreement to the truth. "I hope that I shall meet with your approval."

"I'm sure you will." He stood up, bidding her adieu.

As he headed toward the door, she noted again how his every stride seemed purposeful, deliberate. She watched him walk away, her gaze centering on his rounded buttocks.

He paused halfway out of the room, looking over his shoulder at her. Her cheeks colored. He couldn't tell that she'd been starring at his bottom, could he? No, better to act as though she'd simply been peering aimlessly off into the distance. She blinked, hoping she looked properly distracted.

A rare grin broke out across his lips. He hadn't fallen for her subterfuge, and he knew exactly what she'd been thinking. "Vivian?"

"James?" The flush to her cheeks was now an impossibly hot flame. She met his gaze, trying to convince herself that his amusement at her salaciousness was a good sign. He hadn't been aghast by her impropriety.

Rather, his eyes locked on hers, and for a second, his face was transformed into something softer. His baritone voice had never sounded so rich as in his next words. "Never doubt that it is *you* I want."

He did not give her time to react. He was gone before she could reply, which was probably for the best because she couldn't begin to puzzle out a suitable response to such a pronouncement.

She remained in the room long after he left. This was a good decision. A logical decision. Yet she couldn't shake the feeling she'd just exchanged everything she'd ever known for a life she couldn't begin to fathom.

CHAPTER 9

"YOU WANT TO wed the *governess*?" Elinor shifted on the chaise, her dark eyes fastening on his in a death glare that would have rivaled Josephine Bonaparte's most demanding moments.

James winced. He'd known telling his sisters would be difficult, but if Elinor's voice became any higher, dogs would be the only ones able to hear. At least Korianna was still in London. It had taken two months to repair the damage from the last argument she'd had with him.

Still, he'd chosen the parlor for this conversation because there were fewer things Elinor might hurl at him. A man could never be too careful. Using that same reasoning, he'd sent Vivian down to the village market and asked that the servants not disturb their meeting.

Arden crossed the room, coming to stand behind the plum chaise. Her face shadowed from Elinor's vision, Arden caught his eye and mouthed her apologies.

Not for the first time, James sent a silent prayer of gratitude that he had one sane sister. Because she'd been adopted as a child and raised as a Spencer, Arden didn't have the bloodline's famed hot temper.

"I'm sure Jim has his reasons," Arden began, placing a reassuring hand on Elinor's shoulder.

Elinor in turn grasped at her hand as though she was a life raft in a turbulent sea. "I can't imagine any of them would be valid. I presented you with a list of six appropriate candidates, and you choose our governess? Really, Jim."

James muffled his groan. Of course, Elinor would believe she could arrange his life better than he could. He crossed to the liquor cabinet and poured himself a finger of brandy. Three o'clock in the afternoon be damned.

He downed the glass in one fell gulp, gasping as the burn slid from his throat to his stomach. Schooling his features into a mask of determined resolution, he turned back around. "Ellie, has it occurred to you that you really don't get to have an opinion in who *I* marry?"

Elinor blinked.

Arden exchanged a glance with him, an impish smile curling her rouged lips.

Elinor recovered, draping her hand over the side of the couch as though she had all the time in the world to debate this with him. Once, she'd argued with him for four hours over the guest list for the end of the Season ball. He'd eventually given up and allowed her to invite half of the *ton*. His dislike of Society—and its marriage-minded mamas—was outmatched by his desire to end to the conversation.

"Don't be ridiculous," she sniffed. "You can like anyone you choose. I like the tiger that drives our carriage. I like the cobbler. I do not wish to marry them."

He told himself not to respond, but the words were out of his mouth before he could stop them. "That's completely different, and you know it."

"Is it, really?" Elinor arched her brows at him in

the perfect display of skepticism she'd perfected over years of winning arguments against him.

But this time, he vowed, it would be different. Vivian depended on him. He'd promised he'd protect her, and that was one promise he would never break.

Did you catch the blackguard who killed her?

He remembered Vivian's question that night in his office. He'd been able to *do* something about Louisa's death. Now that Vivian knew who had killed Evan, she wouldn't stop until Sauveterre was either captured or dead. People touched by grief surged onward, forsaking their own safety until their revenge was achieved. Considering her first attempt had brought a likely Bonaparte spy to their door, he shuddered to think of what else she'd encounter.

"Jim is quite capable of choosing his bride." Arden sunk down into the voluminous cushions of the hunter green armchair the Lion had always preferred. "Besides, I like Miss Loren, and so does Thomas."

"I like Miss Loren too," Elinor said. "If she hadn't entered service, I might even support this, though I'd of course think you could do better than the ward of a viscount."

"I was the ward of the duke," Arden reminded her, quietly but firmly.

Elinor's face softened. "Yes, but you were different."

"Why?" Arden arched a single brow at her. "If you're willing to give me a chance, why not Miss Loren?"

James smiled appreciatively at Arden. No matter what, she had always had his back.

"Because our father was already married and settled. Adopting a ward does not draw the same scrutiny as taking a wife." Elinor frowned, peering down her nose at them both. "Don't make me out to be the villain here, you two. A governess has no place as the Duchess of Abermont, no matter how delightful she might be. Our reputations are our best covers."

"You might want to tell Korianna that," James muttered.

Elinor sighed. "I have. Many times. She, like you, doesn't listen to me."

He took a seat on the settee across from her. "I listen, Ellie. I don't always agree with you, but I listen."

Whatever scandal stirred up by his marriage to Vivian Loren would be small in comparison to the attention of a full Season of old biddies cornering him, and the scandal sheets reporting on his every move. There simply wasn't time to find a wife before the Season started, man the Clocktower, manage his other responsibilities with Abermont House, and solve the Sauveterre problem.

Unless he married Vivian.

And he *wanted* to marry her, whether or not his cover depended on it. Even if he knew he didn't deserve a woman like Vivian.

"It will hardly be the worst scandal the *ton* has seen," Arden said. "Just think of Elizabeth Chudleigh, or even Prince George's affair with Mary Darby."

"There you have it, she could be an actress," James retorted with a wry grin at Arden. "That would give you apoplexy. Be grateful Miss Loren is a governess."

Arden sent him a reproving look that effectively summarized as "don't poke the bear."

"'Grateful' and 'governesses' do not belong in the same sentence," Elinor snipped.

"There are other matters at play here too." Advancing to the chaise, he pulled out the notes he'd received from Vivian and handed them to Elinor. She read each one, her forehead crinkling in confusion. When she'd finished with the notes, she passed them over to Arden.

He summarized everything Vivian had told him the day before.

Arden grimaced as she gave him back the letters.

"What do we know about Sauveterre? I don't recognize the name."

"Nor do I," James said.

In tandem, they both turned expectant gazes toward Elinor.

Elinor's eyes widened, feigning modesty. "Why would you think I'd know him?"

Usually, James would have rolled his eyes, but today he'd indulge her, for Miss Loren's sake. "Because you remember every single enemy agent we've encountered."

She smiled drolly. "I suppose that's true. But no, he's not familiar to me either. I could certainly check our records."

As soon as they left the room, he strongly suspected his eldest sister would be rubbing her hands together with glee over consulting her files in the secret room.

And not for the first time, he'd be grateful for her efforts.

"If you can't find anything there, send Korianna to the main archives," he ordered, as he would have with any other agent.

Korianna was already in London, and Elinor's illness had become too unpredictable for her to travel much. One day she'd be fine, and the next she could not move from the pain.

Elinor's posture stiffened at his dictatorial tone. "Of course." Her glare told him that his command should have gone without saying.

"I'm sure if there's a connection, Elinor will find it," Arden interjected smoothly, her eyes flickering from his face to Elinor's and back. As soon as her sister's stance relaxed, the uneasiness left Arden's expression.

Always the peacemaker. As the youngest sibling in a house full of firebrands, Arden had often been tasked with interference. When they were younger, it had been him and Elinor against Korianna and Louisa. Their lines had been drawn, their fights routine. Now that Louisa was gone, they were combatants without allegiances. The rhythm of their family was forever changed.

He'd lost his little sister, but he'd be damned if he lost Vivian too.

"We need to move fast," James said. "No more close calls."

"Always have a contingency plan." A smile ghosted Elinor's lips. "One of Papa's favorite expressions.

"So Sauveterre suspects you," Arden mused. "But not the rest of us?"

James nodded. "From what Miss Loren said, I don't think he knows about any of you, or even the Clocktower. He must have found something that made him think I'm working for the Crown."

Elinor pursed her lips, running her hand down the back of the divan. "Precautions will need to be taken. You are absolutely certain this girl is telling the truth?"

He thought of how damnably distraught she'd looked in the conservatory. How he'd drawn her close, his arm around her, never wanting to let her go. The way her head nestled against his shoulder, as if he was truly a hero. And he knew, with the same level of certainty that he knew he'd never be the hero she deserved, that nothing she had told him was a lie.

"She's telling the truth," he said, looking straight into his sisters' eyes. "I know it. The threat against Miss Loren is very real."

Something in his tone must have stopped her, for Elinor opened her mouth to protest, and then shut it. She settled back upon the divan and waited for him to continue. In the chair beside her, Arden remained silent. Yet without needing to meet her eyes, he could feel her gaze upon him. Observing him. Calculating any minor shifts in his emotion. He'd taught Arden how to interrogate, and damned if she didn't use his own tactics against him.

"The bastard sent her teeth." James's fist clenched on the arm of his chair, a futile attempt to master his rage at the memory.

Elinor's nose wrinkled. "How...odd."

"Her dead brother's teeth."

"Oh," Arden and Elinor said at once.

"It wasn't enough to coerce her. He had to torment and threaten her too." His nails dug into his palm, the sharp stab of pain keeping him alert. Reminding him he was alive, when so many others more deserving than him weren't. "She needs us to protect her."

She needs me.

And maybe, he needed her. Not because of some great love, for he'd long since stopped believing that a spy could ever achieve real happiness. But around her, he began to see glimpses of the man he'd been before Louisa's death.

He needed to be that man again. For the Clocktower. For his own sanity.

"We should help," Arden said, with a plaintive look toward her eldest sister. "We can't allow an ingénue to go up against a murderer."

Elinor let out a loud sigh of exasperation, but James could tell from the sparkle in her eyes that she'd relented. "I suppose a governess in the family isn't the worst that could happen."

No, the worst was another death. Miss Loren's vivaciousness extinguished. Her corpse cast out into the stews of Seven Dials like her brother.

He wouldn't let that happen. She'd be protected as his duchess. Afforded the same rights as any peer— though that hadn't helped to save his sister.

He had to do better. To *be* better. "I want this man captured. Whatever we have to do to get him, we'll do."

THE HOURS BETWEEN midnight and three in the morning had become James's favorite. Every night since Louisa's death, insomnia besieged him; an uninvited guest that long overstayed its welcome. But in his sleepless state, he'd discovered the peacefulness of silence in a house that was rarely ever quiet.

In those magical three hours when he roamed the grounds, he was neither a duke nor the head of the Clocktower. He was simply a man communing with nature.

Tonight, five days after his proposal to Vivian Loren, he strolled onto the front lawn of Abermont House. The full moon was half-hidden by murky clouds, providing moderate guidance for his walk. He did not carry a lantern with him. After so many years of training, he felt more at home under the cover of darkness than he did in the harsh light of day.

James breathed in the crisp night air and said a silent prayer for fortitude in the coming weeks. He stopped, leaning forward to smell the fresh blooms of the rose bushes lining the drive. God, how the flowers reminded him of Vivian. The romantic scent of her soap. The softness of her skin. That delicate flush of her cheeks, so much like the first buds of spring.

The sudden crack of a twig interrupted his reverie. His senses on high alert, James spun around. A figure appeared in the distance. A woman, he guessed. Tall and reedy, her frame was almost boyish—were it not for the outline of her gown in the moonlight, he would have marked her as a man. A peal of recognition sounded in his mind, though from this distance, he didn't want to chance that he was wrong about her identity. She was too far away for him to be absolutely certain, and he believed in caution above all else.

Moving swiftly, she slipped down the tree-lined

drive. She knew exactly what spots would shelter her from the gas lamps. He advanced, keeping sufficient distance between them that he remained shrouded in shadow, yet near enough he could positively identify her. She turned to face him, and he ducked behind a tree for cover, peeking out from behind the trunk.

Of course. *Korianna.* She wasn't due back from London for another two nights, but she'd always loved to make a grand entrance.

It was a trait she'd shared with Louisa.

He frowned as she stepped out into the open, tilting her head up toward the sky. As if she'd ascertained that there was no threat, and she needn't be careful now.

Come now, Kori, you can do better.

All-too-familiar tension seized hold of his gut and twisted. When would she learn not to be so damned reckless? Hadn't they lost enough already? James crouched, in one smooth movement pulling out the knife sheathed in his boot and standing back up.

Countless lectures had done nothing. He could not pull her from sanctioned missions—such was the lone saddle he could put upon this wild horse. While he had retreated inside himself, throwing himself deeper and deeper into the management of the Clocktower, she had come to live for the field.

So he'd use language she'd understand. Violence and blood. He'd remind her that they must always be careful. A simple attack not meant to do more than scare her into being sensible.

He crept closer. He waited until she paused. Her arm moved as though she brushed something off her skirt. Seizing the opportunity, he launched himself onto her, wrapping his forearm around her throat. The blade of his knife pressed into her throat.

He *should* have had the advantage. He had at least fifty pounds on her.

Yet before he could process what was happening,

she'd slammed the ball of her foot into his knee. Pain shot through him. His grip on the knife wavered. Taking advantage of his weakness, she placed one hand above his elbow, the other below it. With one swift motion, she spun around, using his arm as a hinge so she could escape his hold.

Bloody, bloody hell. His attempt at teaching her had been turned upon him.

Korianna fixed her hat back to the proper jaunty angle and smoothed out the wrinkles in her dress. Her brown eyes gleamed impishly, a sardonic smile curling up her rouged lips.

She raised her hand to her brow, executing a mock salute. "You're getting sloppy. Too many hours spent in the office make Jim a very dull boy, you know."

He slid the knife back into his boot, trying to ignore her remark, even though a part of him wondered if she was right. He hadn't been out in the field since Louisa's death. Could he really keep Vivian safe? He swallowed down his doubt. Yes. One failed attack did not negate years of training. He'd beaten Korianna as many times as she'd thrashed him in the past. That's what had made them good sparring partners. She fought with passion, making her attacks harder to predict but oft less effective; he fought with logic, proven combined steps and greater estimated damage.

Still, tomorrow he'd start doubling his mills. A session with Arden in the morning, and his regular one with Richard in the evening.

Straightening his waistcoat, he faced Korianna, keeping his expression impassive. "One victory, Kori. I needn't remind you of the last time we met like this." She'd ended up with a bloody nose and bruised ribs.

Korianna shrugged. "I survived just fine."

He resisted the urge to roll his eyes. "In most circles, it's considered polite to inform the host before you show up on his doorstep. In this family, it's a matter of life or death. I could have slit your throat."

Korianna let out a loud huff of protest. "You tried and failed."

His brows wrinkled. "I'm serious. I knew it was you all along, but you still weren't aware I was sneaking up on you."

For a second, doubt flickered across her face. It was more self-examination than he usually had from her, so he'd consider it a victory.

He took her arm, escorting her down the lane. "Why didn't you write?"

She shrugged, the casual bravado to her motion reminding him more of an insouciant lad than a finely bred miss. "Didn't seem a need to, when it's a day trip by hack. I'd already be here by the time you received the missive. The bloody post's so slow."

"Language, Kori," he replied automatically, though he knew it wouldn't do a damn bit of good.

She rolled her eyes. "Oh, let me be, won't you?"

He suppressed a sigh, reminding himself that however much Korianna irritated him, she was still family and family needed to be held close. All too quickly that age-old pang of loss edged up on him, and he shoved his hands into his coat pockets, trying to ignore it.

The mission, he reminded himself. Talk of the mission would steady him, giving him purpose. Korianna had gone to the records room at the Clocktower headquarters.

"Did you get it?" he asked, beginning to walk back to the house.

Korianna shot him a look. "Of course I have it. When I have ever failed you?"

"Hanover Square." He answered too quickly, for her expression soured.

"That was *one* bomb, Jim, and it wasn't even a large one." She frowned at him, refusing to take the arm he proffered to escort her down the drive. Instead, she strode forward, one full stride in front of him. A difficult task, in her dress and petticoats. But that was Korianna: audacious, infuriating, and highly competitive.

"One bomb in a square the Beau Monde frequents," he reminded her. "The mission was to gather intelligence."

"And I did one better," Korianna said. "Arden and I snagged you the enemy agent you wanted, and we did it without having to involve Wickham."

"Just because it worked in this case doesn't mean it'll always work." He sped up, grabbing for her arm to spin her around so that she faced him. "Listen to me, chit. You could have been caught."

Korianna wrenched her arm away from his grip. "I'm not some child you can order around anymore. I wasn't caught. I'm never caught."

"Kori—" He gave up halfway through another attempt to force caution into her. After they'd dealt with Sauveterre, next on his list was managing Korianna. "What did you discover about Evan Loren?"

"Nine trips overall. I cross-examined the timeline of Miss Loren's brother's tenure at Hoare's Bank against known covert activities at the time." Officially, the Alien Office's main purpose was to monitor entrances and exits into the country by foreigners. Korianna had gone to their headquarters to check their files against the Clocktower's. She tilted her head toward him, a curious expression on her face. "You know, this really would have been a better job for Elinor."

"She's indisposed," James said with chagrin. Elinor could walk into any records room and immediately know the layout, but when her illness flared, traveling became near impossible. The mere act of moving from bed was taxing.

Korianna frowned. "Again? That's twice in the last four months." She dropped back to walk with him, now accepting his arm. They'd made it down the driveway, and now stood at the front of the house. Steering him toward the garden, Korianna opened the gate. "I've spent all day cloistered in a hack. The night air is lovely."

He agreed, and they set off down the path. "Tell me about the trips."

"I copied down the information for Ellie, or as much as I could get without bloody Rupert hanging over my shoulder, peppering me with questions about her." Korianna rolled her eyes. "I swear to all that is holy, if she doesn't put him out of his misery, *I* will."

"Poor Castwell," James laughed. The head archivist was hopelessly enamored with Elinor, though she ignored his attentions. "But at least his fancy for our sister is useful. At times."

"I'd like him much better if he stayed out of my way," Korianna grumbled. "As it stands, it appears Evan Loren went to France six times in the last three years, and Switzerland thrice, under the guise of work for Hoare's Bank."

"Anything match our missions, or French activity?"

Korianna's nod confirmed his suspicions. "Five of the trips match."

"So he's an agent. But whose? Definitely not ours." He and Elinor were the sole people to know the real identities of all the Clocktower agents. The rest of the spies went by code-names exclusively, unless they had prior knowledge of each other, as in the case of Deacon and Richard.

"I suspect the Alien Office," Korianna mused. "If he were French, there would be more crossover with Bonaparte. The events that flagged are British missions."

James let out a sigh of relief. At least Vivian would have the solace of knowing her brother was loyal to his country.

"I didn't make inquiries to Wickham's assistants," Korianna said. "I figured you'd want to do that."

"Good." The spymaster hadn't mentioned Evan Loren when he'd performed Vivian's background investigation for her governess position.

If they went to Wickham now, without the shield of Vivian being his duchess, there was a grave chance that she could be taken into custody. He couldn't risk that. He felt it in his gut that she'd been used by Sauveterre—she didn't deserve to be gaoled as a possible enemy to the Crown.

"After the wedding, I'll contact Wickham myself." They had come to the bench where he'd found Vivian sitting last week. The moonlight shone down on the white-painted wood, silhouetting the alcove. He paused in front of it, his hand on the armrest.

Once he formed an accurate picture of Evan's life, he'd know how the man ended up in Sauveterre's crosshairs. And from that, he'd extrapolate how *he* had come to this Sauveterre's attention.

He carded a hand through his hair, frowning at the bench. Puzzles had never been his favorite. He was a problem-solver, a delegator. The pieces of this mystery whipped through his mind, never fitting together. He knew enough to proceed on his current course. Enough to suppose that Evan Loren really was one of Wickham's, and a damnably skilled agent at that. Wickham wouldn't have protected the identity of a lower agent in Vivian's background check, not to him. The Clocktower and the Alien Office worked together, but ultimately Wickham was the supreme power.

Korianna watched him in a rare moment of silence.

He shifted uncomfortably, not used to her scrutiny. "Is there something else?"

"Vivian Loren. Ellie's letter about your engagement made it all sound so...dispassionate." She spoke with softness unfamiliar to him, more sister than spy now. "But I'm concerned."

For a moment, they could be naught more than siblings, discussing his betrothal as though it affected two lives, and not the fate of the nation. "Because she was a governess?"

Korianna shook her head. "Of course not. In fact, I relish your name appearing in the scandal sheets instead of mine, for once."

James's grimace at that made her laugh more. Though he'd never admit it to her face, he admired her ability to shake off what the rest of the world thought of her.

"Ellie mentioned the threat on Miss Loren's life." Korianna's next words came in a long stream, with barely a breath taken in between. "If you're doing this out of a sense of a duty, there has to be another way we can keep her safe. You shouldn't commit to marrying her because you feel some sort of misguided notion that you have to protect everyone."

"I *do* have to protect everyone." Fist balled at his side, he spoke through gritted teeth. He couldn't expect Korianna to understand, not when she threw herself in danger's way at the drop of a hat.

"She's gone, Jim," Korianna whispered. "Martyring yourself won't bring her back. As for the rest of us, you have to trust we know how to live our own lives."

He turned away from the bench, back down the trail. Back toward Abermont House. Back toward Vivian, who he'd vowed to protect with his life, and who somehow managed to pry out of him the very things he did not wish to talk about.

Korianna followed after him, for once not turning the walk back into a race. As she pulled open the door to the conservatory, he shook his head. "This marriage—it's not just the duty. It's something more. *She's* something more."

A grin stretched across Korianna's face. "That's all I needed to know."

CHAPTER 10

THE NEXT DAY, Vivian remained in the drawing room after the appointment with the milliner. Miss Spencer had placed an order for several dresses last month that were now ready. Lady Elinor had suggested that since Vivian was of similar proportions to Miss Spencer, she could take the gowns instead. A few alternations would need to be made, but by the wedding Vivian would have several gowns suitable for a duchess. The rest of her new wardrobe would arrive in the following weeks.

Swallowing, she ran her hand down her old dress. What would it be like to be constantly adorned in the finest fashions? It seemed extraordinary.

And scary, for it was all so very new.

Elinor had gone back upstairs to her quarters, but Vivian had nothing else planned for the day. She glanced at the clock. Two in the afternoon. Three hours still to dinner. If only she could will the minutes to move faster. The hectic schedule she'd grown used to in the past half a year was suddenly empty, except for any wedding plans or meals with the family. She still made it a point to visit with Thomas after his lessons, but soon he would have a new governess.

She'd go mad from this inactivity. Taking a seat on one of the dainty blue cushioned chairs, she planted her feet firmly on the carpet, resisting the urge to jiggle her legs.

She stood, going to the small group of books atop the mantel. A book would calm her nerves. Selecting a leather-bound volume with the simple title of "Family" embossed on the side, she made her way back to the chair. Flipping open the book, she quickly discovered it was not a work of literature at all, but instead a portrait album. The first page featured a sketch of an older couple in with the caption "Edward and Margaret Spencer, 1583." The book continued on, with drawings of important members of the family.

Should she put the book back? It seemed so personal. But in a few days, she'd be a Spencer too. Shouldn't she learn as much as she could about her new family? "Better to have all the facts before you form an opinion," she'd told Thomas a fortnight ago when he'd asked her why he must learn ancient history. "The past influences the present. Without it, we are lost."

Turning the page again, Vivian decided that since the book was out in the open, it was fit for public consumption. She skipped to the next page. The portraits appeared to be from the reign of Charles, before that unseemly affair with Cromwell. Each stately ancestor of the Spencers was more impressive than the next. *"Lady Henrietta Williams, second cousin to Elizabeth Stuart."* Sweet Mary, James was related to the blooming Queen of Bohemia.

She bit her lip, proceeding to the next page. It became worse from there. Page after page, decades of influential people. She should have used this blasted album to teach Thomas history, since almost every name in it had left their mark on Britain's past.

Her fingers curled around the locket charm she wore around her neck.

She was a Loren. Her name meant nothing to the *ton*. Evan, her dear, sweet, wonderful brother, had been deemed so unimportant by the Runners that they'd left his murder unsolved.

Vivian shoved the book off her lap. It landed upside down on the floor with a plop, somehow fitting when her stomach felt like it was sinking to the floor too.

"Abysmal ending?"

She hadn't noticed James hovering in the doorway. Her cheeks flamed with embarrassment. She bent down to pick up the book as he ambled into the room.

Dash it all.

She couldn't hide the album from his sight, not when he sauntered over to her, leaning over her shoulder.

"I haven't seen that book in years," he said. "It was Elinor's project with Thomas's mother, Juliana. The new duchess wanted to know all about the 'illustrious Spencer clan,' as she called us."

"It slipped from my hands," Vivian lied, hoping she wouldn't have to explain further.

His brow arched as if he didn't believe her, but he let her untruth slide without comment. Sinking down on the cushion next to her, he pried the book from her hands, glancing at the page where she'd left off.

"Ah, Great-Uncle Herman." He held the book out to her, pointing at the stoic man with far more facial hair than could ever have been fashionable. "No one liked him—or so my grandmother claimed when I was growing up."

Vivian scooted back on the settee, turning her body so that she could see both him and the book. "What did Uncle Herman do to that made him so unlikable?"

"If I remember correctly, he liked pickled fish too much. Thankfully, Great-Aunt Matilda had no sense of smell. So she thought he was delightful." James smiled, and she was struck by how handsome he looked when he smiled.

In a few days, he would be *her* James—in name, at least.

Someday, she'd learn how to make him smile often. Someday, when the past did not have such a hold on them, and they could breathe without the ache of loss.

Someday, if Sauveterre did not kill her first.

She shoved that thought from her mind, forcing herself to focus on the story of his relatives. "It sounds as though Herman and Matilda were a match made in heaven."

"Or hell, because apparently Matilda was an appalling jaw-me-dead. Between the two of them, they could clear a room in record time." Passing the book to her, he pointed at Great-Aunt Matilda, a severe woman with a feathered headdress that could have poked out an eyeball if she came too close.

"Well, at least they had each other." She took his story as a sign that the universe promised happy endings for some people—if not all. That gave her hope.

"'Til death did they part," James said with a chuckle. "I personally think they should have buried Uncle Herman with a jar of pickled fish. My grandmother, however, caned me for suggesting so."

She winced. "I suddenly see where your sisters get their fire from."

"That's putting it mildly." He spun the book around again, indicating a small oil painting of a woman with long chocolate locks and dazzling green eyes.

"She's beautiful." Vivian glanced from the picture to his face. There was a definite familial resemblance in James's strong chin, his wavy dark hair and wide forehead.

"My mother," he explained. "Korianna is the spitting image of her. Has her temper too. Why, once in a disagreement with my father, Mama even flung a vase against the wall."

Vivian's brows arched. "It could have been worse."

James paused in turning to the next page. He gave a short nod, this time a prompt for her to continue.

She shrugged. "Your mother could have thrown it at the duke's head instead."

He let out a bark of laughter at that, and she relished the sound. Loved this side of him, so loose and casual. She saw herself spending the rest of her life with this man.

She saw herself in love with him.

And in that moment, tucked away in the drawing room with him with all his family history surrounding them, she wanted so badly for that dream to come true. A marriage built on genuine affection. A marriage where he'd chosen *her* because out of all of the women in England, he adored her the most.

He stood up, going to the drink sideboard in the corner of the room. Soon, he came back with two drinks. He passed the first glass to her, and set the second on the low table whilst he sat down.

Picking the glass back up, he eyed it with disdain. "I hate sherry, really."

"I will confess it is not my favorite either." She took a sip, then placed her glass back down on the low table. "Why drink it, then?"

"Because Elinor insists it is not acceptable to stock the parlor with brandy. Ah well, down the hatch it goes." James drained half his glass in one gulp, making such a disgusted face that Vivian couldn't help but laugh.

She gestured toward the door. "It is a big house. Surely there are other rooms besides your office where you've secreted brandy, away from Lady Elinor's control."

He nodded again, so swiftly she did not doubt he had seventeen bottles of brandy stashed in different rooms. She was about to ask him why he did not drink them instead, when he stopped with the sherry glass halfway to his mouth and he looked straight at her.

"If I was to go get one of those bottles, I'd have to leave you."

Her heart fluttered rapidly. Oh, his grave voice did naughty things to her insides. When his gaze met hers, the sheer *emotion* behind those stormy grey eyes lit the most private parts of her anatomy on fire in the most delicious way.

All she could think of was how his gaze had fastened on her that night in his library, and how rich his voice had been when he'd told her to never doubt that she was the one he wanted.

She matched his honesty with her own. "I don't want you to go."

He reached for her, covering her smaller palm with his massive, tanned hand. Her gloves were thinner today, cloth instead of kid leather. His fingers felt calloused and rough, which made no sense for an aristocratic man. But he was a Corinthian, his athletic body muscled and hard, so she dismissed the irregularity.

"I'm not going anywhere." The softness of his voice caressed her like his hand. "You'll have me by your side for a long time, my dear. Once we say our vows, you'll wish you could get rid of me."

Was it her imagination, or was there a hint of self-loathing in his voice? Releasing her hand, he shifted on the settee. He picked the album back up and returned to his perusal.

"I doubt very much that will be true." She chose her words carefully, lest she admit what was on the tip of her tongue: the idea of a lifetime with him was becoming more appealing the more she knew him.

Since that night in the office when she'd bandaged his hand, he'd treated her with kindness at every turn.

At every turn, he'd proved he was worthy of her trust.

She peeked over his shoulder. A sketch of his mother riding a gorgeous stallion, captured in the moment right before the horse took off over a jump.

"She was certainly fearless," Vivian remarked.

"Yes," James agreed. "I don't have many memories of her, as she died when I was still a child, but I do remember some things. Her favorite color was yellow, so she always insisted we have yellow flowers around the house. She liked carrots, but hated turnips. Specific moments are harder to recall."

She knew all too well what he meant. "When the carriage accident killed my parents, I was seven. For a few years, I could remember everything about them. The sound of my father's voice. The twinkle in my mother's eye when she was proud of us."

He ran his thumb over the sketch of his mother, tracing the shape of her face. "Over time the memories fade, don't they? Until all that's left is a wisp of time. You'll hear a certain melody, or feel a tinge when you eat a meal you know she would have enjoyed."

"Every time I smell gardenias, I think of my mother's perfume. But were it not for sketches of her, I don't think I'd remember what she looked like." Vivian swiped the glass of sherry off the table, taking a long sip. It did nothing to quiet her mind. "It's going to be like this for Evan, isn't it? Already, I can feel the recollections slipping away."

For a moment, there was no sound in the room but their breathing. They were two hearts beating in tandem, but each lost to their own memories.

"You can't bring him back," James said finally. "But together we'll make sure Sauveterre never hurts anyone again."

"It'll have to be enough." She closed her eyes,

trying to recall her last night with Evan. Though she could still clearly picture him, the details were hazy, as if she viewed a portrait where the paint smudged.

Sighing, she took the book from his hands, flipping toward the back. Perhaps there was a sketch of him as a child; something that would make him laugh again. She located a few pictures of Korianna and Elinor, but none of him. Moving to the next page, she read the caption underneath a sketch of a young child she did not recognize with ribbon-tied braids.

Louisa Spencer, age 4.

She tried to turn the page before he noticed. As if by not seeing the picture, she could erase the past—but she of all people knew that was impossible.

"Don't." James placed his thumb on the book, preventing her from turning the page. "I'd like to remember her this way, for once."

Vivian released her hold on the book, letting it rest in his lap. "She looks happy here."

"She was always happy." His voice took on a faraway quality, lost to memories. "Maybe that's what I remember most. Her cheerfulness—the way the atmosphere changed when she entered a room. She was so vibrant. Everyone around her became a bit more animated."

"I'm sorry you lost her." She wanted to reach for him. Wanted so badly to ease his pain. But how could she soothe his hurt when she couldn't stop her own? When everything she did was motivated by the need for revenge?

His sister had been ripped from him, and she couldn't change that. But she could listen, and she could try to understand.

Her hand edged forward, toward his, her pinkie finger grazing the corner of the page. "I would have liked to meet Lady Louisa."

He moved his hand over, so that his thumb stroked her pinkie. "I think she would have liked you."

Warmth emanated from that tiny touch of their fingers. "You think so?"

He shifted on the settee, bringing his thigh in contact with hers. Again, heat filled her—flooding her body as he smiled at her, a bittersweet, genuine smile. She could not take away his pain, but she'd help him to remember the better times in addition to the sorrow.

"If you can fence half as good as you claim, you would have been her favorite sister." He looped his thumb around her pinkie, his larger hand around her smaller one. "Do you have a portrait of Evan? I should like to know the brother who was so important to you."

"In my locket." She pulled her finger from his grasp to reach behind and undo the knot in the ribbon around her neck. The brass locket dropped into her hands, and she opened up the clasp to reveal the portrait of Evan. "This is him."

James took the locket from her, holding the portrait up to examine it. "Ah, I see the family resemblance. Good cheekbones on you both."

"I look like my mother, I'm told," she said. "Evan took after my father."

"It is good to know the man I'm fighting for." He motioned for her to turn around. Then he leaned forward, the family album still spread across his lap, his breath hot against her bare skin. And his nimble fingers tied the ribbon swiftly around her neck, too swiftly, for then he was gone again, back to his side of the settee. "I like that locket."

"Lady Elinor would prefer I replace it." She spoke without thought, regretting it afterward. She should not cause strife between him and his sisters—not when she hoped to become a part of their family.

He shook his head. "Perish the thought. I believe you should hold onto the parts of your past that bring you comfort."

She reached out again, this time brave enough to

take his hand in hers.

THE NIGHT BEFORE he became a married man, James paced through the conservatory, shrouded in darkness. Perhaps a man such as him did not *deserve* the light. For no matter how Vivian made him feel in those moments when they were alone, he could not forget the man he'd been before. He was a spy, damn it, and he was good at it: examining a man's weak spots and gaging where an attack would do the most damage; identifying an enemy's fear and using it against them; finding that one key detail in a series of seemingly unimportant facts.

Soon, that knowledge would be Vivian's too. Imprinted upon her mind, shaping her conduct for years to come. Making her something new, but not necessarily something better. It was unavoidable. Her life was at risk. She'd become a target, and without the Clocktower's help, she would die. He knew that deep in his gut, in the same way he knew that Louisa's death had been his fault.

A few more strides brought him to the bench they'd sat on when she'd confessed to spying upon him. His little ingénue, trying so hard to be covert and failing miserably. After two weeks under his tutelage, she'd know the basics of spycraft. And she'd be safe enough. Safer than she'd be without him.

But after this? After Sauveterre was captured, and Vivian had her justice? Not her revenge, because he'd be damned if he turned her into a killer like him. What would become of them? Would she still want him after she knew every side of him? He was not the dandy duke the *ton* wanted him to be. He'd seen too much, done too much, to be anything but jaded.

He dropped down onto the bench, stretching out

his long legs in front of him. When he was with Vivian, for a few seconds—a few minutes, sometimes—he forgot who he was. The broken man beneath his polished exterior didn't feel so broken. But months from now, once the immediate threat dissipated, Vivian would realize that she hadn't contributed to her brother's death, after all. She would come to terms with her grief, while James would remain mired in his guilt.

"I suspected you'd be here." Arden's voice drifted to him from several paces away.

He turned in his seat, draping his arm over the back of the bench. He'd been so lost in his thoughts he hadn't heard her approach. But that was no surprise. Sometimes he barely recognized the little girl his father had found wandering in the Whitechapel rookery, lost and alone. She was as much a spy as any born Spencer.

Arden stopped behind the bench, resting her hand on his shoulder. He leaned into the weight, grateful for her reassurance. Whenever he'd had a problem in the last fifteen years—sometimes before he knew it himself—Arden had been there. Always.

"Oh, Jim." Her soft voice filled with pity as she caught sight of his expression.

From anyone else, pity made him defensive. He'd learned quickly to project a veneer of confidence, so that people wouldn't think him weak—or worse, ask too many questions. With Arden, he couldn't hide.

"I'd hoped you were finally experiencing some peace." She came to his side of the bench, slowly sitting down beside him.

"As the Lion always said, 'there'll be peace when our work is done, and our work is never done.'"

"You always do that," Arden chided him. "In fact, I can't remember the last time I heard you refer to him as 'Father.' It's always 'the Lion.' Why is that?"

He blinked. "No reason."

Arden gave him one of her characteristic "you're

not going to get rid of me that easily" arch looks.

James ran a hand across his chin. "I don't know. He might have been our father, but he was a legend. Isn't that more important than whatever he was to us?"

Arden shook her head. "We were taught to think that way. You especially, since you're the heir. You don't get a chance to see the smaller picture—to see each life individually. The stakes are so much higher for you, our leader."

"'Lose one life to save a hundred,'" James quoted, recalling the Lion's words when a favorite agent had died foiling an assassination plot against the Prime Minister.

"Yet you punish yourself every day over Louisa's death." Arden laid her hand on top of his.

He thought of the portrait in the family album. Louisa's wide smile, her front tooth missing. The ribbons in her hair he knew were pink, though the sketch was charcoal. He remembered the dirt always streaking her hands, even as she aged—she'd been so daring, never daunted by anything.

But he couldn't recall the sound of her laugh.

"Every day, I remember a little less about Louisa." He did not know if he spoke to himself or Arden. With one foot in the past and the other in his new future with Vivian, he lacked a hold on the present. "I was with Vivian today, going over Elinor's family album. For an hour with her, I made jokes and I laughed."

Arden smiled. "If the memories are becoming cloudy, then that's a sign. Your mind's trying to tell you that it's time for you to be happy."

He sighed. "I don't know."

"I do. When you told me you'd asked Miss Loren to marry you, I thought maybe you'd found a way to be happy," Arden said. "I've seen the way you look at her. If anyone deserves happiness, it's you, Jim."

He didn't believe her, but God, how he longed to. Arden knew him better than anyone else. From the moment the Lion had brought Arden home that stormy night fifteen years ago, they'd been as thick as thieves.

"I'm coming with you," Arden declared, breaking into his thoughts.

"Where?"

"When you take Miss Loren for training," Arden said. "My trunk's already packed."

"Ah." The trip he'd planned to tell Vivian was a wedding trip, but in actuality was Clocktower protocol.

He didn't have the slightest idea how he'd explain Arden's presence on such a trip, yet he couldn't bring himself to ask her to stay away. Having her there made sense, from an instructional perspective. If Vivian were going to learn self-defense, it would be better that she received help from someone of similar build.

"I'm going so you don't always have to be the spy." Arden patted his hand, rising from the bench. "Let me watch your back, while you spend time with your new wife."

It was a nice idea, but highly improbable in practice. "You know the mission comes first."

"For me, yes," Arden answered. "I checked the manifest. We've a good team in place. Elinor scheduled Nixon to drive, and I'll be taking Northley too, of course."

He shuddered at the mention of Arden's maid, who'd picked up more than a few defense maneuvers in her time with the family. He now had a perpetual fear of parasols thanks to that old woman.

Arden smiled at his reaction. "Leave the intrigue to us. Make something real with Miss Loren."

He stayed on that bench long after she left, listening to the silence of the conservatory. Smelling the flowers that reminded him so much of Vivian. Maybe it was time for a new mission. For the last year, he'd held onto Louisa's memory, punishing himself.

He had thrown himself into work and little else. He stopped living.

But every time Vivian entered the room, his breath caught in his throat. She'd somehow managed to demolish his walls. He felt *alive* again. And that feeling centered him, gave him purpose. Whatever Sauveterre tried to bring to them, he'd fight, and he'd win. For Vivian. He might not be the man she deserved, but he was the man best suited to guarding her.

And he would not fail this time.

CHAPTER 11

PRECISELY FOURTEEN DAYS after the Duke of Abermont had proposed to her, Vivian stood beside him at the newly constructed altar in his family's parlor and prayed to God that she was making the right decision.

The old grandfather clock in the hall chimed eight in the morning, signaling the beginning of the wedding. Vivian grasped the bouquet of lilacs tightly in her hand, her knuckles no doubt whitening from the force of her hold. The flowers were the same color as the silk dress she wore, with its lavender netting, spangles, and long train.

She glanced over her shoulder at the assembled coterie. James's friends and family, for the ceremony had been arranged too swiftly for her to write to her old friends in Devon. She shouldn't have been surprised by the efficiency with which the Spencer family had arranged the wedding. Everything they did was quick and well organized, with nary a detail forgotten.

Still, she wished she had *someone* from back home. Someone who'd help her remember that she could remain largely the same person she'd always been, even when surrounded with such opulence. Someone who would console her when the threat on her life made her doubt the wisdom of staying instead of running.

Upon a nod from James, the minister opened his common prayer book and began to read in a sonorous tone, "Dearly beloved, we are gathered together here in the sight of God, and in the face of this congregation, to join together this Man and this Woman in holy Matrimony..."

Surreptitiously, she peered out from behind her veil at the duke, standing on her left side. Her eyes traveled from his startlingly black crop of hair, those smooth waves she wanted so badly to run her fingers through, to his wide forehead and his rounded chin. This man, with his hawk nose and his serious eyes that seemed to track her every movement, would be her *husband*. She'd see him every morning and end her days with him.

It had been so long since she'd been excited by the prospect of anything so truly scintillating, she'd almost forgotten what it felt like.

As the minister addressed the congregation, explaining that the purpose of marriage was primarily to procreate, Vivian's nails dug deeper into the ribbon around the bouquet. She let her eyes drift down James's frame, her cheeks pinking at the mere thought of being that close to him.

Of being *with* him. He stood with his strapping shoulders back, his kerseymere coat expertly tailored to display his muscular chest. And his pantaloons, God help her, his pantaloons were skin-tight, the drop front hugging that private area of his body she most certainly should not be pondering.

The masculinity of him almost took her breath away. How positively sinful, to have these stirrings of desire for him when she ought to be focused on pledging her obedience to him.

"I require and charge you both, as ye will answer at the dreadful day of judgement when the secrets of all hearts shall be disclosed..." The minister's eagle-eyed glare zeroed in on her, as if he could sense the tawdry turn Vivian's thoughts had taken. "If either of you know any impediment, why ye may not be lawfully joined together in Matrimony, ye do now confess it."

Vivian gulped. Would anyone offer a protest? It would make sense if the Spencers didn't want a lowly governess sullying their aristocratic bloodline. She chanced a glance at Abermont's three sisters, who flocked her on the right. Lady Elinor schooled her features into absolute blandness. Beside her, Lady Korianna appeared amused by everything she saw. And Miss Spencer simply smiled at Vivian as though she couldn't wait to welcome her into the family.

Vivian decided she liked her the best.

When no one spoke up, the minister continued. "Wilt thou have this Woman to thy wedded Wife, to live together after God's ordinance in the holy estate of Matrimony? Wilt thou love her, comfort her, honor, and keep her in sickness and in health; and, forsaking all other, keep thee only unto her, so long as ye both shall live?"

James didn't hesitate. The surety in his voice fortified her. "I will."

The minister repeated the same questions to Vivian, but her focus wasn't on his words. She saw James. The reassurance in his eyes. His crooked smile. Somehow his presence made her feel stronger—though certainly not more at ease.

And so when it came to be her turn, she said resolutely, "I will."

When the priest asked who would give her away, Vivian's heart tugged. She'd always thought Evan would be the one to give her away. If only he could be here!

Instead, Lord Haley came forward, presenting Vivian to the minister. Perhaps that was fitting, for Haley did so remind her of her own brother, with his glib grin and his sandy brown hair.

The minister gestured for her to hold James's right hand in hers. Silk to the softest kid leather, their palms touched, leaving her wondering what it would be like to feel his hand on hers without such impediments.

"Repeat after me," the minister indicated. "I, James Alexander Spencer, take thee, Vivian Eloise Loren to be my wedded Wife, to have and to hold from this day forward, for better for worse, for richer or for poorer, in sickness and in health, to love and to cherish, till death us do part, according to God's holy ordinance; and thereto I plight thee my troth."

James's deep voice rang out through the crowded room, rich and clear. His eyes shone with intensity, while the set of his mouth was earnest. He meant every word he said, if Vivian was as adept at reading him as she wanted to believe.

I plight thee my troth.

They loosened hands. She missed the solidity of his contact, the way he made her feel like she wasn't alone.

As the priest repeated the vows for her, she tried to conquer the anxiety waging war within her. If she said those vows, if she pledged her soul to him, there was be no going back. She'd be his.

Quickly, so quickly she would have missed it had her gaze not been locked on him, James winked. Her heart beat faster, and for a minute, she wished she could speed up time. To get to the point where they were alone—free of this pomp and circumstance. Where they could be simply two people.

She reached for his right hand, covering it with hers. As she promised to love and honor him through all eternity, she gave herself to this marriage. Even though it was a marriage of convenience, even though she didn't know if they truly would suit as he claimed, even though all the odds were against them...she'd be his wife and devil take it, she'd be loyal to him.

He dropped her hands, drawing from his coat a ring, which he laid on top of the prayer book. The priest handed him the ring, which James held out to her.

"With this Ring I thee wed, with my Body I thee worship, and with all my worldly Goods I thee endow," he murmured, slipping the ring onto her finger.

She stared down at the gold band. Sapphires twinkled back up at her, shaped to look like leaves encircling a diamond flower bud in the center. It was majestic, surely, yet there was no way she could ever deserve such extravagance. Would she ever feel like this ring was supposed to be hers? Or would she continue to expect another woman to pop out from the woodwork and exclaim that all along Vivian had simply been a placeholder for her?

James caught her eye as the minister bid them both to kneel so that they could join in prayer. *You needn't worry*, his eyes seemed to be saying. *You are the one I want.* Vivian had begun to think his eyes could say as much as his expressive nods.

The prayers became a blur. She repeated the words without fully registering them. With her eyes focused on the ring on her finger, Vivian held onto that unspoken promise.

THE WEDDING BREAKFAST had ended. The fifty or so odd people that had descended upon Abermont House to attend the ceremony had left to continue celebrating at the neighboring Haley estate. Ostensibly, Richard had agreed to host the house party to give the newlyweds some privacy, but really, he'd always been far better at entertaining.

Normally, James would have breathed an immense sigh of relief at the absence of his guests. Relocating the party meant there was less chance of one of the guests discovering his family's covert activities, and he'd be able to read his newspaper and drink his morning coffee in peace, the two things he required to start his days off properly.

None of that mattered when compared with the fact that he was alone in the parlor with the woman who had become his wife. The woman he'd sworn to protect.

The woman he'd now whisk away to a safe house under the pretense of a wedding trip.

He ruffled a hand through his hair, resisting the urge to jump up from the settee. That morning, before the ceremony had started, he'd received a letter from Deacon Drake, who he'd left in charge of the organization's headquarters. His agents had located Sauveterre—but they'd been too late to catch him. The villain was on the move again, possibly to Maidstone.

Which meant he had to get Vivian away from here as soon as possible.

Nixon, another agent with the Clocktower, prepared the coach and four. Arden had packed their tools the night before, and arranged for the necessary bags to be loaded while the rest of the house was distracted with the wedding. A trunk of knives, truncheons, flintlocks, and then Korianna's addition: enough supplies for three small black powder bombs or one huge explosion. Northley had packed Vivian's trunk with her old gowns. There was no point in ruining the finer dresses Elinor had ordered for her when they'd be out in the wilderness, far from prying eyes.

Or so he hoped.

The safe house in Guildford had never been

compromised. Only twelve agents knew of its existence. For all the servants knew, they were heading toward the shores of Brighton to celebrate their new union.

So now all he had to do was wait. He opened his mouth to speak, but no words came out. What did a man say to his wife? Surely, not that she was in even more danger than they'd originally thought. There was no point in worrying her, not when the plans were already underway.

He tried to think about how his father and mother had acted. Mama had died shortly after Louisa's birth, so his memories were hazy at best, but he thought his parents had been amiable with each other. He remembered the Lion's second wife, Thomas's mother, better. Though the two never had a great love, Juliana and the duke had been partners. The best of friends, supportive of each other.

One look at Vivian and he wanted more than simple companionship, even if he knew he didn't deserve it. Even if he wasn't certain he could ever be enough for her.

Vivian saved him from sitting there for the next half hour silently. "It was a lovely ceremony."

She spoke as though she was commenting on the weather, not her wedding day. This was absurd. If this was how proper husbands and wives discoursed, he wanted no part of it.

He shifted on the settee so that he was next to her. "Vivian."

She held his gaze. "James."

He'd been many names over the years. Abermont. The Marquis of Silverton, prior to inheriting the dukedom. Edouard when he'd spent a summer undercover in France. Dupont during his time assisting the Swabian Agency in Switzerland. Falcon to his fellow Clocktower and Alien Office agents.

Prior to today, he'd always felt more at home in

these secret identities—free of responsibilities, the past, and societal pressure.

Now, he did not want to be anyone else. He would not be Abermont to her, or even Falcon. He was just James. He had not anticipated how musical his true appellation would sound on her lips. Bollocks, he hadn't anticipated *any* of this. She'd changed everything.

"Vivian," he said again, partially to focus his thoughts, and partially because he wanted to feel her name on his tongue once more. Her name became a commandment in itself. "With God as my witness, I'll keep you safe. You needn't fear anything."

"I know." Those two simple words packed more of a punch than any long-winded declaration, for she spoke as though her faith in him was a given. "And I do trust you."

As a spy, missions depended upon his ability to get a target to trust him. In the past, he'd always been successful. In the past, he'd always been someone else.

He did not know if he—James Spencer, not Falcon, not Edouard—deserved her trust.

She watched him, her wide eyes never leaving his face. Under her scrutiny, he felt exposed, as though she could see inside to the depths of his soul. He was transfixed by the delicate curve of her high cheekbones, juxtaposed with the sharpness of her chin. Everything about her was a contrast. Her dainty, petite frame against the strength of her willpower. Her excellence in the more typical occupation of governess against her unconventional love of fencing and mysteries.

"Evan used to say that people were mostly good," Vivian said.

Evan Loren had only been an agent for the Alien Office for a few years. Long enough that his idealistic bent would have started to wear off—but not long enough that he'd be truly jaded by everything he'd seen.

James had been on missions since he was fifteen. His optimism had been stripped away, little by little, until all that was left was harsh reality. Good people were often driven to do bad things—and bad people often triumphed. He fought for a world he sometimes wondered if he should let burn.

But he kept fighting because he knew no other way.

"I guess I always believed him," Vivian continued. "We were sheltered in Devon. And when we moved to London, I thought everyone was nice. But my brother was murdered by a madman, and I don't know why. So how am I supposed to believe the world has good in it?"

He'd asked the same questions after Louisa's death. God, he *still* asked those questions.

"The world may not have good in it, but some people do," he said. "It's not enough to make up for Evan's death, I know. But it's all we have."

"*Revenge* is what I need for Evan's death." She met his gaze, and the simmering rage he saw in her blue eyes shook him to his core.

He'd been there before. In the moment when he'd hunted down Nicodème, he had felt good. Justified. But he was already so far gone—taking one more life was immaterial to the state of his soul. For Vivian, killing Sauveterre might change her irrevocably. It could take away her chance at healing from her brother's death. He'd do anything to make sure she still had that chance.

He shook his head. "Revenge won't bring him back."

She smiled, full of bittersweet sadness. "I know. But it'll taste sweet."

He could think of many things that would taste sweeter and be far more pleasurable. But he tried to shove those thoughts to the back of his mind. She was an innocent, and he had a job to do.

"We are working on getting him justice." He went to the teacart, picking up the silver tray and carrying it to the table. At least it gave him something to do besides pacing the room. "You will see in time that justice is much better than revenge."

She picked up the teapot from the tray, pouring tea into the two china cups. "Cream? Sugar?"

"Both."

She fixed his tea, and he accepted the cup she handed him.

She added a lump of sugar and a splash of cream to her tea. "Revenge is what Sauveterre deserves. I want to make the bastard pay for what he did to Evan." She paused, her nose wrinkling. "I want to make him pay for what he did to me."

"And I promise you, we'll catch him." He took the tea tray up from the table, bringing it back to the cart. The more space he put between them, the easier he found it to think. Should he tell Vivian what he'd learned about her Sauveterre's whereabouts earlier? Korianna's suspicions about her brother being a spy would have to wait until he could safely confide in her about the Clocktower.

He'd promised her they'd work together on this. Though he couldn't tell her everything about his work, he could at least share the parts that related to her brother's murder. Enough truth to fulfill the arrangement they'd agreed to, but not enough to put her in further danger.

He turned around, leaning against the cart. "In fact, I've already found several leads on Sauveterre."

Vivian burst up from the settee, coming to stand by him. She carried her teacup with her. "You've discovered something?"

"My contacts went to the tavern where you used to write Sauveterre. They interrogated the innkeeper." He didn't specify that he'd sent his own agents. Until he moved her somewhere secure and could tell her his true occupation, it was better to let her think that the Runners were doing all the work.

"I wrote that innkeeper," Vivian said. "He claimed he didn't know Sauveterre."

He shrugged. "Let's just say the Chatham Boar and Deer won't be receiving any awards for their honest customer dealings any time soon."

"What did he say?"

"A Frenchman was staying at the Boar and Deer, but he left two weeks prior to their visit."

Vivian leaned forward, the mug grasped between her two hands. "Do they think it's Sauveterre?"

"Nothing was left in the room for them to search, but yes," James said. "The innkeeper remembers him often receiving mail at that point, and the times coincide with your letters."

"Two weeks." Vivian deposited her cup of tea on the cart and pushed off, going toward the door. "*Two weeks.* If we'd just been two weeks earlier…"

He followed her, stopping her mid-step. His hand on her arm fixed her to this one point, though her nostrils still flared, indicating she might flee. So he reached for her hand, the lace of her gloves against his bare skin unnerving him. Whatever wise pronouncement he'd been about to make died on his tongue when she slowly slid her thumb up and down the ridge of his index finger.

He gulped. A futile attempt to calm his racing pulse, for her thumb kept stroking. Her slight touch aroused him more than it should have. More than he'd ever experienced from the connection of their joined hands.

"We are not certain it was Sauveterre," he managed to gasp out. "And if you'd gone there two weeks ago, without my help, who knows what would have happened to you. The man is a murderer, Vivian."

Her thumb ceased moving against his. "You don't have to remind me of that. I'm well aware."

"I'm sorry." He hated the sharp stab of pain that crossed her features. The fact that *he'd* caused that, when all he wanted to do was bring her happiness. His grip on her hand tightened, and he wished he'd never have to part from her. "The idea of you going up against a murderer, unarmed and unprepared, terrifies me. I meant every word of those vows I said today. I'm going to honor and cherish you, but I can't do that if you're dead."

She let out an exasperated sigh, but she did not pull away from him. "I suppose you're right. Going off half-cocked will solve nothing. But I don't understand why you didn't tell me this immediately. We're supposed to be partners. In more than just this, now."

"I received the letter today. There was no time to tell you before the ceremony." He did not move—could not move, for her gaze held his in thrall. "Vivian, we *are* partners. We're in this together."

"Good. Because that's the only thing I want." She scooted closer, her hand still linked to his. She was so close now; the hem of her lilac dress skimmed his buff pantaloons. So close her sweet floral scent filled his nose until everything smelled like roses.

Any moment now, the carriage would be ready, and they'd be forced to leave this house. How would she react later to his confession? He didn't know. But right now, with her so near, he couldn't hold back any longer.

He leaned down, cupping her chin in his hands. God, how soft her skin felt against his bare hands, softer than he'd ever imagined. He brushed his lips against hers. Gave her a moment to adjust to the feel of his lips on hers, and when she leaned into him, he increased the pressure. She was tentative at first, but she learned his rhythm quickly. She returned his kiss with an equal passion, slanting her lips over his. He couldn't think of a single reason why he hadn't spent the last six months doing just this. Kissing Vivian became as natural as breathing—his body moved on its own, a creature of desire and longing.

He broke apart from her long enough to tug her flush against him. Her supple frame fit perfectly between his spread legs. He'd meant to taste her, nothing more. But then her hands slid upward, grasping at his shoulders as though he was the one thing separating her from a shipwreck, and he was powerless to resist her. He hadn't felt such all-consuming need in years, if ever, for he'd never been one to give himself fully to passion. The women he'd been with before had been experienced, widows or courtesans, as jaded as he was. They'd gone through the motions, each knowing the worth of their own bodies.

Before tonight, he'd always claimed that was how it should be: a trade of information for pleasure, set expectations for an encounter.

He hadn't been prepared for Vivian. How her sweet innocence could drive him wild. She kissed without artifice or ulterior motive, and it was bloody wonderful. He dipped his tongue out between her parted lips, seeking entry. She opened her lips to him, and he thrust into her wet mouth. Her body shook as he teased her, his tongue toying with her own until she moaned with pleasure. The sound shot through him. He was rock hard, yet he hadn't even touched her intimately—couldn't touch her, because if he did he'd lose himself completely. So he kissed her, kissed her until he'd memorized the arc of her lips, until his mouth was numb, until his chest burned with the lack of oxygen.

When they finally broke apart, he stepped back from her. He dared not touch her while his body warred with his mind. His breathing ragged, he exerted every last bit of his willpower to keep from tossing her skirts up and burying himself inside her then and there.

If he didn't get them on the road soon, he'd stay in this parlor, kissing her. Learning the rhythm of her breaths and the meaning behind every one of her sighs. He ran his hands down his pantaloons, willing his body to calm.

All the bombs he'd disabled, the traitors he'd arrested, and the assassins he'd thwarted in the past would never be as dangerous as Vivian was to him. She was changing him, a little bit at a time, prying away the falseness of his identity and leaving only the real man beneath.

CHAPTER 12

HE'D KISSED HER.

Vivian's mind sputtered back to life. She raised a hand to her lips, swollen from his kisses. Her eyes barely focused as he rubbed his hands against his legs, as though he needed to keep his hands busy because if he did not, he'd touch her again. Sweet Mary, how she wanted him to touch her again.

He had kissed *her!*

She ought to say something flirtatious. Maybe express her appreciation of his prowess? She didn't know. This was another area of etiquette that thoroughly boggled her. What was the proper reaction to being kissed senseless? Vivian could only rest her weight against the back of the settee, her ring finger still poised on her lips.

She still tasted him. She still felt him. The tight muscles of his arms as he held her to him, that particularly intriguing bulge in his pantaloons as he leaned into her, his body perfectly fitted to hers. She still heard the sound of her own pleasure-soaked moan in her ears. She'd been so wanton, thinking nothing of the other people in the house who might overhear them.

She sneaked a glance over at him. He appeared as stunned as her, eyes wide, jaw jutting out, lips as red as her own must be. He battled against the passion that had seized him—she noted it in the raggedness of his breathing, as if each gasp was an endeavor in its own right; in the clench of his fists at his sides, making her think of a warrior preparing for battle. So much about him reminded her of a fighter. The rigidness of his sculpted muscles, so hard and well-formed under her questing fingers. That determined flicker in his eyes whenever he made her a promise. The rawness in his voice when he spoke of his sister.

He was a man who'd never give up.

He was a man of honor.

And he was *her* man. Perhaps more than in name only, if that kiss was any indication. She ought not to feel so blastedly elated, as she hadn't accomplished her true goal yet. Sauveterre lived. But that weak, romantic part of her wanted to run back into James's arms and relish being his duchess.

She must crush that part of herself as ruthlessly as Sauveterre had crushed her brother's windpipe. This was not about her, or even them. It could not be. Not yet.

A knock sounded on the closed parlor door, and then the door began to swing open. Miss Spencer entered, her calm green eyes taking in the distance between them, perhaps even noticing the way Vivian's hair looked mussed, and how James's coat was no longer so straight. Vivian had the sinking suspicion the quiet Miss Spencer observed far more than she ever let on.

"The carriage is ready," Miss Spencer said.

"Ah." James nodded, but Vivian didn't have any idea what this nod meant. So much for reading him well.

Miss Spencer made no move to depart. "We need to leave in the next five minutes."

James gestured for her to go. "Tell the jarvey we'll be right out."

Miss Spencer exchanged an enigmatic glance with her adopted brother before she closed the door to the room again.

Vivian pounced, seizing the opportunity before he had a chance to deflect her questions. In the chaos of the wedding plans, she'd forgotten about the trip Elinor had discussed during the fitting. "Lady Elinor mentioned a trip. Where are we going, James? And why? If you've already taken precautions to fortify this estate, why would we leave? The start of the Season isn't for another month, so it can't be for that."

She came to stand beside him. As close as she'd felt to him mere minutes before, doubt crept back into her. Why did it always feel like he was hiding something? He'd sworn they were partners—in more than finding her brother's killer—but she could not shake the thought that she'd married a man she would never truly know.

"And don't tell me it's merely a celebratory wedding trip."

James opened and shut his mouth, the briefest flicker of surprise in his eyes before he regained control of his emotions. "The staff believes we are going to Brighton."

Her eyes narrowed. "But we are actually going to where?"

He strode to the door, and she was momentarily distracted by the power and speed behind his gait. Even his *walk* was authoritative. It would be so easy to throw her fate in his hands. To believe without question in his ability to keep her safe. Yet she'd spent enough time under the thumb of mysterious men.

She followed him, stopping him before he could open the door. "I'm going to ask you one more time: where are we going? If you want me to get in the carriage with you, I need answers."

He turned back to face her, letting out a resigned sigh. "You're awfully aggressive, did you know that?"

"It has been pointed out to me before, yes," she said. "Evan preferred to call me 'domineering,' but you may use whatever term you see fit."

"How benevolent of you," he noted dryly.

She shrugged. "I can be magnanimous when the situation calls for it."

"There are certain precautions that need to be taken," he began, with a pointed look toward the door. "If I tell you where we're going while we're still in this house, that will put your safety at risk. I refuse to take that chance. So we can argue about this when we're in the carriage."

"No, we can argue about this now." She stepped in front of the door, blocking the door with her body. A flawed idea, since he'd had no trouble touching her moments prior, but it was all she had. "Why do we need to leave so hurriedly? What aren't you telling me?"

"You're impossible, woman." He gave her a beleaguered look that *almost* made her feel sympathetic. "I didn't want to worry you, because I've taken measures to ensure your safety. There was more to the letter. The innkeeper at the Boar and Deer thought that Sauveterre might be coming to Maidstone."

He did not need to say anything more. She knew from the alarm in his eyes that he suspected Sauveterre was on his way to Abermont House. To her.

"He's figured out that I can't get the information he wants, so he's going to kill me." She clasped her hands together to keep from shaking, but that did not stop the frantic racing of her mind. She'd been a duchess for exactly one hour and already her death warrant might as well have been signed. "You're taking me far, far from here? Somewhere he can't find me."

"That's the general idea, yes." James reached for her, but she shied away from him, stalking over to the teacart.

"Why?"

"I should think that obvious. If he can't find you, then he can't kill you."

She leaned her hands on the cart, her back to him. "But then we can't find *him*."

"A secondary goal when compared to keeping you alive." James advanced on her, spinning her around so that she faced him again. He laid his hands on her shoulders, and she did not want to admit how much his grip steadied her.

She jutted her chin out, refusing to give in to the fear. This was a chance to accomplish what she'd vowed. Nothing else mattered. "Let him come for me. I will rip out his heart."

If only her voice did not waver when she made that declaration. If only she believed she was truly capable of going up against a sick, twisted killer and surviving.

"No, you will die in the process." James leaned forward, resting his forehead on hers. The certainty in his voice whispered across her face, a soft touch when it should have been a slap. "We are not ready, my dear. Let us prepare to take him on first. My contacts found him once, and they'll find him again."

"Do you really think so?" It seemed impossible that the Runners could find Sauveterre again. But wasn't it better to be prepared? Every step she'd made had been based on false assumptions. "How will we become ready?"

"I'll teach you how to fight," he said. "I have not always been duke, you know. As a boy, I was as rough and tumble as you and your brother. I'll teach you how to shoot and how to defend yourself."

"And then we'll end Sauveterre." She needed to hear him say it. She longed for a time when this was over, when the guilt of failing Evan did not consume her soul.

"And then we'll *catch* Sauveterre." He pulled back from her, but only to loop his arm in hers as he guided her to the door so they could both change for the trip. "Justice, Vivian. Justice before revenge."

GUILDFORD.

James had said they were going to Guildford, somewhere in Surrey. She wasn't familiar with the place. On three fingers she could count the places she'd frequented in the last twenty-four years: Devon, London, and then Maidstone. Yes, she'd traveled through various towns on the way to each destination, but she'd never paid much attention to the scenery going by the mailcoach. Each trip, she'd been too eager to start out on her new life.

Now, she didn't know what she felt. Anticipation warred with fear until her stomach roiled, and she had to fight to keep down the stew she'd already consumed at this stop. She didn't know what scared her more: the idea of going somewhere unknown with her new husband, or the fact that every mile took her further from Sauveterre and her chance at vengeance. Though James was right that they weren't prepared, that didn't make leaving the one lead she had any easier.

She let her spoon drop from her fingers, the metal clinking against the ceramic bowl. The sound barely made an impact in the crowded main room of the Jester and Trader Tavern in Otford. They'd stopped for dinner, but none of the food was appetizing to Vivian's queasy stomach. She'd managed to eat a third of the beef stew served up to her by an alarmingly buxom serving wench—who James never looked at again after he'd delivered his order, granting her a small measure of happiness—because James and Miss Spencer kept watching her expectantly.

"Something wrong, dear?" Concern laced Miss Spencer's tone.

"No," Vivian answered without hesitation. How much had James told his sister about her situation? She didn't know, and she certainly wasn't about to volunteer information that made her appear to be a lying thief. "I fear I'm a bit fatigued with all the traveling."

"It's been a busy day," James agreed. "You can rest in the carriage."

"I shall do that," Vivian said, though she doubted she'd be able to sleep with him so near to her. "Thank you for your concern, Miss Spencer."

"Arden," she corrected with a grin. "We are sisters now, after all."

Sisters.

She'd been alone in the world since Evan's death. Suddenly, she had three new sisters and another brother, a brother she'd spent the last six months watching as his governess.

And most importantly, now she had a husband. She let her gaze drift over to James, hunched over his stew. He'd asked for a booth in the far corner of the tavern, closest to an exit, shadowed by the low hanging eaves. His cravat was tied in a simple fashion, and he wore a black coat that was neither extravagant nor too cheap to draw notice. He'd traded his Hessians for top boots, dusty from their travels. His tanned, handsome face was as inscrutable as ever—but did she detect the smallest furrow of his bushy black brows? Her eyes traveled down, to those firm, chiseled planes of his chest, and her cheeks warmed at the memory of him pressed up against her body, all sinewy muscle and strength, those wicked lips supple against her own.

He might be duke when at Abermont House, but here outside the estate he was a much more intimidating creature. When a grizzly, haggard man passed by their table, his roving eyes stopping on Vivian with more interest than she would have liked, James turned swiftly in his chair, his glower alone sending the man running. Had that been not enough, she had no problem believing that this version of him, rough and rugged like the road they traversed, would have reached for the knife strapped to his side. Perhaps he had one in his boot as well; Evan had often done that.

Her husband's equipped state brought her some comfort. If Sauveterre did happen to find them, James could protect them.

He'd better, because she had no weapon.

Not from lack of asking. When James originally attached his holster, she'd asked him for a knife too. He'd told her he had enough to worry about without her accidentally stabbing herself. She glanced at his waist, frowning into her stew. The nerve of the man! As if she was useless. While she might be unskilled with a blade, she could fathom which side of the blade was supposed to go into a ruffian and which one went in her hand.

Partners, my blooming arse.

He'd been this way since they'd climbed into the carriage late that morning. What had happened to the man who'd held her in his arms as if she was precious to him?

During the first hour of their journey, she'd attempted to make conversation. James had told her the name of the town they were going to, and then fallen silent as he'd reviewed a seemingly endless stack of files brought forth from his portmanteau. Eventually, Vivian had grown tired of only talking to Arden, especially when she still wasn't sure why the duke's youngest sister accompanied them on this trip. Most newlyweds didn't need a chaperone.

But most newlyweds weren't fleeing from a threat

on their lives, so there was that.

Ignoring her ire, James stood and brushed his hands off on his breeches. He went to find the tavern wench so that he could pay the bill, as she'd disappeared once she'd realized James had no interest in her. Vivian's scowl deepened. That was definitely a second knife sheathed in his holster too. Why should she have to rely entirely upon him for protection? It didn't seem like good sense to keep her unarmed.

Arden caught her eye and winked. "Don't worry. I have a knife you can use."

She didn't have time to express properly her appreciation, for James returned to the table.

"Let's go," he said. "Still a few hours left, and I want to be there before dark."

A few more hours trapped on the same bench as him, while Arden read her book on the bench across from them. Vivian couldn't ask James the questions she wanted to with Arden present, and so the need to know chafed at her like an uncomfortable itch she could not scratch.

Their small party proceeded out into the courtyard toward the carriage. Vivian eyed it suspiciously. Every postchaise she'd ever seen had been a yellow bounder, but this one was painted black with no defining markings. Distinctly different from the Spencer's usual coach and four, which bore the Abermont crest of arms. Distinctly covert.

She was beginning to wonder if Sauveterre had been right. Even their jarvey appeared barbarous, a mammoth of a man with broad shoulders and a chest that reminded her of a tree trunk. There was so much about the Spencers that didn't add up—yet she was certain she'd never found any indication that he was financing a revolution in France.

Perhaps Sauveterre had the right *idea*, but the wrong *execution*...

She pressed her lips into a thin line. As soon as

they arrived at their destination, she'd get answers, even if it meant she had to smack some sense into James.

He helped her into the carriage, holding the door open for Arden too. Through the open curtains of the carriage, Vivian saw Arden shake her head, instead accepting the reins of a bay mare from the jarvey. The driver helped Arden up onto the horse.

James slid onto the bench next to her. "Arden is going to ride alongside the hack. Apparently she longs for fresh air."

"Understandable. Had I known that was an option, I might have considered the same." Vivian remembered Arden's earlier wink. Maybe having a new sister could be beneficial after all.

James frowned. "We can't have you out in the open."

She gave him an arch look. "Hence why I said *might*."

The door to the carriage slid shut, and a moment later they were off again.

CHAPTER 13

VIVIAN LEANED HER head back against the crimson brocade squabs and wondered if this was what her life would be like. While the black Padua silk-lined walls and soft bench seat were an improvement on the hired hacks she was used to riding in, at this moment she would have given up any convenience for some certainty. Some security.

James drew out yet another folder from his portmanteau, signaling that the next three hours would be spent in silence again.

Vivian snatched the folder from him, holding it up and out of reach. She did not, however, account for the fact that he was taller than she was and had longer arms. He easily reached past her, his hand covering hers on the file.

But she would not be defeated so easily. She dug her nails into the paper, refusing to let go.

"Vivian," James said warningly, and if she weren't so bloody frustrated she might have done the proper thing and released the file.

She didn't. She gripped it harder, because if she were to do the proper thing, she wouldn't be in this carriage as a new duchess. "All I want is for you to spend one hour of this trip actually conversing with me. Do you realize you haven't said more than two words to me since you told me where we're going? I swear to you, James, if you intend for the rest of our marriage to be passed in silent observation, I will go mad. Silence causes slow deaths, I am sure of it."

"The last thing I would want is for you to die slowly," he said dryly, dropping his hand from the file. He held his palm outstretched. "At least allow me to put the folder away properly."

She considered this. He was a crafty man. If she handed him the file back, he'd probably move to the bench across from her and continue reading. So she lowered the file and slid it underneath her, sitting back down on it.

"Don't think that'll stop me from getting it." His gaze swept from her to the file and back to her again, his lips curving into a slow smirk. "Especially since I've been aching to put my hands on your delectable rear since the first night I saw you."

"Oh." Her cheeks pinked again—maybe more than just her cheeks, for she felt warm in certain areas that had been unexplored until he'd kissed her. "So that kiss was not a chance occurrence?"

That wasn't the question she'd meant to ask. She ducked her head, avoiding his eyes. It was so much harder to think properly when he looked at her.

He shifted on the seat, nudging her with his leg. "No. Do you really think I would have asked you to marry me if I wasn't attracted to you?"

"You said, and I quote, 'Marriage is like an equation. You and I are both variables.'" Her voice dripped with sarcasm, the full strength of her frustration on display. "How was I to know one of the variables is also your attraction?"

"I told you to never doubt that I wanted you." His voice was coarse, like the late evening stubble on his chin.

He cupped his fingers underneath her chin, bringing her eyes up to meet his. The desire reflected back at her surprised her; he was a coiled beast, ready to strike if she gave him permission. And oh, how she wanted him to strike.

The sapphire ring on her finger glinted in the sunlight, reminding her who she was now. A duchess—*his* duchess. When he'd kissed her before, her fear over Sauveterre had quieted. She'd felt safe in his arms, and she wanted to feel that way again.

She started to reach forward, but stopped herself. What would his hair feel like without her gloves? Stripping off one glove and then the other, she felt his eyes upon her, tracing her movements hungrily. She ran her hand along the curve of his cravat, the starched linen stiff against her skin. He kept his hair shorter than the fashion. Up her fingers traveled, the black locks slipping through her fingers. He let out a groan of approval. The satisfaction on his face emboldened her. The rocking of the carriage had taken on a rhythm that heightened her, and she moved with it.

"You've said you didn't want to talk about where we're going." The huskiness of her own voice surprised her. "But we have much time to pass..."

He pulled back from her, scooting further down the bench. "We shouldn't."

Her eyes narrowed. "Well, you *could* tell me how you managed to procure an unmarked carriage so readily. Or, you could tell me why your sister is on this trip with us. Or, you could tell me exactly where in Guildford we're going. Or, you could tell me—"

James's left eye started to twitch with her first question, increasing as she continued. He held up a hand to silence her, and she shut her mouth. But only because she'd run out of questions, not because he'd told her to.

"When I kissed you before, it was because all I'd been able to think about for the last two weeks was kissing you." He made this sound as if it was a very bad thing, and she was hard-pressed to follow his reasoning. "My thoughts should be about keeping you away from danger, not about how bloody perfectly your lips fit mine, or how you manage to smell like my blasted garden and home all in one. I need to focus, Vivian. When I get distracted, bad things happen. People die."

The intensity behind his words took her aback. How many near-death situations had he been in, exactly? She filed that as a query to make later, because the rest of his statement was infinitely more interesting.

"James," she began, edging closer to him, the corner of her traveling habit brushing against his buff breeches. "I know I may not have given you the best impression of me, given that I ended up on your doorstep under...let's say nefarious purposes, but I've been taking care of myself for a long time."

"Never against a foe like this." His jaw clenched, and his eyes found hers again, pain and sadness and longing, too. For her.

She nodded, hoping it conveyed as much as his mannerisms usually did. "That's why I have you. Together, we're a force to be reckoned with."

James swallowed. "I can't lose you. Not you too."

Of course. How could she not have seen it? He'd already been through so much loss.

She came even closer, until she was almost sharing the same space with him, her leg so near to his. "Nothing is going to happen to me. I'm not going to die. Not with you here and certainly not with that brute of a coachman you seem to have dragged from a traveling act."

That brought a small smile to his lips. "Nixon is a good man."

"Good man or not, one look at him and Sauveterre will run for cover."

"That was the idea."

"I think you've accomplished that goal quite well, then." Her hand drifted to his arm, her fingers running up and down his coat sleeve. "But we're still alone in this carriage for a while."

James watched her fingers track, his eyes darkening. He ran his tongue across his lips, those lips she wanted so badly on her own, stripping away her apprehension and leaving pleasure in their wake. "You make it very hard to say no to you."

Vivian trailed her hand up further, tracing the curve of his ear. "So you've said. I believe you also called me impossible."

"And aggressive," he reminded her, leaning into her touch. "When we are together the first time—and we *will* be together, Vivian—I want it to be right. It should be you and me, no worries, no doubts."

She dropped her hand, her meager attempts at seduction now seeming tawdry compared to the real connection he described. But he caught her fingers, intertwining them with his own, and he brought her hand to his lips to lay a sweet kiss upon her skin.

"I want that too," she murmured. "A proper wedding night, if one can still call it that when it isn't the night you marry."

"So much about us is already unconventional. Who says we cannot defy the calendar too? Our wedding night can be whenever we please."

"How rebellious," she said. "I like it very much."

When he released her hand, she went to make her way back to her side of the carriage, but he stopped her. In one quick movement, he'd dropped down to the floor of the carriage and knelt in front of her at eye level. "I'll make you a promise."

"Another one?"

He'd already promised to save her life, to cherish her, and to call her his wife forever. How much more could he give her?

He leaned in until they were almost nose-and-nose. "If you're willing to follow my instructions exactly as I'm showing you how to fight, as well as teaching you other certain skills you might need to learn—"

She bristled at his demand for obedience, but she was intrigued enough to let him continue.

His expression became grave. "I'm serious. Complete focus. I can't take the chance that something will happen to you."

"Fine, I agree," she said because he refused to continue until she did.

"Then I think we can explore whatever...this is." He waved to the tiny space in between them. "Within reason, of course."

"Kisses, then," she put forth helpfully. "And some touching."

His eyes settled on her breasts, covered by the thick fabric of her traveling habit. "A lot of touching. Because when I see you all I want to do is run my hands down every inch of your body."

Her mouth suddenly felt quite dry indeed, but he seemed to be waiting for her to say something. For her to grant him permission. Damn his chivalry, for now she had to think of a suitably hoydenish remark. "I would not be opposed to a lot of touching."

"Good." Another nod, so quick this time she almost missed it, for then his lips were on hers, and the world was spinning.

He kissed her deliberately, thoroughly, as if he'd made it his objective to tear out any thought in her mind that wasn't related to him. His lips crushed hers, demanding her obedience, but she gave it all back to him in a kiss that was neither gentle nor refined but was in itself an unstoppable act. She'd lacked control over almost every aspect of her life in these six months, and she lacked control in this kiss.

But his hands gripped her shoulders, anchored

her, and suddenly the loss of control wasn't a problem. She gave herself in to this, into the unruliness, swaying as the carriage moved.

She darted her tongue out, tasting the smooth plane of his lips. He opened to her, his own tongue thrusting forward to toy with hers. They tangled like this, an intricate dance she did not know the steps to beforehand, yet seemed to follow intrinsically. And through it all, the heat in her body rose, rose, rose in the tips of her breasts, in that private juncture between her thighs, but it was a welcome, wonderful warmth that made her feel safe. She was not alone. She had him.

He drew back from her, kissing her neck. His tongue dipped into the hollow of her ear, then behind her lobe. Tingles shot through her, first in her hands, then traveling through the rest of her body as he nipped at the bottom of her ear. She had never imagined such pleasure could be found in this. He kept at her, alternating between licking and nibbling, until she was panting with desire. Her head lolled back against him, exposing more of her neck.

"God, you are so beautiful," he murmured against her throat, his nimble fingers undoing the top buttons of her dress to give him more access. Her collarbone was now bared to him, and he ran his fingers swiftly against her skin, leaving trails of fire wherever his fingers lingered.

"What next?" She barely managed the question before his hand slid forward, cupping her bosom.

Once, she'd seen him when he was bare-knuckle boxing with Lord Haley, and she'd watched as his fists inflicted pain. But now all they did was cause her bliss. He kneaded her breast, holding her and then caressing her in turn. Her nipples hardened to peaks under his touch, straining against the confines of her stays. The traveling habit that had seemed so loose this morning now felt too tight and far too hot. He switched to her other breast, giving her the same attention until her belly tightened with want and she thought of nothing else but his hands gripping her. His tanned skin against her traveling habit. The scars on the backs of his hand from too many fights.

"More," she whispered, though she could not breathe without the smell of him, the feel of his presence. Still it was not enough.

"You are a flippant minx." She felt his grin against her neck, heard the approval in his voice, though she could not see his face. Climbing up on the bench next to her, he leaned her forward. His fingers made hasty work of her buttons, despite the rollicking of the carriage.

She should have cared that her bosom was on display for him. She should have felt revealed. Yet when she glanced up at him, the heady desire streaked across his face made her feel...empowered. Delightfully wanton. She leaned back against him, helping him to shove the fabric down to her waist.

Somehow, he managed to turn her around, so that she now faced him. It was the quickest of movements, his deft precision reminding her of how smooth he'd been executing his defense maneuvers. He was a man who could keep her safe at all costs, a man who knew exactly how to go after what he wanted.

And what he wanted was her.

She wouldn't question it. Wouldn't breathe a word of denial that she was too plain, too wallflower, too anything but interesting enough for his attentions. Today she would pretend she had the confidence of a woman who could catch his eye. Today she would pretend she deserved everything he'd done for her so far, because God she wanted to believe she did. He saw a better version of her, and she wanted to be that person.

She wanted *him.*

"You're killing me, woman," he ground out, at the

sight of the pink ribbon tied underneath her breasts, in the same shade as her garters. Judging from his reaction, Vivian no longer considered extravagant undergarments as a needless expense.

"It will be a wonderful death," she found herself saying, as his fingers worked deftly at the knot.

"If I can but die with you naked before me, I'll reconsider my stance on living long." He plucked at the last knot, unfastening her stays. She sat before him now with her chemise and her stays spread wide, her gown pooled around her waist. He helped her remove the stays, tossing them aside.

Before she had time to protest, his hands were on her again, molding her breasts against his palms. If she had thought the contact before had been good, she'd not expected this. He teased and played with her, exerting pressure where she needed him most, until she was crying out from how *good* it all made her feel. He dived down, taking her breast into his hot mouth. As he tongued her, circling her nipple until the dusky peaks of her nipples were almost painfully stiff, she reevaluated her previous ideas on just how much bliss the human body could take. Because she was soaring, her mind hazy, all her senses overloaded with pleasure, and he didn't seem intent on stopping.

Until the carriage hit a bump in the road, jostling them forward. Then the postchaise halted entirely. Nixon's shouts echoed from outside.

A second later, there was a knock upon the door, and Arden's voice echoed. "James, the wheel is stuck in a rut. You're going to want to come and help Nixon push it out."

"Damnation. Damnable, damned, damningly damnation." The black look he sent the door alleviated some of her disappointment—for he was just as upset by this interruption as she was.

"James?" Arden called again.

"I'll be out in a minute." James cursed under his

breath, fetching her stays. "This is not the way this is supposed to work, you know. Once these stays come off, they're supposed to bloody remain off for *at least* a half hour, do you understand me? We should make this a rule from now on."

She turned so he could lace her back up. "At least a half hour. Duly noted in the marriage charter."

He chuckled, even as he scowled at having to do up the back of her dress again. "So we have a charter now?"

She leaned into his touch, unable to help herself. "Absolutely. I believe in order above all things."

He brushed a kiss on her neck, then moved away, going to the carriage door. "Stay inside. This isn't over."

For once, she was only too happy to obey his command.

CHAPTER 14

Guildford, Surrey

THE JOURNEY FROM Maidstone to Guildford took approximately eight hours by postchaise. Two stops at inns along the way to eat, stretch their legs, and select fresh horses. In the past, he'd always completed this trip with little delay, unable to risk more than a ten-minute stop to change his steed.

In the past, he'd always been running from enemy agents, not taking his new wife for training. In the past, he'd never spent part of the ride pleasuring the most intriguing woman he'd ever known.

This trip, though it took all day and the better part of the evening, was infinitely better than the rest.

Blackness swathed the sky, the thick forest blocking out the moonlight. They'd stopped half a mile back from the hunting lodge, for the carriage could not easily travel through the densely wooded drive. Nixon unstrapped the matched pair from the carriage, running his hand down each horse's body to make sure that there were no injuries. Satisfied with what he felt, he took the reins of both of the horses. While the postchaise would remain in the forest, James preferred to have the team kept closer to the lodge in case of emergency. He'd learned the hard way that a good agent always needed a plan of escape.

Nixon started forward, holding his torch high to guide their way. He knew the lay of the land almost as well as James did, for he was the Clocktower's usual whip for the safe houses within driving distance of London.

James toted his own portmanteau, as security demanded the barest minimum of servants. Arden followed in his wake, leading her mare. Northley lagged behind, carrying the rest of Vivian's things.

He slipped his hand into Vivian's, not wanting to chance that he'd lose her in the packed thickets. He breathed easier when her small fingers dovetailed between his. Though the location of this safe house was heavily protected, there was always the chance that ruffians might take advantage of the sylvan setting.

She was safer where he could see her. Safer with him.

The party picked their way carefully through the woods, stepping over downed logs and steering around puddles. He'd expected some form of protest from Vivian, for the lodge wasn't visible from the roadside, and for all she knew he was leading her into danger. But with her hand securely in his, she matched his stride. Her boot-clad feet picked nimbly over the roughest of the terrain, and even when the top of her cloak snagged on a tree branch, she freed the fabric and continued onward.

Her braveness impressed him. At every turn, she'd exceeded his expectations. And the hunger he'd felt in her kiss—he hadn't been prepared.

She brought out something unrestrained in him.

They entered a clearing, where the moon shone bright without the cover of trees. He sneaked a glance at Vivian. Her pale skin silhouetted in the moonlight, the hood of her cloak pushed back and her golden locks glimmering, she reminded him of Selene, the goddess of the moon. For a second he stopped completely, enchanted by her beauty. The swell of her breasts, the camber of her hips, and the vibrant red of her bow-shaped lips all combined to leave his mouth dry with want.

This was not the time—not now, when they were exposed out in the open. Yet the impulse fired within him, quickening his breath. He, who had been so long ruled by logic and action, could not fathom the pull she had upon him. It was almost elemental, the way his body craved hers, the inexplicable draw of his mind to hers. How he felt at ease with her, able to be completely himself. He was not sure he even knew who *he* was anymore.

As they approached the lodge, his hand tightened around hers. Although the Clocktower owned the lodge, he felt a special kinship to this place. Built in the latter half of the sixteenth century, over the years the interior of the cottage had been updated, while maintaining the original front. It was a humble timber framed house, with a domed upstairs loft and a dormer window. The gable roof was made of red stone, with two stone chimneys.

Abermont House eclipsed it in luxury, yet the simplicity of this little safe house appealed to him. Here, he thought better. He breathed without the spectral presence of his father in every nook and cranny. He was Falcon.

Vivian's eyes lit up. "Is this where we're staying? It's charming." She dropped his arm to approach the house. Northley trailed after her, tutting.

His breath released in a loud whoosh of relief as he unlocked the house. She liked it. He hadn't anticipated that her opinion would matter so much. Nevertheless, it soothed his anxieties, giving him confidence. Maybe, just maybe, if she appreciated the house—she'd appreciate what it meant to his profession.

Spies came to this out-of-the-way copse seeking respite from the darkest missions, often wounded and scared of detection. A rival agent had terrorized her under the auspice of "safe harbor," but this place was a true haven for those with the Alien Office. Within these four walls, the best spies of England had recovered and recommitted themselves to the Crown.

If he had any chance of turning Vivian into a capable agent, it would be here.

If he had any chance of winning her heart, it would be here.

He shouldn't want her love. Her respect, and her tolerance, yes. Admiration, unlike love, did not muddy the waters. Love made a man do foolish things, and a spy could not afford to be foolish.

But no matter how much he knew this, he could not change how he felt about her. Nor could he so readily dismiss his maddening craving to taste her again. She'd worked her way into his bloodstream, and now every thought he had was saturated with Vivian. Her laugh. Her smile. Her sweet rose scent.

While Nixon prepared the horses for the night, he followed Vivian into the house. Arden came after them. The caretaker had been there before they'd arrived, for the sconces were lit, giving the vestibule a homey glow. Off of the entrance hall was a drawing room, a library, a small study, two smaller bedrooms, and, further back, the main bedroom. A larder and a dining room were situated to the back of the house. Northley would stay upstairs in the loft, which was divided into two tiny rooms.

With a perfunctory nod, Northley took Vivian's cap and set off toward the bedroom with her trunk. Arden bid them adieu for the night, claiming she wanted to retire early.

He set his portmanteau on the floor to handle

later, and surveyed the room. Little had changed in the house since he'd last been here. Dust cloths no longer covered the dark wooden furniture; basic pieces constructed more for serviceability than aesthetics. Against the far corner of the wall rested a sturdy desk with knotty mahogany wood and a straight-backed chair with a threadbare purple cushion. A deep violet geometric tapestry adorned the wall. An overstuffed leather couch and two leather armchairs centered on the stone fireplace. Rust-colored rugs hid some of the scratches on the wooden floorboards, yet still James could feel the presence of the agents who'd been here before.

Elinor wanted to redecorate this safe house, claiming that it showed signs of serious wear. James refused. There was no glamour to the reality of what they did. The information they obtained often ruined lives. Men and women died in the interest of national security. It was bloody and it was necessary, but that did not make it easier.

He plopped down on the couch, hoping that Vivian would sit by him, but wanting her to have the option to refuse. He could not grant her a choice in adopting this new lifestyle—her life depended on the training she'd receive here—but he could at least give her this. She'd be as close to him as she wished.

She came to him. Her movements were far more graceful than his. Where he'd flung himself onto the couch, spreading out his legs wide and draping his arm over the side, she sat daintily, her hands folded in her lap. Waiting.

"I suppose you're wondering why I've chosen this place."

Great effort, you dolt. He should have prepared a speech. Something to ease him into this conversation. Because instead of knowing precisely what to say, he stumbled about, finding words that did not fit. He tugged his gloves off, cursing his own ineptitude.

She blinked. Once, twice, her eyelids fluttering shut and reopening in the space of a second—though the moment seemed much longer to him. Her chin lifted, her gaze drifting around the room, taking it all in. He ached to know her thoughts, when he ought to be able to read her without effort. His own whirlwind emotions kept him from a clear picture.

"I like it here," she said finally. "I'm reminded of the cottage Evan and I shared in Devon, before he took the position with the bank. At first, being so far out in this forest concerned me, but..." She hesitated, her eyes coming to rest on his face, interest flickering in the crystal blue of her gaze. "Now I think it is exciting. An adventure."

"It is, indeed." Soon she'd know exactly how different her life would be from now on. "I'm sure we can muster up something more thrilling to do than your usual routine in the schoolroom. I know for a fact that there are two rapiers in the hall closet. Perhaps tomorrow I'll finally know how skilled you are at fencing."

Her eyes sparkled with delight as she laughed merrily. "You would not be able to handle me, Your Grace. What would the Beau Monde say if you came back from your wedding trip wearing an eye patch?"

He placed a hand to his heart as though she'd struck him. "You wound me with your disbelief, my dear."

She started to reply, but then paused as if reconsidering. When she spoke again, her voice was much more subdued. "It wouldn't be proper. I may know little about being a duchess, but I am rather certain your sisters wouldn't approve of me fencing."

He let out a loud snort. "I take it you have not spent much time around Korianna. Just last month she planted a facer on Lord Mawkesbury." Korianna had been either on mission or in London for much of Vivian's employment.

Vivian's eyes widened. "You're bamming me."

"I absolutely am not." For once, Korianna's wild exploits actually had use outside of espionage. He'd thank her for helping him with Vivian, but then he'd never hear the end of it. "You'd think I would have known when I taught her the haymaker that she'd use it against the next blighter trying to steal a kiss."

He did not have to fake his put-upon sigh. The horror at his peers knowing he'd been beaten by a girl had sealed Mawkesbury's lips, but next time Korianna might not be so lucky.

"Serves him right then," Vivian proclaimed with a grin.

"*You* didn't have to spend a half-hour holding up a handkerchief to Mawkesbury's bloody nose while he blubbered drunkenly," James replied. "I assure you, fencing with you would be the highlight of my experiences with unconventional women. As long as you don't deliberately try to topple me, we'll be much better off than any match I've had with my sisters."

She giggled, looking far too amused by the idea of him being hurled to the ground by his siblings. "I do so enjoy their company. I hope they'll still like me, now that things have..." She pressed her lips together, searching for the right phrase. "Changed between us."

"They like you fine," he reassured her. "After all, Arden is here so you have some female companionship."

A partial kernel of truth.

"I like Arden," Vivian said. "She has been kind to me, letting me borrow Northley."

He smiled. "Arden's a true gem. Not a day goes by without me being glad my father adopted her."

Vivian nodded. "It was good of the duke to take her in."

He shifted in his seat so that he faced her. "People always make it sound like we did her an act of charity, when in truth, it's Arden that's brought us together.

Without her, I'm certain we all would have killed each other by now."

Vivian laughed. "I'm sure it's not as dramatic as that."

He shot her a disbelieving look. "You've met my sisters. Elinor alone is enough to make a man drink."

"Lady Elinor is quite resolute," Vivian said, taking obvious care with her words.

That brought of a bark of laughter from him. "That's a nice way of saying it. Ellie means well, but the problem with being correct all the time is that people grow to resent you for it."

She swept a hand down her traveling habit. "Well, I think Lady Elinor has impeccable taste."

He tracked her movement keenly, soaking in every aspect of her frame. Instead of looking away bashfully, she met his gaze, a mischievous smile toying with her lips. In her eyes, he saw the same desire he felt.

"Tomorrow morning we could fence," she suggested, and he found the breathy quality to her word entirely arousing.

"I don't know about that. We might wish to sleep in after such a rigorous journey." The huskiness of his voice made everything sound like an innuendo.

She caught his meaning, pink flushing her cheeks. "I suppose there's that possibility. Afternoon, then." Her lips parted, just begging to be kissed again.

God, he couldn't resist any longer. He leaned forward. She kept still, her eyes drifting closed. As he narrowed the distance between them, his lips about to brush hers...

The door opened. Nixon and Northley entered. Although Northley had the good grace to look sheepish, Nixon arched a brow at him with a sly grin. Bloody, bloody spies—cocky bastards, the lot of them. If Nixon wasn't the best damn driver he knew, he'd have the bounder reassigned to Russia.

By the time Northley collected his portmanteau

and Nixon finished smirking, the moment had broken. Vivian eased back against the couch, the faint color to her cheeks reminding him of the opportunity missed. She yawned, raising her hand to her mouth to cover it too late.

"You must be exhausted." He rose from the couch, extending his hand to help her up. Together, they walked down the hall to the bedroom that would be theirs for the next week.

He opened the door. This had always been his favorite room in the house, with its red brocade wallpaper and the two gray wingback chairs positioned by the fire. An eight-paneled fire screen depicting scenes from a foxhunt stretched across the hearth. But the object that drew his attention was the large four-poster bed, enclosed by crimson velvet hangings that both gave the room a gothic feel and kept out cold draughts.

The sheets were ivory satin, underneath a silver grosgrain counterpane. Their bags were already unpacked by Northley, and Vivian's nightdress lay across the bed for her, in case she decided she didn't need the maid's help in undressing. James stared at the flimsy concoction, edged in white lace, his powers of resistance fading the longer he imagined Vivian wearing it. The longer he remembered the tantalizing pink bow at the center of her stays, hiding the most perfect pair of breasts he'd ever beheld.

Dropping his hand, Vivian took a seat on the black cushioned bench, unbuttoning the tiny fasteners on her walking boots. As she did so, her eyelids drooped, her shoulders slumping. Guilt plagued him. The last thing she needed was him acting like a stallion sensing a mare in heat.

"I'll get Northley."

She let out another yawn, louder this time, as he stepped out into the hall. Within a few minutes, he'd managed to locate the maid and send her back to their room. He remained in the parlor, going over the files he'd brought with him on different Clocktower cases, until enough time had passed that Vivian should be ready for bed.

When he reentered the room, she was curled up underneath the covers, sound asleep. After changing into his own nightclothes, he crawled into bed next to her.

He brushed a kiss across her cheek and turned over, blowing out the candle. He'd attempt sleep, though he had no real hope it would come to him.

Tomorrow he'd confess everything to her—and hope to God she understood.

WHEN HE AWOKE the next morning, his arm was slung about Vivian's waist, his right leg swung over the top of hers. The faint scent of roses drifted from her blonde locks splayed out across her pillow. How did she smell so good after a day's worth of traveling? He doubted he smelled as fresh, after helping Nixon to fix the carriage wheel.

Her scent was doing wicked things to him. Making him far too aware of the lushness of her curves, the way her body fit against his like the perfect key to his locked up heart. He swallowed, trying to will his erection down. Yet he couldn't help himself—snuggled up to her, he felt he was right where he should have been all along.

He hugged her tighter to him. She dozed peacefully, her breathing steady. A primal part of him recognized that as an achievement. His woman slept soundly by his side, confident that he could protect her from harm. She'd felt safe in his embrace. Comfortable.

Would she still feel so content when he told her the truth?

He grimaced, that reminder dimming his sultry thoughts. He'd always considered it a point of pride that he'd never had to reveal his real identity to an asset. There were missions that required such exchanges of information, but his cover had always been deemed too valuable to expose. But such competence in his profession meant he had no point of reference for a conversation like this. Every opening line he thought of sounded trite to his ears.

Gently, he extricated himself from the bed, careful not to disturb her. His arousal would decrease, as long as he kept away from her. By the time she awoke, he'd be able to look her in the eye without his mind being a lust-addled jumble.

The main bedroom had no windows, which made it easier to guard but much harder to ascertain the time of day without the rays of sunlight. He lit the candle by the bed, looping his thumb in the handle of the brass chamber candlestick and carrying it over to the dresser. He did a double take as he caught sight of the clock face.

Six in the morning.

He'd slept until dawn. Christ, he hadn't done that since Louisa's death. Setting the candlestick down on top of the dresser, he tunneled his fingers through his hair, trying to remember if he'd stirred at all during the night. He couldn't recall dreaming. Only the soothing blackness of night, the reassuring hum of Vivian's breathing.

He spun around, facing the bed again. Lost in slumber, she looked almost angelic, her golden hair a halo. Yet he knew her to be more salacious than her appearance dictated, and he found himself loving the real version of her far more than the visage. Her hand curled around the counterpane, the sapphire ring on her finger flashing in the candlelight. He didn't need a ring to mark the claim she had on him. She'd done what no other woman before her had managed. She'd broken through his carefully constructed walls.

And that scared the devil out of him.

He allowed himself one last look before turning back around. Sliding the dresser drawer slowly to minimize the noise, he pulled out his clothes for the day. He dressed behind the privacy screen, not wanting to shock her in case she awoke. Without a valet, his toilette was much simpler by necessity.

He pressed his fingers to his lips and blew a kiss to Vivian's sleeping form, then crept from the room.

CHAPTER 15

JAMES DIDN'T SEE Vivian until after breakfast. He'd spent the early hours with Nixon, going over potential scenarios of attack. On the very remote possibility that the bastard managed to locate their safe house, they'd be prepared to fight Sauveterre. Between Nixon, Arden, and himself, he felt confident that they'd be able to defend Vivian. Still, he would remain vigilant. Never again would he underestimate his opponent.

When he came back to the house, he followed the sound of voices to the parlor. Vivian was talking with Arden, a steaming cup of tea in her hand. For a second, he stood in the doorway, observing their interaction. Vivian smiled, laughing at something Arden said. He loved the way she laughed—freely, unrestrained, so genuine. He'd forgotten what it meant truly to laugh without a gambit to follow until she'd sauntered into his life.

Arden caught his eye, raising one brow in question. He nodded, and her grin widened.

"James, do come here," she called. "We were discussing Robert Burns's poetry, particularly *Auld Lang Syne*. I'm sure Vivian would love to hear your diatribe."

Grimacing, James sat down on the couch next to Vivian. "The man can't write."

"Really? I thought it was quite lovely." Vivian chuckled, resting her hand on top of his. The ease of her gesture soothed him—she was comfortable around him. Comfort he was about to destroy.

"Burns took much of the first verse from James Watson." He spoke without passion, unable to summon up the energy that normally accompanied this lecture. "And Lord knows who Watson took his from; as yet another version of the poem was compiled by Allan Ramsay. I detest how Burns has made his fame off the work of others."

Arden and Vivian continued discussing Burns's work, but even the prospect of ranting against his least favorite poet could not interest him when his chance for a happy existence might shatter in a few moments. These last few days with Vivian had given him hope that maybe they could have a marriage based on more than friendship. He wanted that with every fiber of his being.

His right leg jiggled as he sat on the couch, his foot tapping against the carpet. He couldn't be still. Vivian's hand had not moved from his left knee, yet her touch did not reassure him as it usually did, for it reminded him of how relaxed she'd become around him. Was all that about to change? He rubbed at the back of his neck. Kept his eyes on the clock, ticking away the minutes until he could get Vivian alone.

Finally, when five minutes had passed and still they showed no signs of stopping their conversation about literature, he cleared his throat, interrupting them. They both turned as one to look at him.

"Would you mind giving us a minute alone, Arden?" His voice came out smooth, but his hands were clammy.

Christ, he'd faced off unarmed against four assassins with less tension. Still his heart thumped against his chest.

"I told Nixon I'd help him with the horses, anyhow." Arden directed an inquisitive glance at him, but she stood up, smoothing her hand down her skirt.

Once Arden closed the door to the parlor, he turned on the couch so that he faced Vivian. But that didn't help. All he could think about was how her eyes met his, such trust in her expression. He didn't merit her faith. He jumped up from the couch. His boots ground into the carpet as he paced the width of the room.

Vivian's teacup clinked against her saucer as she set it down. The sound made him turn his head, but he did not stop moving.

Her brows furrowed. "What's wrong, James? Have you found Sauveterre?"

That would have been an easier conversation. Locate the target. Identify their weakness. Strike in an opportune manner. He was trained for that.

Honesty was another matter entirely. Already, he could think of seven convincing falsehoods that would ensure she fancied him. For too long he'd been cowardly, hiding behind lies because the truth was more complicated and unpleasant.

But it was not just about him. Vivian deserved to know that her brother had died protecting the nation. He hadn't told her when they were at Abermont House because the servants could easily overhear. Here in Guildford, in the middle of the bloody forest, he didn't have that pretext.

"When I married you, I promised I'd honor you. You deserve the truth, or as much as I can tell you without endangering your life or the lives of others."

She crossed her arms over her chest. "I don't understand."

He forced himself to slow. To face her. "What I'm about to tell you, you can't tell *anyone*, do you understand me?"

Her eyes tapered. "Who would I tell?"

"*Touché.*" He crossed to the couch, but he did not sit, too restless for such torpor. "In my investigation into Sauveterre, I have come upon information about your brother."

"Evan?" She leaned forward, the anxiety in her features replaced by eagerness. "Do you know why he was in Seven Dials that night?"

"I do." He scrubbed a hand through his hair. "Evan was a courier for the Alien Office. He relayed documents or messages from one place to the next."

"A courier for the Alien Office?" She repeated, blinking up at him. "The Alien Office keeps records of all foreigners who enter the country. Why would they have business in the rookeries?"

This was the part of every interaction with an asset he hated—when he was about to turn their world inside out. But Vivian wasn't just an asset he could forget about once the mission was over.

Whether she wanted to be or not after this conversation, she was in his life forever.

He took a deep breath. "Because that's not all the Alien Office does. After the revolution in France, all espionage personnel were routed through the Alien Office, under the control of William Wickham."

Her jaw fell. "Espionage? Are you saying Evan was a *spy*?"

He leaned against the arm of the couch, wanting to stay near to her, yet still trying to respect her space. "That is exactly what I am saying."

"No, no, that can't be true," she sputtered. "Evan worked for Hoare's Bank. He got the job because I wanted to relocate to London. If I hadn't asked him to move to Town, he'd still be alive today."

If nothing else good came from tonight, at least he could persuade her she wasn't responsible for her brother's death.

"Your desire to move was but a happy

coincidence, for the Alien Office had already recruited your brother," he said. "All those trips he made for the bank he worked at when you were in Devon."

Recognition dawned in her eyes. She remembered her brother's travels; now he simply had to give her the rest of the pieces to put the puzzle together.

"Just as he did in Devon, Wickham used Evan's banking career as a cover for their missions. I began to suspect it as soon as I saw how many of Evan's trips overseas overlapped with known Alien Office missions."

She drew back from him, reaching for her teacup. Her hands shook as she raised it to her lips, buying time to process what he'd said in silence.

He thought she might agree with him. She was quick-witted. James wouldn't be surprised if she had noticed something was off about her brother. About *him*.

"You're wrong," she declared. "We lived together. If Evan was spying, I would have known."

"He traveled often, and you didn't accompany him on those trips. Nor were you with him when he went to his supposed work place every day." He wanted to reach for her, to take her hand in his, but he knew from her icy blue eyes that she'd refuse the contact. "I'm sorry, Vivian. Evan did not deserve to die. I know it is little consolation, but he died defending this country."

"How dare you talk as though as you know him." Her voice trembled, but he felt every ounce of venom aimed at him. "You never met him. I'm done listening to you."

She set her teacup down so fast that liquid streamed over the sides, sloshing onto her saucer. She burst up from the couch, trying to go to the door.

He stopped her, his hand on her shoulder. She tried to shrug him off, but he held firm, anchoring her in place. The worst was still yet to come, but they would get through it. They had to. This was their life now. No more lies. No longer would they allow the gloom to hide their true selves.

He'd stand there as long as it took her to understand.

THIS WAS MADNESS.

Lies piled on top of lies until there was no space in her mind for veracity. Were it not for his hold on her arm, she would have thought this was some sort of waking nightmare. But no, James stood in front of her, the bulk of his body positioned against the door. She'd tried the same tactic when arguing with him about leaving on this very trip, but unlike her, he was effective. She could not skirt around him. She could not tug him away from the door.

He blocked her exit. Not that she had anywhere she could go. Even if she had transportation to take her from Guildford, she didn't know the way back to home.

Sweet Mary, she didn't *have* a home anymore. She'd given up her independence when she'd married him.

She whirled on her heel, stalking back to the couch. She ignored her abandoned cup. Tea wouldn't make this better. Nothing could make this better. She'd gone from being controlled by a madman to being married to one.

She parked herself on the couch. Closed her eyes. Tried to slow the hammering of her heart. Evan couldn't have been a spy. She knew him better than herself.

Yet she couldn't quiet the niggling doubt at the back of her mind. How quickly Evan had agreed that they should move to London, when he hated being in

Town. How he'd never wanted to talk about his trips once he returned. He'd always claimed that reflecting on the past accomplished nothing—he wanted to live in the present. The time he'd come home with a jagged cut down his cheek, which he'd said he received in a scuffle with some footpads.

She opened up her eyes, letting out a long, tremulous sigh. "I want to see some evidence. If Evan was truly a spy as you claim, surely there must be some sort of record."

James did not move from the door. "It doesn't work that way. Spies depend on anonymity. Any records kept are heavily guarded. If I could, I would show you the files, love."

She let out a derisive snort at that term of endearment. "Do not patronize me. I'm not your love, for if I were, you wouldn't insult me with such lies. There's no way you could know all this about Evan."

He pushed off from the door, making his way to her. "I know because I work for Wickham too. In a top-secret division of the Alien Office called the Clocktower. I'm a spy, Vivian."

"What? How? What?" Her chest hitched. She could barely hold her head up. She sagged back against the couch, the soft cushions offering her no relief.

Sauveterre had been right.

James Spencer worked for British intelligence.

She stared at James, her glassy eyes barely registering him when her ears rang so loudly. "You work for the organization that got my brother killed."

"*My* work did not do this. The Clocktower may be a subset of the Alien Office, but your brother was not one of my people." He said that distinction as if it mattered, as if she shouldn't be angry with every damn British spy that still lived. "And even if it had been my organization, we are not the ones who ended Evan's life. That was Sauveterre."

"Who he only came into contact with because he was spying." She reached up, running her thumb against the locket she wore around her neck. Evan's locket. He'd be here to give her a new ribbon for it himself, if he hadn't been a spy. "You know how much he meant to me."

"I do," James said again, such a simple phrase that she had begun to loathe. He knew everything, while she fumbled for clarity. "And that's why I'm going to make damn certain Sauveterre pays for murdering your brother. I catch bastards like him. I may not love the things I've had to do over the years to protect my country, but people are safer because of our work."

She hadn't married a madman. That would have been better—at least madmen had their mental degradation to excuse their actions. James Spencer was in full possession of his faculties, so much that he'd managed to manipulate her into marrying him. Though he might look remorseful right now, with his posture so slack and his hands in the pockets of his coat, she no longer trusted that he felt anything genuine for her.

Lord, she'd been such a fool.

His rough, calloused hands. The soundless way in which he walked. The guards at his house. How he always seemed to know what she was thinking—the cool, logical way in which he assessed everything. She'd seen all of these things, and she'd dismissed them, because she'd wanted to believe he was different from what Sauveterre claimed. Because she'd wanted to believe he was good.

Because she'd wanted to believe that a woman as inconsequential as her could attract a duke as influential as he was.

He was an expert at reading people because he'd been trained in coercion. Probably, all those little things she'd assumed were signs of his affection were just cleverly perpetuated tricks to win her over.

"Why are you telling me this now? You had plenty of opportunities to tell me before we were married. Instead you waited until we were completely secluded." Damn the quiver in her voice, the way her head felt so blastedly light.

He came closer, stopping in front of where she sat. He towered over her, all muscles and brawn. She remembered how he'd glowered at that rogue in the Jester and Trader Tavern. Her bottom lip quaked as she recalled watching him bare-knuckle box.

She swung her gaze back to the door. There was no way she could escape without him following her. So she brought up her chin higher, looking him in the eye. If he wanted to hurt her, he'd have to do it without her cowering. "Did you bring me here to kill me?"

He reared back from her so abruptly he stumbled over the low table, barely managing to right himself before he toppled to the ground. When he stood back up, the whites of his eyes were eerily visible, reminding her of a spooked horse.

"Christ, Vivian," he grated, the sheer anguish in his voice seeping into her body whether or not she wanted it to. "How could you think that? I *married* you! I pledged before God and my family to cherish you and you think I could kill you? I would rather cut out my own heart and devour it than harm you. Bloody hell, woman, I love you, can't you see that?"

Of all the times she had dreamed that a man would profess his undying devotion to her, it had never been in a profane shout. She shouldn't believe him—everything he'd said and done told her she shouldn't—but still her heart soared.

This man would consume her. He'd leave her wrecked. All because he loved her.

She forced herself to tear her gaze from him. "If this is how you show your love, I don't want it. Take it back."

"I can't." His voice broke, agony lancing through

his words like the blade of her favorite fencing foil. "I love you, Vivian. It's why I asked you to marry me. It's why I brought you here, so that I could teach you how to protect yourself. It's why I'm telling you what I actually do."

"You married me when you knew we were going to spend our life deceiving each other." She couldn't comprehend how that equated with love. "Why didn't you tell me before? I deserved to know what kind of man I was marrying."

"I wanted to. I wanted to so damn badly." He hunkered down on the couch beside her, moving farther over when she glared at him. "The organization I work for has rules governing who can know a spy's true identity, especially one as high up in the organization as me."

"Ah yes, because you are the Duke of Spies, head of the Clockbridge."

"Clocktower," he corrected.

"Sauveterre would have *loved* that. I would have been his favorite little helper if I'd sent him that tidbit." She threw her back, releasing a loud, barking laugh. "I wonder if he'd still be trying to kill me."

"Yes." The certainty in his voice made a shiver crawl up her spine. "A good spy takes care of the loose ends, and you would have been able to identify him."

"Aren't I a loose end to your organization then?" She was suddenly cold, so very cold. She hugged her arms to her, running her hands up and down to stimulate warmth. No matter how she examined this situation with Sauveterre, it always seemed to end in her death.

"If I had told you before I married you, yes, you would have been." Again that conviction of his brought her no comfort. "My superiors would have claimed your loyalty couldn't be ascertained, when you were so willing to trade information about me in exchange for the name of your brother's murderer."

She swallowed. This just kept getting worse. "And now?"

"Now you are not only a peer, but *my* wife. No one that I would work with would dare take you into captivity. And as for my enemies, the smart ones wouldn't risk infuriating me. Those foolish enough to try, I can dispense with easily."

"Because you're such a bad, bad man." She ought not to taunt him, but she could not resist.

"Darling, I'm the worst." His voice lowered, that husky quality doing wicked things to her core. Almost as if he'd made her another promise. "But my savage reputation works in your favor. There is not a man on this green Earth that will protect you better than I can. If you have another agent assigned to you, it'd be about duty for them."

Devil take him, for she found herself leaning forward to catch his every syllable. "What is it about for you?"

His intense regard made her heart tumble. "Love."

There was that damn word again.

"How can I trust you when you say you love me? I asked you if you were a spy." She sat up straighter, channeling every ounce of ire into her tone. "After I had bared my soul, you looked me in the eye and you *lied* to me. At least when I lied, I had the decency to confess before you entered into any partnership with me."

"I never lied." His chin dipped to his chest, but his voice remained level, and she hated him for that. "I might have allowed you to form incorrect conclusions, but I never lied."

She couldn't believe his audacity, lying to her now still. "You must be unclear on what the word 'lie' means. I directly asked you if what Sauveterre suspected was correct, and you told me no."

He shook his head. "You asked me if I had financed a revolution. I told you I preferred to take a more active stance, and I do. As head of the Clocktower, I oversee all our missions. Before that, I was a field agent. But never, in my entire lengthy career as a spy, have I *ever* been the bankroller."

"Semantics," she spat at him. "You knew what I meant and you chose not to tell me the whole truth."

"Never underestimate the importance of semantics," he said solemnly. "I told you that my contacts would help you find Sauveterre, and they did. My agents went to that inn."

Her head spun once more from trying to keep the facts straight. "I thought the Runners were investigating."

"The Runners are bloody useless." He sneered. "Even if I'd applied pressure to them, they'd just muck up the entire investigation. They're lionized thief-takers, in it for the money."

"While your agents are in it for...what? The glory?"

He blew out a loud puff of air. "Hardly. You can't be glorified when your entire profession depends on no one knowing what you've done."

She'd been about to retort something else, but something about his tone stopped her. For a year and a half, she'd been consumed with making sure Evan was remembered. As if by slaughtering Sauveterre, she could ensure that Evan lived on forever.

"I want to know why you do it." She turned on the couch so she faced him. "Why are you a spy?"

"Because it is what my family does." He sighed, stretching his legs out underneath the low table. "Some families build orphanages or hospitals to improve their country. My family serves the Crown by spying on our enemies."

"Your whole family?" She thought of his sisters. Impulsive Korianna, coldly rational Elinor, and quiet yet undeniably strong Arden. They certainly didn't fit the typical ideal of a prim, docile woman, but she'd attributed their eccentricities to that of the obscenely wealthy.

Of course, if they were spies, that made a lot more sense.

James nodded. "I come from a long line of spymasters and field agents."

"And I thought it was imposing that you had an ancestor directly related to Elizabeth Stuart," she remarked dryly.

"It saddens me deeply that you weren't impressed by Uncle Herman," he retorted with a smile, that same damn secret smile she'd thought he used only with her.

How her heart ached at that grin. He stirred up something deep within her, unable to be contained by logic or survival instinct. She ought to remain focused. Gather as much information as she could from him.

"Arden is not here to keep me company, is she? I thought that was odd." But she'd dismissed that too, so keen to be with him. No more. She would not dismiss her uncertainties. "Earlier, you spoke of training me to fight. I imagine it would be easier to demonstrate suitable self-defense techniques using someone of my size."

His smile grew, becoming one of pride. "I love the way your mind works, Vivian. You find the conclusion without me having to lead you to it."

"I would arrive at the conclusion much quicker if you didn't hold back basic information," she retorted acerbically. "Who else knows you're a spy? Our servants? I bet they were all laughing at me, marrying a man without knowing a single real thing about him."

"Only Mrs. Engle, Caldwell the butler, my valet and my sisters' maids."

"*Only*?" She scoffed.

"Mrs. Engle and Caldwell grew up at the estate. My father told them about our organization." He crossed one long leg over the other, angling his body toward her. "My valet and the ladies' maids need to know because we often return home at late hours, but they all knew of the Clocktower long before they came to work at Abermont House."

"The maids and your valet are former spies? *Northley* is a former spy?"

"The most I am at liberty to say is that they were involved in the organization." When she frowned at him, he smiled apologetically. "There are many things I won't be able to tell you, Vivian, and I'm sorry for that. You need to know that when I leave out certain things, it is not because I don't care about you. It's because telling you would either put you in danger, or risk another's life."

He placed his hand on top of hers, his touch bolstering her more than it should.

"Your brother was still the same man," he said, in that basic way he had of speaking, when the truth stung so much more because he did not couch it behind polish and veneer. "As am I. Spy is our vocation, not our soul. There are secrets we might have to hold back to keep you safe, but it does not change our feelings. Your brother loved you, and nothing will change that."

He locked gazes with her. She felt that dynamic pull to him again, as though he were an elemental force drawing her in. And even though she was not entirely certain she agreed with him, his words salved some of her hurt.

"Sometimes people lie for good reasons," she murmured, more to herself to than him.

"And sometimes the lies do not determine who that person is," he said. "Or what they truly need from life."

She did not know what she needed. She knew what she *wanted*—him, James Spencer, duke, spy, whatever title he chose to call himself. Her heart clamored for her to take him under any circumstance. But too many things had changed so quickly, and she feared making another ill-informed decision.

"When I lied to you, it was to avenge Evan."

"And when I withheld information from you, it was to protect the country." The smallest smile toyed with his lips. "Both are equally valid reasons."

"How do we proceed from here?" She didn't know to be a duchess, let alone the wife to a spy. "Has everything between us just been one giant subterfuge?"

He snatched her hand in his, raising it to his chest. She felt the throbbing of his heart, fixed beats while her own heart raced.

"When you start to doubt us again, I want you to remember this." He ran his thumb across the sapphire ring on her finger. "Most husbands and wives have secrets from each other. They pretend their hearts are engaged while they hide away, taking another lover."

She listened to his heartbeat, her eyes fixated on the ring. "I don't want that."

"And I will *never* allow us to become that way," he vowed, his gaze never leaving her features. "No matter what I do as a spy, what lies I am forced to tell, the information I must hold back from you, know that it will never reflect on how I feel about you as my wife. You need never worry about me being constant. You have my heart, Vivian. Always."

CHAPTER 16

WHEN ARDEN TOLD James that Vivian was outside the next morning, he had not expected to see her with a thin metal blade clasped in her right hand, the point of her foil directed at the tree opposite him in the glen. She darted forward, thrusting out her blade before skipping back. Clad in wide-legged trousers and a white linen blouse that did nothing to hide her womanly curves, she was temptation personified. Her current position, standing with her back turned to him, presented him with far too much opportunity to compose any number of obscene ditties about the view.

His cock twitched as he watched her, just longing for the chance to cup her rounded buttocks in his hand, maybe even give her a solid smack. Tingles started in his hands at the prospect, and he ached to tug her into his arms and teach her exactly what a roguish spy did with his lascivious wife. Of course, given how they'd left things yesterday, he doubted she'd allow him to touch her hand, let alone her rear. More's the pity, for what a fantastically glorious arse it was.

He watched her for a minute longer, as she swept her blade out, then assumed the first position of parry. Her form was good, but that didn't mean she'd hold up as well against an opponent. Or that she'd even want to fight when she was equally matched.

Christ, *he* didn't want her to have to fight. He'd give anything he had for her to get to lead a normal existence. But the day Sauveterre targeted her she'd lost that chance. When one French spy was involved, another was sure to follow—the bastards were like lemmings. Crazed, deadly lemmings that followed the orders of a man who wanted to remake Europe in his own image, no matter whose freedom he had to destroy. In this war against Bonaparte, agents were needed. People with quick minds and even quicker moves.

As he observed Vivian practice her footwork, he sent up a silent prayer that she would eventually agree to join the Clocktower. He'd bring it up later with her, when she was more receptive to talking with him. He wasn't sure how their marriage would function without her being a fellow spy; she knew the truth now.

He carded his hand through his hair. If she didn't want to share his life after Sauveterre was captured, then at least Abermont House would be a safe place for her. He'd see her in Town during the Season, but there would be so much he wouldn't be able to tell her. Their entire marriage would become like last night. He hadn't returned to their bed until well after midnight, when he'd known she'd be asleep. He'd crept out before dawn again.

This couldn't continue. He wanted more for them.

He advanced upon her, tapping her shoulder. She spun around, the button tip of her rapier inches from his chest. Her brows winged up at the sight of him, but she did not take a step away from him. Allowing her this show of strength, he decamped first, though her blade scared him little. He knew the foils Arden had packed for their trip were not sharp enough to pierce flesh, even without the covering over the top.

Her lips curled into a smirk. "Come to duel, Your Grace?"

He bristled at her use of his title. What was respect from others was a step back in intimacy from a woman who had moaned his given name in pleasure. "You're displeased with me."

"Nothing trouncing you in a match wouldn't fix." She shrugged, and the movement made her breasts jounce against the fabric of her white shirt.

His mouth watered, even as he tried to shake off the haze of attraction. If she wanted to funnel her aggressions into her foil, then he'd grant her a worthy opponent. After, perhaps they could have a sound, logical conversation about their relationship. He suppressed a groan. When had he started to *want* to discuss his feelings? Damned woman.

He turned to head back to the house. "I'll go retrieve another blade."

"No need." Vivian gestured toward the tree she'd originally faced, and he saw another blade tucked to the side of the trunk. "I had a feeling you might find me here."

"I do so like a woman who prepares." He winked at her, and her cheeks pinked delightfully—reassuring him that though she was irritated with his reveals, she still desired him. He'd take that as progress. Undoing the buttons of his coat, he tugged it off, folding it up neatly and setting it on the grass. His waistcoat came next. As he rolled up his sleeves, she watched him, unable to veil her interest. He may have flexed his muscles, just for a second. A man had his pride, after all.

She handed him the foil, and he assumed the position. Driving her blade up, the metal of her foil clanged against his, their blades meeting in the shape of an "X." She stretched out her left arm behind her, improving her balance. "*En garde.*"

The atmosphere between them changed, as if a

curtain had been pulled back. The air became tighter. Every sound amplified, from the chirping of the birds in the woods to the whisper of the river behind the cottage. Seconds felt like minutes, as all his senses sharpened, readying for battle.

She lunged for him, her blade aimed at his shoulder. But he parried her attack with his foil, sliding into a riposte as he whipped his rapier up and went for her chest. He almost had her, but she was too swift on her feet. She jumped back, his foil swishing uselessly above the space she'd occupied a second before.

"Impressive," he said, as they both retreated and resumed beginning stance.

Hurt flashed in her cobalt eyes. "I told you I defeated my brother often. You remember him, the brother your supervisors didn't protect?"

He flinched at the bitterness of her voice. The accusation. Perhaps the Alien Office truly had failed Evan Loren. Until he knew the exact reasons why Sauveterre had killed the man, he couldn't for certain declare that the agency hadn't taken the proper precautions. There was still a chance that Evan's death had been brought on by his own failure to observe caution.

But James had known every single guideline for a mission. Hell, he'd written half of them. And still Louisa had died on his watch.

So he'd take Vivian's blame. He kept his lips pursed firmly shut, his gaze steely.

She lifted her chin, challenging him. "You shouldn't underestimate me."

He brought his foil up, clashing it against hers. "That is a mistake I shall not make again, wife."

She appeared pleased by his promise. He took advantage of that, catching her off guard as he charged forward. The side of his foil swiped her gut. She winced, but he suspected it was her pride that was wounded, and not her stomach, for in the next second she was back in position again.

"No point. You must hit me with the tip of your foil, not the side," she declared, her tone begging him to differ. "You may have played dirty in the past, but when I fence I follow the *rules*."

He was unsurprised she'd placed such emphasis on established codes of conduct when her whole world had shifted without her approval last night. She'd want to cling to what was familiar, as he had with running the Clocktower in the wake of Louisa's demise. For her, fencing must be that same comfort zone.

So instead of arguing with her, he simply nodded and reset his stance. "Shall we go again?"

She crossed blades with him, and then they were off again. He swung at her; she dashed out of the way. She cut her foil through the air, but he dived away, avoiding her tap. They continued on for a few more swings, each narrowly missing the other, their blades clinking together until he felt the smack of the tip of her foil against his chest. She'd nicked him.

Dancing back, triumph washed over her flushed face. He knew then he'd take any number of hits if it meant she'd grin like that again, so utterly pleased with herself. She waggled her brows at him, the outward signs of her ire beginning to fade, replaced with the joy of successful exertion.

"Go again?" she asked.

"If you think you can handle it." He goaded her, knowing that she'd rise to the bait. She needed an enemy to fight against, so that she'd feel like she was in control of at least a part of her life again.

She lifted her foil. "I'm the one who gained a point against you, old man."

"I'll have you know I am only four years older than you," he retorted, raising his own foil.

She squinted. "Is that a gray hair I see?"

He blinked, and in that instant, she almost hit him

again. He parried her attack just in time, carrying through with a riposte of his own. The button of his foil notched her shoulder.

He grinned back at her. "Point, even."

She returned his smile, her eyes sparkling. "I'll give credit where credit is due. You're a good fencer."

"As are you," he said, wiping the sweat from his brow. "I haven't been this well matched in years."

"I thought you'd take it easy on me," she said, her voice softening as though she was admitting a dark secret to him. "But I'm glad you aren't."

He came toward her. "I want to protect you, Vivian, not cage you."

"Sometimes they are the same thing," she said.

He knew that firsthand. In the past, the Clocktower had felt like a prison, keeping him from embracing anything normal. But these past two weeks with her had made him wonder if he could be both spy and husband. He'd existed with dual identities for so long the mere possibility of having someone in his life who understood all the aspects of his personality seemed like paradise.

"Again?" He queried.

She nodded. They fought longer and harder, each scoring points against the other. When finally they were both straining for breath, she pushed forward, pinning him back against the tree. Her foil crossed over his chest, his own thrown up to fend off her thrust. The cool metal did not abate the burn of his body at her closeness. She leaned forward, and he breathed in the welcome scent of roses. For a minute, they remained poised like this, their eyes fixed on each other, as if they could see into the depths of each other's souls. She dragged in another breath, her kiss-worthy lips quivering.

Just as he would have brushed his lips against hers, she lowered her foil, sighing. "I'm sorry. I shouldn't have said that before. About Evan and your superiors."

He followed her lead, dropping his blade as well. "You should say whatever you feel. You need time to accept all of this."

She tapped the side of the blade against her leg, her expression pensive. "I don't know what I feel. Confused, I suppose."

"Might I help?" he asked gently, not wanting to pressure her. "Perhaps I could explain things more thoroughly. Give you some clarity."

She shook her head, giving him a sad smile. "There are some wounds only time can heal. I've spent so long blaming myself for Evan's death—thinking that even though I didn't kill him directly, I was still the reason we were in London. Now I know the blame lays nowhere other but with Sauveterre."

"You couldn't have saved him," he said, the familiar line bursting from his lips before he could stop it. It felt as false when he said it to her as it had every time one of his friends repeated it about Louisa. Perhaps guilt knew no sense. The heart attributed culpability, whether or not the mind knew it to be false.

"I know." She turned, walking away from the tree, back toward the house. "Which makes me even more determined to find and gut Sauveterre. If your grand 'spy senses' can help me to do that, then I'm grateful not just to you but to your training."

He trailed after her, resisting the urge to fold her in his arms. Her brother's true vocation was something she'd have to come to terms with on her own. "My skillset does make me extraordinarily useful in this case."

She tilted her head toward him, her foil still in her hand, but pointed downward. "I'm not surprised about you, James. I think a part of me always knew you were involved in something dangerous. I'm not happy you didn't tell me before, but I do understand your reasons."

He let out a sigh of relief. Maybe there was hope for them after all. "Thank you."

"Evan always said to fight fire with fire," she said. "Well, I'm bringing a damn inferno to the party, then."

THAT EVENING AFTER dinner, Vivian curled up in an armchair by the fire in the library. Her body ached from their rigorous fencing, but it was a good ache—a reminder she'd done something for once. She'd fought James on equal footing. She hadn't given in to the urge to flee far from here.

She still couldn't make sense of what their relationship would become, but at least for now, her mind was clearer. That was the beauty of spirited exercise. She resolved to challenge him to another match tomorrow, and the day after that, onward until she could find the right words to express the tumult of her thoughts.

Untucking her locket from underneath her gown, she lifted it up, surveying it. The gold was dingy, burnished. She flipped the clasp open to the portrait of Evan.

"How could you?" She murmured. "How could you lie to me for so long?"

But she knew the answer. It was the same reason James had kept the truth from her too. To protect her—not just from enemies of the nation, but their own people. She closed the locket, dropping it back underneath her gown. Fine, so she understood *why* they both had lied, but that did not make the revelations any easier.

This new knowledge did not bring Evan back from the grave. Nor did it show her how to continue with James. All she could see was a lifetime of him holding back a part of himself from her. He'd do his spy work—whatever that was—and she'd stay home, raising their children.

She'd gone from the lonely existence of governess to perhaps an even lonelier one as duchess; married to a man she wanted desperately to know. But when he'd spent his life perfecting fabrications, she was scared to trust that anything with him was genuine.

Even if it *felt* realer than anything else she'd ever experienced.

Just as she was about to pick up her book again, James poked his head in the doorway. "May I join you?"

She nodded.

He sidled in, taking a seat in the chair across from her. "I have another proposition for you."

Her eyes narrowed. "Will I get to know all the facts ahead of time?"

"Yes. As long as I can say it without endangering anyone, I will tell you everything you want to know."

She leaned forward. "You have my interest."

He grinned, his enthusiasm catching. "We will begin your defensive training tomorrow, but there's more. I want to instruct you on how to be an agent with the Clocktower."

"You want me to be a spy?" Perhaps she should reevaluate her previous assessment of him as sane. "I can't be a spy. I haven't a stealthy bone in my body. If you hadn't been gone from the estate so much, I'm sure you would have found me earlier."

"No one's ever taught you how to be furtive." He propped one elbow up on the arm of his chair, resting his head in his outstretched palms. "It is a skill, learned and practiced like any other. After I am through training you, I swear to you that you'll be able to creep through any room unnoticed."

She closed her book, setting it on the table. "And I would take orders from you, yes?"

"Yes. I assign the missions." He nodded. "I took over after my father's death four years ago. For almost a hundred years now, a member of the Spencer family has run the Clocktower."

"So many rules and regulations you must have to learn," she said. "How do you ever keep track of what you can say freely?"

His lips turned up slightly, the barest hint of a grin. "Lots and I do mean lots, of practice."

She stood, going to the teacart and pouring herself a cup of tea. Northley had just refreshed the pot, and preparing the cup would give her time to think. She held up another cup, but James refused her offer.

She splashed cream and sugar in her cup, and then took the tea back to the chair. "I don't know if I'm comfortable with more lies."

"The most important things are true. You and me. Our marriage." For a minute, he paused, his gaze resting on her face. "I confess to some selfish desire in wanting you to join our ranks. We'd be together far more often, and I'd be able to share basic information with you that I would have to keep to myself otherwise."

She imagined nights spent with him in some shadowy corridor, forced to wait there until their opponent left the vicinity. They'd put the time to good use, finding all the right places to touch, the threat of possible exposure fueling their passion...

She took a drink of tea, coloring as she realized his eyes were on her. "What would becoming a spy entail?"

"For now, it would be simple missions. Reconnaissance, eavesdropping, and evaluating the intelligence received by other spies. Document retrieval, if you're with a more experienced agent. Largely, the same thing you've been doing in the last half a year. Nothing too perilous. The last thing I want is to endanger you further, but you're already in this life." Having completed a full circuit of the room, he retraced his steps anew. "There are other spies who will handle the more dangerous missions, like persuading an asset to our side or..."

He stopped himself in time, but she did not need him to finish the thought.

She peered over her teacup at him, widening her eyes in faux doe innocence. "Or elimination?"

He stopped his pacing, turning on his heel to meet her gaze. The muscles in his throat worked as he swallowed. "Or elimination."

"You who speak so highly of justice," she murmured, setting her teacup down on the table.

He came to her, finally plopping onto the seat next to her, his long legs stretched out before him. "It is *because* of the terrible things that I have done in the name of my country that I caution you against vengeance. Once you take a life, you're forever changed and not for the better. You're a good person, Vivian. I don't want to see that stripped away from you."

She didn't feel like a good person. Hadn't she burned that bridge the day she accepted a position in his employ under false pretenses? Yet he still saw something worth championing in her.

"This spy proposal of yours," she began. "Would I have to answer now? Or could I have time to think about it?"

"You may have as long as you need," he said. "But what I've told you has to stay between you and me alone."

She nodded. "I understand. Would you still teach me self-defense?"

"Absolutely."

She breathed a sigh of relief at that. The idea of being unprepared for Sauveterre's attack ate at her. "Good. Because I need time to think about this."

"You are my wife, Vivian." He rose from his chair,

crossing to the door before turning around. "I am never going to take your choices away from you. You must find your own path--but I hope it's with me."

CHAPTER 17

THE NEXT MORNING, Vivian stood in the center of the small clearing, waiting for James. Nixon had escorted her to the copse after breakfast. While she still found his brute size intimidating, she'd discovered that Nixon was quite nice. He'd told her a few stories of his past work with James as they walked into the forest, though she suspected the names of their associates had been changed to protect their identities. *A rose by any other name would smell just as sweet,* Shakespeare wrote. Maybe it didn't matter what name James went by—as long as his feelings for her remained the same.

She ran a hand down the sea-green muslin of her simple day dress, one of her old gowns from when she'd been a governess. Northley had smacked her hand away when she'd reached for her fencing trousers, claiming that if she was going to fight, she ought to learn to do so in the clothes she'd normally wear. She supposed Northley had a point—though it was slightly disconcerting to have the maid speak about fighting so authoritatively.

Though her old dress still fit the same, it didn't feel right on her anymore. In a little over a fortnight, her life had changed so much. She was constantly spinning, readjusting as another new bombshell hit her and disrupted her hard-won equilibrium. Her brother had been a spy. Sauveterre was an operative. James was one too, and his sisters. At this point, she'd started to wonder who in her acquaintance *wasn't* a covert agent.

She took a deep breath, lowering herself down on an overturned log toward the end of the enclosure. Nixon's eyes narrowed, but he didn't comment. She liked that about him. He'd told her earlier that they were going to be training in self-defense today.

Which would put her one step closer to being able to defeat Sauveterre.

She reached up, untying the knot that tied her bonnet under her chin. The most important thing was stopping Sauveterre from hurting other people. And making him rue the day he ever met her brother. That goal had not changed—perhaps it was the only thing that still remained the same.

Arden emerged first from the woods, James on her heels. Vivian's heart soared at the sight of him. He held back, surveying the thicket, his Roman nose wrinkling as he thought. Scruff dotted his chin, giving him a rugged appearance. He wore no coat, his white cambric shirt straining against his broad shoulders as he strode forward, content there was no immediate threat of danger.

And though she could not explain it, though he'd dealt a vicious blow to her established order two days prior, she felt safer now that he was here.

He came toward her, brushing a kiss across her cheek. She leaned into him, but in a second he was gone, standing in the center of the grove with Arden and Nixon.

"First, we'll demonstrate the moves, and then you can try them out," he said. "I want you to feel confident that you'll be able to defend yourself in any given situation."

She nodded. "I understand."

To start with, he led the group through a series of stretches to prepare them for the exercises. Once they were ready to begin, he gestured for Arden and Nixon to face each other, while he took a seat next to her on the bench. "The point of any self-defense technique is to give you a chance to escape. The agents you're fighting with—or against—have years of experience. They can take care of themselves. I don't want you to put yourself in unnecessary danger. Do you understand, Vivian?"

"Leave the gallantry to the professionals?" She did not tell him that she'd already started imagining making Sauveterre bleed.

His eyes narrowed, and she suspected he knew she'd lied. Her emotions were too transparent around him. If she did accept his offer, how would she ever be a proficient spy when she couldn't lie effectively? It seemed impossible.

"First, we're going to discuss soft targets. Do you know what those are?" Upon her negative response, he tapped his left eye with one finger, then his ear. "I want you to remember this: eyes, ears, mouth and nose. Throat, groin, fingers and toes. Say it back for me."

"Eyes, ears, mouth and nose. Throat, groin, fingers and toes," she repeated, cocking her head. "It sounds like a nursery rhyme I'd teach Lord Thomas."

"Good, then you'll remember it better," James said. "Those are the areas of your body that no matter how strong you are, remain susceptible to attack. So if you're in a confrontation, you want to go after the soft targets."

Vivian surveyed her hands. "But how will I possibly have a chance against someone who is, say, twice my size?"

"No matter how strong you are, it still hurts like the dickens when someone hits those softer areas,"

Arden replied. "Say Nixon comes at me from the front. I divert him with both thumbs jammed into his eye sockets."

"What will that do?" she asked.

Nixon grimaced. "It'll bloody hurt."

"It'll send a sharp jolt of pain through him, and gives her enough time to either combine that with another move—like a knee to the groin, or a strike with her elbow to his mouth—or leave the area entirely." James reached forward, tapping her ear.

"I could also have slammed my palms upon his ears," Arden added. "That would daze him, again giving me a better chance at escape."

Vivian touched her eyes, then her ears, and onward. "So the main goal in any attack is to get away."

The main goal in any attack against Sauveterre would be to strike him dead, but somehow she didn't think James would agree with her.

"There are three most likely attacks: a sudden onslaught from the front, a throat grab, or an approach from behind," Arden said. "Watch what I do when Nixon tries to attack me from the front."

Nixon came at her, crowding her aggressively. Arden slapped him in the neck, stunning him. Nixon reeled back, landing on the ground. Arden extended a hand, pulling him back up.

Vivian's jaw dropped. "How was that possible? You hit him once and he went down."

"It's about knowing *where* to hit." Arden ran her finger down the back of Nixon's neck. "There's an artery here, you see? If I slap with the palm of my hand, it affects Nixon's ability to breathe. When he falls, I have a chance to get away."

She demonstrated it again with the same result. Nixon fell to the ground, and Arden ran.

James reached for her hand, helping her up from the bench. "Now it's time for you to try. And don't hold back—no matter what you do to me, I've had much worse. I will gladly take whatever pain you deliver it means you'll be safe."

One glance at his face told her he meant it, too. This man, this spy, had dropped everything to defend her. He was not the man she'd believed he was. Perhaps he was better. His words of protection were not empty promises. She knew undeniably as he rolled up his sleeves and stood back from her that he'd rather die than let her fall into the hands of a villain.

For all she knew, she'd be dead now if he hadn't intervened.

She gulped.

Clenching her fists at her side, she took a step forward. James approached her, swinging his arms and getting into her space. She reached up, slapping him. When at first, she didn't hit the right area he had her repeat the move. It took her several tries, but finally she slapped him with her palm out, and he went down.

"Oh!" She exclaimed, running to help him up. "That *does* work."

He grinned at her, brushing the dirt off his breeches. "You did marvelously. You remind me of Arden when she first started training."

She blushed. "Thank you."

"Songbird's the best we have," Nixon chimed in, heading back to the middle of the makeshift ring for the next exercise.

Arden laughed. "Flattery will not gain you reprieve from arse-kicking."

Nixon shrugged. "'Twas worth a try."

"A noble effort," Arden agreed. "Fruitless, but noble nonetheless."

They taught her how to break a throat grab by wrapping an arm around her adversary's neck and forcing him backward. The time passed quickly, as they practiced each move until she could complete it successfully. By early afternoon, she understood the basics of evasion. Slowly but surely, she became more at ease with the steps, gaining fluidity in her movements.

When it came to show her an attack from behind, Arden and Nixon reassembled in the center of the clearing. "Say I don't notice that Nixon is behind me. Ideally, he'd stay still after grabbing me and I could stomp on his foot and then run. But most likely, your assailant will be focused on trying to grab you and move you to a different area."

The icy hand of fear twisted her gut. If Sauveterre captured her, he'd try to transport her somewhere else, away from Arden and Nixon. Away from James. She'd known this would be hazardous, but to hear the likelihood expressed so flatly made her doubt her course of action.

And it was not just the peril, but the idea of being apart from the man who sat on the log beside her, his thigh pressed against her own. She'd thought originally that the nearness of him muddled her mind because around him, she could not help but want things she'd never imagined possible. A future filled with sensual encounters like their embrace in the carriage. An equal partnership where she could make her own choices but never be alone.

But now she wondered if that hope for a better day was the only thing separating her from being an animal like Sauveterre.

James leaned forward, whispering in her ear. "We'll keep practicing this. You don't need to be scared. You're safe here with me."

She believed him. So many things had changed, but that one fact remained. She'd always be safe around him.

She needed to know how to stop Sauveterre from taking her away from James. Though she might not understand his spying, she did know that she wanted to be with him.

She laid her hand on top of his. "Let's do it."

Nixon winced but assumed the position. He came at Arden, his arm across her throat. Holding onto his arm, she threw her head back, smacking into his jaw. When he was stunned, she stuck Nixon's groin as hard as she could, then elbowed him. Once he faltered, she slammed her foot into his knee. Nixon fell to the ground, groaning.

Vivian yelped, as James winced in sympathy. "That didn't look pleasant."

"It wasn't," Nixon groaned. He lay on the grass for a moment longer, his face contorted in pain. "If they didn't pay me so bloody well—"

"Well, we do," James reminded him. "Besides old chap, you've kicked our arses plenty of times."

Pushing himself up from the ground, Nixon's snickered. "That's true."

"We call that move the Albatross," Arden said.

"Why's that?"

"Because once you've been hit there, it's worse than a shackle around your neck," James answered. "Worst impediment ever."

Though pain still darkened his face, Nixon spared Vivian a slow wink. "Plus, it was more proper than calling it the Nutcracker."

Arden rolled her eyes. "You'll have to excuse these boys. After a few years, they simply shouldn't be allowed to socialize."

Vivian smiled. "You don't need to watch your language around me. I don't mind."

"Korianna will be so pleased," James remarked drolly. "Back to work, everyone."

He had her demonstrate each counter-attack multiple times, until they were both sweating and exhausted. Around noon, they recessed for nuncheon. Northley had packed a picnic basket for the occasion with cold meats, cheese, and bread.

Arden exchanged a glance with James. Vivian

couldn't tell what silent communication had passed between them, but Arden took Nixon's arm. "There are a few documents I'd like to go over with you back at the house."

"But, nuncheon—" Nixon stared longingly at the picnic basket.

"This can't wait," Arden insisted, tugging on Nixon's arm.

Giving one last languishing look at the basket, Nixon allowed himself to be led away from the grove. In a moment, they were gone.

Vivian took a seat on the log, pouring out the tea into two cups. She handed one to James. "What an interesting man."

"That's certainly one way to put it." James dropped down next to her, sandwich in one hand and cup of tea in the other. "I've known Nixon for about ten years now. Never met a better whip."

"I like him," she decided. "He called Arden 'Songbird.'"

"All spies have code-names to keep their identities safe. Nixon is a special case in that he knows both who we really are and our codes."

She nibbled on her bread. "What's your soubriquet?"

He sipped at his tea. Perhaps he debated whether or not he should tell her—or perhaps he let the silence drag on purposefully to create a dramatic pause. "Falcon."

"Ah." She suspected she was supposed to attach some great import to his disclosure, but the name itself meant little to her. The man behind the name, however, had managed to imprint his name upon her heart. "Thank you for telling me."

"When I can, I will always answer your questions," he said.

They finished their lunch in silence, but after a while, prickles began to creep up her neck, indicating she was being watched. She turned her head toward him, arching a brow. "You're staring."

"I'm doing no such thing," he claimed slyly.

Holding her hands out, she frowned at the dirt speckling her pale skin. Her gaze traveled to the long grass stain on the side of her skirt, then down to her boots, coated in mud and torn-up sward. "I must look frightful. No wonder you're gawking."

"I think you're beautiful." He snatched a leaf from her hair, gifting it to her. "The foliage adds character."

She peered down the bridge of her nose at him, as she did when Thomas misbehaved. "You're mad, you know that?"

"You married me," he jested.

She attempted to adopt a stern expression, yet she couldn't stop the corners of her lips from turning up. "Under duress."

"Come now, I wouldn't classify a single assassin as duress," he said. "Now if it were *three* assassins..."

She laughed. "Three assassins would change things, indeed. It is quite fortunate you have an army of spies at your disposal, my Spy Duke."

His eyes darkened with desire. Her words must have done that. He liked being called Spy Duke, for whatever reason. She leaned forward, resting her elbows on her knees. Would he like to hear his code-name as much?

"So, Falcon," she purred, darting out her tongue to lick at her lips. She remembered one of the servant girls back at Abermont House claiming that men liked that. Of course, said servant girl had stopped talking once she'd realized Vivian was listening, but not before she'd passed on a few very helpful seduction tips.

His gaze narrowed directly on her lips. She'd expected to affect *him*, not the other way around. But a vision of him above her, his muscles straining as he thrust deep within her secret place, overtook her and she could barely think straight. She gulped the rest of her tea, willing her pounding heart to return to normal. She'd always heard that a woman's first time would be painful, but if their kisses in the postchaise had been any indication, James would know how to make it a marvelous night she wouldn't forget.

For a charged second, their eyes met, and he smiled as if they shared a joke only they two could understand. *Partners*, she thought as he laid his hand on her left knee. Slowly, so slowly it was almost painful, he ran his fingers across her knee. Her breath sucked inward as he slid his hand further up, from her knee to the bottom of her upper thigh. Wherever he touched, he left a trail of fire.

She would burn from the inside out because of him, but she could not bring herself to care.

He let his fingers sink into the fabric, ruching it in his fist. The hem of her dress moved up enough to reveal the curve of her ankle, then as he glided higher with the fabric tight in his grip, her gown continued to move with him. There were her ivory silk stockings, stark white against his tanned hands. Virginal, when she felt so deliciously wanton.

Birds chirped. Insects buzzed. The wind rustled through the trees. All these things should have made her tell him to stop. They were too out in the open. Too exposed. But aside from Arden and Nixon, she didn't know of a single soul who would encounter them in this glade. The remoteness of their setting lulled her into a sense of security—yet the outdoors made her feel untamed.

James caught her eye. He did not move his hand. She nodded, her breath hitching in anticipation as he inched his hand higher. While her dress remained in place on her right side, he'd pulled her gown high enough on the other side that he glimpsed her garters, held just above her knees with fine metal springs and buckles. Instead of plain, maidenly white, she wore soft pink ribbon, embroidered with roses.

The sight of those garters drew a groan from him. She'd have to thank Madame Celeste for insisting a new bride needed pretty garters. He feasted upon her with his eyes, as his fingers brushed against the satin, tracing the little flowers. He edged up her gown a bit more, taking in the bare expanse of her leg, right above her knee where the garters ended. She shuddered at his touch, shuddered because she made her feel beautiful and wanted, nothing like the bluestocking matron she'd always considered herself.

"You have the best legs," he told her, his voice low and raw. "Bloody gorgeous legs. Go on for yards, these legs."

"Your sister's *modiste* hated them," she murmured. "She said my silhouette is all wrong for today's fashion. My legs are too long and my torso is too short."

"Remind me to have words with that wretched shrew. No one will ever tell you again that you aren't desirable." He ran the flat of his palm across her bare leg, her skin goose-pebbling under his caress.

She couldn't think of a coherent response. She'd moved past words on to sensations. Pleasure. Delight. Craving. But he didn't seem to mind, for he'd dragged her closer to him, his arms wrapping around, one hand on her back and the other splayed across her neck. He lowered his mouth to hers, kissing her thoroughly.

Then he was gone, standing up. She reached for him, but he'd already made it to the picnic basket, pulling out the blanket Northley had packed and spreading it out on the ground. He came back again, and she accepted his hand, never wanting to let him leave again. He motioned for her to sit down on the blanket, and he dropped down beside her.

She lusted for the excitement he provided, the exhilaration of something new. In his strong arms she felt treasured, protected. The only threat was the building of pressure within her, begging to be sated.

His kisses had left her ragged. She wanted more, even though she wasn't entirely sure what more would mean. Still, she knew it was there, felt the sensations rising in her core, flooding her body with bliss.

He moved to sit behind her, his breath hot on her skin. His tongue danced across the sensitive flesh of her neck before dipping lower. His hands came up around her, encircling her breasts. He squeezed and kneaded until she gasped eagerly, a flood of warmth through her body.

Breaking from her momentarily, he undid the buttons of her dress, pulling the fabric down from her shoulders. He made short work of her stays too, only stopping for a moment to run his finger across the bow underneath her breasts.

"Someday, I'll take proper time to appreciate these," he murmured. "But all I can think about now is how the last time we were like this, we were interrupted. Not again."

"A half hour, I promised," she grinned slyly. "You'd best be quick. The clock starts now."

He scooted around to the other side of her, helping her out of her dress. She sat before him in her chemise alone, yet she did not feel ashamed. Outside in this wilderness she could be equally uncontrolled. She had no time to care for the restrictions of society, for his mouth was on her again, her nipple poised between his two teeth. And oh God, those things he did with his tongue—she didn't want to stop, ever.

"Do you trust me?" he asked, the intensity of his words breaking through the dullness of her passion-soaked mind.

"Always," she murmured without thought, grabbing hold of his hand.

Gently, he pushed her down on the blanket, crawling between her thighs. He grabbed hold of the hem of her chemise, dragging them up to her waist, leaving her legs bared to him. "I do not think—"

He slid one finger inside her, in the very place where she felt so slick, so desperately in need of him. And he stroked and stroked as her hips bucked against him. She no longer cared about her unclothed state, about the danger surrounding them when they returned to Maidstone, about anything other than him and his thumb rocking against that little button of wonderful nerves. Squirming against him, she slid her hand down, holding him in that point. The most glorious sensations built up within her, taking her higher and higher, and she wanted to see this through—to see what she'd become at the other side.

She could not think—she could barely breathe—the pleasure was too much. She could not take it. She would explode at the seams, leaving only shattered bits in place.

He pulled from her, quickly opening the clasp to his breeches to give himself room. Experimentally, she reached out, touching her hand to the bulge. His breath hissed in, his eyes rolling back in an expression of half-pleasure, half-pain.

"I should like to explore you too," she insisted.

"You don't have to," he panted, but the beseeching way in which he watched her hands perch on his shaft told her he'd like it very, very much if she did.

She undid the clasp of his breeches, sliding them down his hips. For a second she stared at him, her eyes as round as the gilded dinner plates at the manor. He was so large! She stretched her hand out, amazed by the hardness of his shaft. Tilting her head, she examined him from all angles, cupping his balls in her hands, and then touching the pad of her ring finger to the tip of his rod.

"Like this," he urged her, readjusting her hands. He showed her how to handle him, not too rough, yet not gentle either.

As she pulled upon him, moving him up and down, she observed how his eyes closed, his head falling to one side. His mouth went slack, joy etched in every line on his face. She watched him as she pumped, pride surging through her at his reactions. His cock became granite in her hands, intriguingly hard and yet still supple.

This was James, disarmingly charming James, who sometimes was too autocratic for her tastes but still made sure her needs were met. And she was the one who made him moan, his breath coming out in jagged gasps, his eyes rolling back in his head.

Then, as she ministered to him, his hand slipped back down to her core. He knew just where to touch to get her higher. His thumb flicked against her most sensitive spot and she exploded, fireworks springing before her eyes. She bucked and arched and screamed, caring not who heard her as she rode out this wave to completion. A second later, he groaned, pulling from her and spilling his seed on the grass.

When it was over, he held her in his arms until her breathing slowed. Finally, when she could think again, she sat up. Her cheeks flamed as she pushed her chemise down.

James stretched out on the blanket, his arm crooked behind his head, the picture of indolence. She found it hard to match this well-sated, idle rogue with the driven spy who could flip a man twice his size with one cleverly executed movement. If she'd learned anything about her new husband, it was that he was devilishly hard to characterize.

He caught her eye, nodding. She decided this was her new favorite of his many expressive head tilts: one of approval, of utter contentment, of even masculine satisfaction. She glanced at the bodice of her chemise, free of stays, and suddenly she did not feel so embarrassed.

She felt...proud.

Vivian grasped her short stays between her thumb and forefinger. Hesitating for a second, she ran her finger over the fabric-covered wooden busk at the front. The busk forced her into good posture, reinforced by the laces in the back. In this short corset, she was supposed to be a proper lady. Refined. Polished.

She closed her eyes for a second and listened to the birds chirping in the trees. A few minutes ago, she'd been as wild and free as those birds.

Opening her eyes, she slipped the corset on over her chemise, turning around. "Would you mind assisting?"

James snapped to attention, bolting upright. With adroit fingers, he laced her back up. He handed her dress, helping her into it, sliding the straps of her dress back up onto her shoulders. His touch lingered a little too long. He laid a soft kiss against her neck, his mouth hot against her already heated skin. But it was a welcome warmth, chasing away the coldness of the last year.

She let her body go slack against his stalwart frame. He was a bulwark against the darkness, albeit temporarily.

She didn't want to be alone anymore.

"That was...incredible," she murmured, thinking that the English language didn't have proper words to truly convey how magnificent that had felt.

"I shall include that in my report," he quipped, as his fingers trailed down her arm.

She pulled back from him. "You wouldn't."

He grinned. "While I think that wouldn't be the most salacious thing my superior has ever read, no, I most certainly wouldn't. The idea of another man knowing how to summon those delectable moans from you makes me want to challenge him to pistols at dawn."

She flushed. She'd never found violence attractive before. It had become necessary once Evan was murdered, but she did not relish the idea. Yet the prospect of James fighting a battle in her honor was strangely arousing. God, it had been so long since someone had supported her. Cared about her.

Loved her.

She saw a million futures before her eyes, and she dared hope that someday he might truly be enamored with her. For now, what they'd just done—the way he'd made her writhe with ecstasy—perhaps that was enough.

"As much as I'd like to stay here with you forever, it's time to go." James stood, extending a hand to her. "But don't fret, love. That was only the beginning."

CHAPTER 18

THREE DAYS PASSED. Three days of fighting, fencing, and shooting, a constant surge of excitement through his body. Vivian progressed well with her training. She'd picked up shooting with the flintlock as though she'd been born with his Bedford pistol in her hand. Her combat was becoming fluid, the steps to each defensive maneuver now rote. Tomorrow, he'd start to add more complex moves into her exercises.

It was not enough.

He could not shake the feeling that something bad was coming. No matter how much they prepared, this sensation kept him wide-awake at night. He pushed open the door to their bedroom, intending to creep quietly inside so he wouldn't wake Vivian. She had gone to bed early, while he'd stayed awake to review more files.

But the candle burned in the lamp, casting a golden glow. Amber flames burned in the fireplace, bathing the room in comfortable warmth. The fur rug had been brought out from the armoire and spread in front of the fire. It was a cozy, convivial scene—made even more welcoming by his wife curled up on the rug in a thin white nightdress that left little to the imagination. Her blonde hair trailed down her back in a thick braid, while a maroon shawl draped over her shoulders.

He shut the door, and she looked up at the click of the handle, a slow smile crooking her lips. She sat up on the rug, her legs tucked beneath her. Reaching behind her, she held up a bottle of brandy. "Care for a drink?"

He didn't remember leaving brandy here; one of the other spies must have forgotten to take it with him. "We seem to be missing snifters."

She gave him a playful look. "Why must we be civilized? This is not a grandiose social event. We are in the middle of the woods, James. There's a bottle and there's your mouth. For a man so skilled in *equations*, I think you can do the mathematics."

He leaned down, removing his boots and setting them by the door. Then he came toward her, sitting down on the rug beside her. "I shall never make amends for that dashed proposal, shall I?"

She laughed. "You are a duke and a master spy, a combination bound to swell your head. It is my duty to keep you grounded by reminding you of the most unromantic proposal in history."

"How benevolent of you," he said. "Years from now, you'll be telling our children how 'Papa said we were like equations.'"

He hadn't meant to say that. He hadn't meant to speak about the future at all. He'd wanted to live in the moment, with no thoughts of the danger the upcoming weeks would bring them.

She raised the bottle to her lips, sipping. "So you think we're going to live through this."

"Yes." He grabbed the bottle from her and imbibed. "We are survivors, aren't we?"

She snatched the bottle from him, taking another drink from it. "Everyone must end sometime. I doubt Evan ever expected to die, but there you have it. He's dead."

"Ah." He now knew why she drank tonight. "I won't let you die before your time. I made you a promise, darling."

This time, I will keep my vow.

She passed the bottle back to him. He took another long sip, brandy splashing down his throat, the sweet, nutty bite saturating heat throughout him. Combined with the warmth of the fire, it was almost enough to cut the chill settling in the base of his spine. The unsettling dread that he'd fail again.

"Even you, with all your eminent skills, cannot predict the future." She ran her hand across the rug, her pale fingers a stark contrast to the dark brown fur. Once this wooly shell had been a bear—a living, breathing animal with power and ferocity.

"I do not need to predict the future." His fingers curled around the lip of the bottle, but he did not drink again. "All I need to know is what I am willing to do to ensure that you live a long and healthy life."

She lifted her eyes to him, her long lashes flitting against her milky skin. "And that is?"

"Anything," he answered without reluctance.

Her lower lip quivered. He'd hoped to reassure her, not scare her further. She needed to know the truth: he was in this fight until the end. No matter what he had to sacrifice. She would live.

She shook her head. "I don't want you to do that. You know I appreciate all you've done to protect me, James, but there has to be a limit. My life is not so valuable that it would justify the loss of yours."

Another swallow of brandy, smaller this time, just enough to fire his body again. "I disagree."

"This is my problem," she reminded him. "*I* accepted Sauveterre's proposition. *I* spied on you."

He tucked the brandy bottle behind them. "And my organization failed Evan, and by extension, you and everyone else. Sauveterre is my problem, too. He was looking for me, Vivian. He used you as a vehicle to get to me."

"That doesn't mean you get to die for me." Taking his hand in hers, she wrapped her fingers around his. "Because even if you don't say exactly that, I know that's what you're thinking. I see it in your eyes. That dark, haunted look you get when you think I'm not watching you."

For a second, he could do no more than gaze into her eyes; breathe in her rose scent and pretend that a lifetime with her was not as elusive as he believed. With her free hand, she drew the shawl tighter around her, as though it might keep her safe.

Nothing so trivial could ensure her security. Nothing—no one—could do that but him.

"I'm not going to let you." Her determined tone matched his. "We will fight Sauveterre together, and if it comes to the point that there's no way out, you will run."

He released her hand, shifting so that he sat with his legs straight out on the bear rug. The fire made his socks and the hem of his breeches warm. "I can't do that."

Something in his tone must have intrigued her, for she leaned forward, her eyes searching his face. "I can't help but wonder if there's something more to this than self-preservation or the standard heroism of a spy."

He wasn't a hero. He was a callous killer—that he'd slayed in the name of the Crown did not change the fact. And those murders weren't the worst things he'd done.

Vivian's features took on the contemplative cast he knew too well. "That night in your office, on the first anniversary of your sister's death, you said she died in a hunting accident. But knowing now what I know about your sisters, I cannot help but wonder…was Louisa involved in the Clocktower as well?"

The temperature in the room seemed to drop by

ten degrees at the mention of Louisa's name. No amount of fire or brandy could staunch this cold. Still he shifted closer to Vivian, pressing his thigh against her leg, as close as he could get to her without pulling her into his lap.

She laid her hand on his knee. "I told you all about Evan, about the life I had in Devon. You know everything about me. Tell me what really happened to Louisa."

He stiffened. He did not want to discuss this.

Her voice grew quiet, barely audible over the lapping flames of the fire. "I know honesty is not in a spy's vocabulary normally, but I am your wife, James. Whatever you tell me, it won't change how I see you."

He did not want her to view him as weak. Or worse, to know that he had forfeited his sister's life by underestimating his opponent.

But she leaned her head against his shoulder, and her touch quieted his mind the way no liquor could. He'd promised to tell her what he could, and Louisa's death was common knowledge amongst other Clocktower agents.

"When I said someone was hunting—that was the truth. But what I didn't specify was that *she* was the one doing the hunting. There was a mission." He rested his head against hers, counting her breaths. Anything to distance himself from this story. "We have the Clocktower. Bonaparte has not only Fouché's secret police, but also his own special group of assassins called the Talons. We received word that one of the top Talons, an agent named Nicodème, would be in Paris at a concert held for members of the First Consul's court."

"So you wanted to capture him."

He nodded. "It wasn't just the information he might give us on other Talons. Nicodème ran one of the worst prostitution rings in all of France, aimed at men with violent proclivities. Every day, our inside agents delivered reports of women being raped and beaten in his brothels, sometimes to death."

"That's horrible." She burrowed deeper against him, as if through their closeness she could lessen the woes of the world. "Why didn't the police do anything?"

"Nicodème was a Talon, and he had ample blunt to pay the police off." James's voice grew cold, remembering how the ruffian had boasted of his influence. "But then he made the mistake of kidnapping several British citizens for his bordello. Once I determined that intelligence was solid, I formed a team. It was supposed to be Arden and me, but Louisa demanded to be included."

"What happened?"

"We managed to rescue the women he'd taken, but something went wrong. Somehow Nicodème knew Louisa worked for the Crown. He kidnapped her, took her to his torture chamber." His voice broke, but he continued, for Vivian rubbed circles on his hand, soothing him. "By the time we got to her, she was too far gone to save. Arden and I took her back to our temporary hideout, and she died that night."

"I am so sorry," Vivian murmured, clutching his hand. "No wonder you were in such a state that night. I wish I'd known—I wish I'd been able to do more for you."

"You did more than you could ever know." He pulled her closer against him, his hand gripping the curve of her waist. He held onto her as though she were his salvation, the light to chase away the darkness of the last year. "You gave me a chance at something more."

"I am glad for that, then," she said, squeezing his hand too.

He let out a long, shaky breath. "But nothing we do can change the fact that I sent my sister to death. I knew the mission would be difficult, and still I sent her in."

Vivian tilted her head to look up at him. "Was she a capable agent?"

He deliberated. "She was at times too impulsive for my tastes, but yes, she was an excellent agent."

"And did you have any intelligence that said Nicodème would know who she was?"

"No. They'd never met before." For the last year, he'd gone over the missives they'd received until he memorized the contents. Every asset they had on sight had indicated that Nicodème was unaware of their plans. "But what does it matter? She was twenty-one, and I sent her to her grave."

"You assessed the situation given the information you had, and you made a decision that was logical. Your sister *asked* to be added to the mission, so clearly she thought she could handle it." Vivian's calm voice lulled his tired nerves, until he wanted nothing more than to believe that she was right.

That everything he'd done could be absolved by Vivian's support.

She needed to know the real man she had married. Could she accept him then?

"When you asked me if I'd achieved justice for her, I let you think that I handed Nicodème over to the police. But I slit his throat. He died in my arms and I felt *good* about it." He dropped her hand. He would not sully her skin with his touch. "How can I ask you to be near me when this is a part of my everyday life? The things that I have done for my country..."

She did not draw back from him. Instead, her fingers cupped his chin, forcing him to look at her. "I have spent the last year and a half vowing to slay the bastard who killed Evan. When I have the opportunity, I will take it." Her eyes held his with steadfast scrutiny. "So do not expect me to condemn you for the things you have done. You protected people, *innocent* people, while all I want is to hurt Sauveterre. Of the two of us,

I assure you my goals are far less noble."

He did not know how to respond. Perhaps he should have anticipated this—she was never typical in her reactions to things. But her acceptance when she knew the truth about him still stunned him.

"You may have vowed to kill Sauveterre, but you do not know what you will do if the opportunity arises."

She shrugged. "I do not know many things. But I *do* know that you are an honorable man, James Spencer. Even though I gave you every reason not to, you trusted me. The man I see when I look at you is one I'm proud to be married to, a man I love."

Love.

That last word repeated in his mind. He had dared to hope that she could love him, yet a part of him had never believed she would.

She readjusted her position so that she was at eye level with him. Her lithe body leaned into his as she placed a soft kiss upon his lips. That gentle, sweet kiss grew more ardent the longer his lips connected with hers. Like everything else she did, Vivian kissed with passion—fervently, with reckless abandon.

She was perfection in his arms.

He parted from her, keeping his gaze locked on her. Gently, he caressed her cheek. "I love you too, Vivian. More than I ever thought it possible to love someone. You're my everything."

HIS HAND RESTED on her cheek and she leaned into his touch. She stared into his gray eyes and she found strength in the steady weight of his gaze, the respect he offered her as his equal. His wife. His duchess.

A month ago, she had been Vivian Loren, wallflower and bluestocking. Unnoticed and unloved by most. She had gone through every day as though she were slumbering, trapped in the same spiral of thoughts. Evan's murder. Sauveterre's control. Lie upon untruth upon misery until she believed she would never know anything but bitterness and hatred.

James had changed that. From the moment she'd confessed her wrongdoings, he'd been there. Navigating behind the scenes, ensuring her care. She could not fathom all he had done—how his agents had unearthed traces of Sauveterre, or how he'd discovered that Evan was a spy too. There was so much about his profession she didn't comprehend, and she still wasn't sure if she wanted to accept his offer to join the Clocktower.

But she understood *him*. The man behind his many names. He was intelligent and resilient. His devotion to those he cared about had drawn her in from that first night in his office. The way he spoke of his sisters with such affection, and how he'd always made sure Thomas received the best tutelage possible. She pictured how dedicated he'd be to their own family someday.

He knew how to fight, but he also knew how to love.

She did not know if she was special enough, beautiful enough, tough enough to deserve him. But he made her want to take that chance.

She ran her thumb across his lips, letting her touch show him that though she doubted she could become a proficient spy, she never doubted him. She would work to become a woman worthy of him.

Slowly, day by day, he was teaching her that she could be his partner, but remain independent in her decisions.

She sat up straight, pushing the shawl off her shoulders. His gaze fastened immediately on her plump breasts. The almost translucent material of her nightdress left her little modesty. A quick glance down confirmed that the dark, dusky circles of her nipples were visible.

"You're gorgeous." The low huskiness to his voice made her shiver with need.

She wanted him. There was no question of that in her mind. She wanted him above her, the corded muscles in his arms straining as he thrust into her again and again. She wanted to be naked and gasping beneath him, striving to meet that devastating bliss once more.

Laying her hand on his chest, she gave him a gentle push, and he dropped to the bearskin throw. He pulled her down with him, and they fell together in a jumble of limbs, his back against the rug and her legs between his thighs.

He unbraided her hair until the fair strands fell loose against her shoulders. His fingers entangled in her curls, massaging as he brought his mouth upon hers in a long, scorching kiss. One kiss became another, and then another, mouths meeting in a desperate rhythm. He was hers. She was his. His tongue breached her lips, plunging into her mouth, filling her with the sweet taste of brandy, the spice of him.

Then his hands were on her hips, lifting her up so that she straddled him. Her nightdress fell about her, and he helped her yank it up higher.

"So beautiful," he murmured with reverence that made her wet in her core. Under his watchful gaze she *felt* beautiful.

He ran his thumb across her breast, her nipples pebbling beneath his touch. Her breasts felt heavy, receptive to the slightest drag of the thin fabric. Pleasure rocked through her as he leaned forward, taking her breast in his mouth, his tongue dipping out to taste her through her nightdress.

It was not enough. She wanted more. She wanted *him*, with no impediments between them. Naked.

In one fell move, she whipped the nightgown off

of her, tossing it aside. He had seen her with only her chemise on before, but she had never been bared to him. A moment of discomfiture raced through her, cut short when his eyes roved down her frame with such apparent hunger.

"God, Vivian," he groaned, cupping her bottom and bringing her down on his erection. He guided her against him, the rub of his hard arousal against her mons the most delicious hint of what would come soon.

She ground against him, each stroke adding kindling to the fire that burned within her. His hands gripped her rear, holding her steady, allowing her to hit that one glorious point—that secret spot that had sent her reeling before.

Then he rolled them, and suddenly she was between his thighs, his muscular arms resting on either side of her. He ducked his head, taking her lips in a kiss that branded her as his. He'd left a mark on her soul. Pleasure coursed through her as he moved his attentions to her neck, running his tongue against the crevice of her ear. She had never known that an ear could be so devilishly erotic.

He moved down, taking her breasts in his mouth and sucking upon the tip of her nipple. "Your breasts are wonderful. Firm, yet soft."

Her hands somehow found their way to his head, diving into his black locks and anchoring his head to her chest. This was magnificent; this was perfect; how it had been with them before. That spark, now a full-fledged firestorm. He bit her nipple, scraping his teeth against her sensitive skin, making her squirm underneath him.

Yet he was far too clothed. She clawed at his cravat, ineffectively attempting to undo the knot. Laughing, he separated from her, tearing off the cravat and undoing the buttons of his shirt. When he slid the material off his arms and tossed it onto the blanket, she could only stare open-mouthed at the expanse of his hard, muscled chest. One long scar ran across his right pectoral, while an old burn marred the flesh above his left hipbone. Half a dozen other smaller marks littered his rugged physique.

She trailed her fingers down that long, windy scar. "What happened here?"

"Enemy in Brussels," he said, clasping his hand over hers. "His knife might have left its mark upon me, but in the end I had the best of him."

She leaned forward, placing her lips over top of the old wound. Gently, she kissed him, her tongue darting out to lick his skin.

He moaned underneath her, and she became more adventurous, her hands exploring the strong planes of arms, then his chest. And then down to his arousal— but he stopped her, his hand closing over hers and lifting it. "Not yet, my love," he told her. "Not if you want this to be any good for you."

She arched a brow at him, but he ignored her challenge. He stood up, and then he lifted her up in his arms, taking her over to the bed. He grinned as he laid her down. That mischievous grin of his drove her wild, for she knew she was the only one who ever got to see that side of him.

He parted her legs, situating himself in between them. His lips found her neck, her breasts, her stomach as he explored her, hands roving, leaving trails of heat wherever he touched. She wriggled underneath him, reaching down to try and direct his mouth to where she needed him most, but he was determined to torture her. He proceeded at a slow, leisurely pace, as though he had all the time in the world to win.

"James," she gasped. "I want you. Please."

He stopped his downward glide. "Tell me what you want."

The sight of him was nearly enough to undo her. His half-naked body, his mouth poised right above the thatch of curls that led to her center. His eyes sparkled roguishly, and he held that pose, even as his bulging arousal told her exactly what he'd like to be doing.

He was mad, really, to expect such coherent thought from her.

"I want you to kiss me," she panted. "Down there."

"Not as specific as I would have liked, but we can work on that." He flashed her that heart-stopping grin again before his head dipped between her thighs.

Her hands fisted in the sheets, for the short stubble of his day-old beard against her intimate flesh created a sensual friction she had not expected. Then his tongue flicked out, tracing her inner lips. Toying with that bud until she was moaning with need, slowly shattering under his ministrations.

"You are so wet." He nibbled at her pearl, his teeth lightly grazing her, until she was flying, screaming out her release.

He made her forget about Sauveterre, about the possibility of joining the Clocktower, about everything that had passed in this last year and a half. There was only him and this blessed sense of rapture.

And when she was finished, when her body lay languid against the silk sheets, she looked up at him through heavy-lidded eyes, her gaze coming to rest on his hard arousal. Her climax had been powerful, but it wasn't all she sought.

"I want you." She reached for the band of his breeches, flipping open the clasp. "I want you inside of me."

"Are you sure?" His gaze flickered over her face.

She knew that if she did want to wait, he would—whether or not it made him greatly uncomfortable to go without release. That made her love him more.

"Of all the things in life, I am most sure of this," she told him.

He shucked his breeches and small clothes swiftly,

coming back to her. Nudging her legs apart, he positioned himself between her thighs, bracing himself above her. Her breasts were crushed against his chest, his hard muscles against her own curves, the woodsy scent of him permeating everything.

"I swear, this shall only hurt the first time," he promised her.

She nodded. Pain would no longer scare her away. She'd vowed to be fiercer.

There was the weight of his arousal against her folds. The pressure as he entered her, breeching her maidenly barrier. She grasped his shoulders. Stiffened at the discomfort, but it was fleeting. Her body stretched, accommodating his girth.

His gaze locked on hers, and she gave a push of her hips to let him know she was ready. He thrust, unhurriedly at first, his speed increasing as they found a rhythm that worked for them both. The fire that burned so bright within her before glimmered again, but hotter this time, for he was within her, filling her to the brim. He drove into her, so in tune to her, knowing immediately what pace she needed.

Passion thrummed through her, winding higher and higher, until suddenly she had nothing left to hang onto. The fire burned in the grate, their breaths comingled, but all she could focus on was this pleasure. It built and built within her, becoming almost too much to handle. Just when she feared she couldn't take much more, she came apart at the seams, in an explosion of light and warmth. James crested after her, groaning out his release as he spilled within her.

He broke from her, falling to the side of her. For a few minutes, they simply lay there, cradled in each other's arms. His hand came to rest upon her hip, and she placed her own on top of it, entwining his fingers in hers. Once her mind finally cleared enough to speak again, she turned her head to his, placing a kiss on his forehead.

"That was brilliant," she breathed.

He grinned. "Not incredible?"

She stretched languorously, luxuriating in the feel of the silk sheets against her skin, combined with the warmth of his body. "Better than incredible."

Her heart was bound to his, the last shreds of her uncertainty falling away as he held her close to him. As Vivian Spencer, she would be a different woman, free of the fears that had constricted her before.

CHAPTER 19

HE AWOKE WITH a start. Someone was pounding on their bedroom door. In one fluid movement, he swung off the bed, his feet hitting the ground solidly as he stood up.

"James!" Panic saturated Arden's yell, dowsing the last dredges of sleepiness in his mind. "Come quickly! Someone's approaching!"

He reached over, rousing Vivian with a shake. "We have to go."

She sat up, holding the sheet up to cover her bare chest. Yawning, she blinked up at him. "What's going on?"

Before he could answer, Arden hit the door, shouting once more. Vivian's grip on the sheet tightened.

"Get dressed," he told her, swooping up his breeches from the floor. He tugged them on, then his shirt, ignoring his waistcoat and other accoutrements. He located Vivian's dress and chemise, slung across the bench at the foot of the bed.

"Where are my stays?" she asked, as she accepted her clothes from him.

"No time." He pulled his boots on, grabbing the

three small knives on the bedside table and sliding them into the lining. On his way to the door, he grabbed his holster, strapping it on around his waist and loading two daggers into it.

His heart beat a little slower whenever he was properly equipped, alarm no longer clogging his throat. He could breathe again.

"He's here, isn't he? Sauveterre." Vivian's voice shook as she tossed her dress over her head. She came to stand next to him, and he did up the back of her gown in record time.

"Maybe." He didn't sound convincing, even to his own ears. "In the closet, there's a rapier. All those fencing lessons over the years? They're about to mean something."

The color drained from her face as she rushed to the closet, her fingers wrapping around the cup hilt of the straight-bladed sword. "No button."

"No, love," he murmured. "No button."

When thrust properly, the two-edged blade would slice through flesh, reducing it to ribbons. Now that she might actually have to exact that revenge she'd spoken so much of, she hesitated. He recognized that mien of dread; the slump of her shoulders, for it was the same way he'd looked before his first mission.

But there was no room for second-guessing.

He opened the door, stepping out into the hall. Vivian peeked out around his arm, still holding the rapier. Arden came to them, her hands poised on opposite ends of a long staff. Northley trailed behind her, clutching a parasol that James suspected had a knife built into the tube, for the tip was a bit too pointy. In this circumstance, he was glad the maid was armed. Taking in the lines etched in Arden's wan forehead, he had a feeling they'd need all the help they could get.

"Is it Sauveterre?" Vivian asked.

Arden lifted her chin, her gaze fastened on him. "That is the most likely scenario."

He caught the unsaid meaning behind her words. The list of enemies to the Clocktower was expansive—without knowing what Sauveterre looked like, they couldn't positively identify the threat. They had to be prepared for anyone.

"Where's Nixon?" he asked, following Arden toward the front door.

The hall was wide enough they could walk two abreast. Vivian made a move to walk beside him, but he shoved her back behind him. Protecting her was the priority. If anyone attacked, he'd be able to better shield her with the bulk of his body.

"Outside watching," Arden said.

Her short answers sounded another alarm in his mind. Yes, time was of the essence, but Arden didn't suppress the details unless there was a reason.

He reached for her arm, halting her. He refused to leave the stronghold of this house without knowing what he was facing. Not again. "What's out there, Songbird?"

The use of her code name snapped Arden's head up, her breath sucking in an audible hiss. Good. Her mind was back in the game.

"Five men, possibly more," she said. "All armed. Looks to be clubs and knives, mostly. One gun. Nixon thinks it's a rifle with a bayonet attachment. French military is our best guess."

"Blast," he muttered. "I do so loathe bayonets. Still, that's doable—not even two men for each of us. We've fought worse odds before."

He heard the intake of Vivian's breath. Stretching out his arm behind him, he laid his hand on her arm. Her body relaxed slightly under his touch.

Arden watched them, her lips setting into a thin line. "We can't leave Nixon alone much longer," she suggested gently, as if she hated to intrude, but duty called.

"Go. I'll meet you outside." He nodded, turning

around to face Vivian. How he abhorred the whiteness of her face, the tremble of her hand against the rapier. This place was supposed to keep her safe, not endanger her further. "Listen, I want you to take Northley and go back in our bedroom. It's the safest room in the house. Position something heavy in front of the door, and don't move it for *anyone*. You understand?"

"I can help," Vivian protested.

Her assuredness did not reach her eyes. Before his mind's eye flashed an image of Louisa, as she'd been the night she begged to take on Nicodème.

He said what he should have said then to his sister. "No."

Yet compliance without question was not in Vivian's blood. "You've trained me. I'm ready."

"It'll take years of training before you're ready," he said gruffly. "I don't have time to argue with you. Just do this for me."

She grasped his hand, her touch like a lightning bolt through him. "I don't want to leave you."

And he broke at the seams. This was not a mission like any other. This was her life.

"Please love, I can't lose you too," he murmured.

Her resistance faded at the crack of his voice. His weakness, on display again for her.

She stood up on her tiptoes, planting a kiss on his lips. "You better come back to me."

"Always," he said as she turned, heading back down the hall to the room. Northley glared at him, and then she was gone too, after Vivian.

He strode forward, his body loose. Alert. Vivian had claimed she was ready, but he truly was. Reprieve lay outside this house, in preventing the death of another one he loved.

By the time he pushed open the heavy wooden door and joined Arden outside, not more than ten minutes had passed, but it felt like an eternity. He stood by her side, waiting. Watching. Nothing appeared in the distance.

Until Nixon burst out from the forest, his arms undulating, clumps of grass churning up underneath his well-worn top boots. He dashed to them, leaping up onto the porch. He swung his flintlock off from his back, hurriedly loading the gun and getting into position.

The enemy breeched the tree line, seven armed men descending upon their secluded retreat. James drew out his knife. Arden rocked her left foot forward, her fists outstretched in a fighter's stance.

The shot from Nixon's flintlock pierced the air, the percussion still echoing in James's ears a moment later. The bullet found its target—one of the men flung backward, as the ball lodged in the tender flesh underneath his right shoulder.

"One down, six to go," James muttered.

The French agents fired off a shot, but it swung wide and landed in the porch railing. But James did not breathe a sigh of relief, for the accosters picked up pace, advancing quickly.

Nixon reloaded the gun as Arden and James jumped down as one from the porch, onto the level ground. They raced toward the French spies, each taking opposite sides. For a second, their opponents hesitated, all looking toward the man in the middle of their group: a gargantuan man armed with a rifle, who outweighed even the brawny Nixon. The leader nodded. The men fanned out, two going toward Nixon on the porch. Nixon began to use his flintlock as a truncheon, for the gun would not be as useful in close range. Another man went after Arden, expecting that as a woman she would be easy to take down.

James's lips curved into a sinister sneer. They'd soon find out how wrong they were about her.

That left only the leader and another of his men, a tall, wiry man with an unruly thatch of red hair. James held his ground; knife outstretched in his most forward hand. The leader stood back, as if he wanted to see if his man could finish the job without him needing to be involved. Abstractly, James noted his egotism—it could be used against him. Was this man Sauveterre? He did not know.

The thinner man charged, swiping upwards to the left with his knife. James darted to the side, avoiding the blow. He swung out with his own blade, but Red Hair moved at the last second. They traded attacks like this, blade notching at cloth, never doing more than nicking their skin.

Until the swipe of Red Hair's knife cut James's forearm. A piercing pain shot through him, but he ignored it, just as he ignored the sluice of blood down his arm. A sick grin twisted Red Hair's lips, and he leaned in for the kill.

"You're going to die, English," the Frenchman spat, as if being English was the worst insult he could think of.

"Not likely," James rejoined.

His hand whipped out, grabbing the other man's weapon hand. Striking out with his fist, James connected with Red Hair's nose. The move threw him backward. James took advantage of this. He thrust hard with his forearm, slashing into the operative's lung with one long, deep stroke. The assailant's muscles tensed, catching the blade before James tugged it out. Blood poured out from his chest, his mouth, and he plunged to the ground.

But James did not stop. The carnage barely registered. These invaders were coming for Vivian— and they'd kill anyone in their way as quickly as James had dropped their man. Out of the corner of his eye, he could see that Arden had dispatched the man she was fighting and joined Nixon's battle.

His people remained in danger. Vivian was safe for now in the locked room, but that might not last.

The leader surged toward James, hunched over, the bayonet of his rifle outstretched and gripped between his two hands.

Of course. Always the damned bayonets.

The larger man jabbed the bayonet upwards. James jumped back, narrowly avoiding a gash to his neck. He scurried off the side, using his free hand to block the butt of the leader's rifle. He thrust with the knife at the man's flank. The man dodged. Though he had a good fifty pounds on James, his steps were slow and sloppy—he staggered, instead of moving on the balls of feet.

James needed to outmaneuver him. He must be swifter.

He swiped outward, the blade of his knife skittering against the man's sleeve. The man came at him with the stock of the gun, trying to throw him off balance. Once James was stunned, he'd follow that up with a stab of the bayonet.

But not today. Expecting his opponent's next move, James scurried out of the way. When the heavier man crowded him again, James seized the opportunity of the closer quarters—he drove the knife in his hand upwards at an angle, stabbing from beneath the man's jaw. The blade sliced through, buried in the man's skull. He fell to the ground with a disturbing thud, the knife still stuck.

If indeed the man was Sauveterre, he was dead now. Perhaps he'd spared Vivian from becoming a killer yet.

James did not waste time with further recollections. Instead, he threw himself into the fray with Arden and Nixon. The man who had been shot in the shoulder had risen, rejoining the fight.

Three men against three—he liked those odds.

NOT MORE THAN a quarter of an hour after Vivian left James, a sharp, loud crack penetrated the windowless bedroom where she huddled with Northley. Vivian recognized the sound instantly from her practice sessions with James earlier that week.

Gunfire.

Oh God, what if James were hurt? She held tight to the counterpane, her knuckles whitening. No, James was strong. He was smart and skilled and he knew how to fight. As a spy, he'd been trained for these very circumstances.

But so had Evan.

That thought stole the remainder of her composure. Dropping the quilt, she burst up from the bed, intending to go toward the door. Northley's hand snaked out with more speed than she thought the old woman possessed, snagging the back of her dress and anchoring her to the spot.

"You're not going anywhere, mite," Northley stated.

"Let me go." Vivian slapped at her hand, attempting to walk forward. The maid hauled her back, her grip tightening on the muslin of her dress.

"His Grace said you ought to stay here, and so here you will stay," Northley replied, the levelness of her tone surprising Vivian. As if this was all habit to her.

"You don't understand," Vivian snapped. "I have to get to him. I can't stay in here."

James was out there fending off a group of armed villains because of *her.* How could she have been so shortsighted? In these last weeks, James had become her everything. He'd made her feel normal again.

And she'd in turn sacrificed him for a chance at revenge.

The snapping sound of another gunshot ripped through their chamber. Fear snatched at her gut, twisting until she felt like her entire body was being contorted and maligned. Her heart pounded furiously against her chest, her breath coming in pants instead of measured exhales.

No, no, please no. Not James.

He'd risked everything for her.

She'd save him, or die trying.

Vivian wrenched her dress from Northley's iron grip, racing toward the door. On the way there, she grabbed the rapier James had given her. She ignored the maid's call for her, her hand on the door. Her ears strained for any sound of the outside fray, anything that might indicate whether James was hurt.

There was nothing. She didn't know if she should be relieved or not. In the past year, she had come to dread the unknown. Stealing herself for whatever she might find outside this safe room, she opened the door.

She almost slammed straight into a short, portly man with a round face and a receding hairline. His brown hair was streaked with gray, whilst his ears stuck out, seemingly too large for the rest of him. He dressed all in black—except for the white neckcloth adorning his thick neck.

He appeared wholly unthreatening. Until his almost black, beady eyes set upon her with such coldness that it sucked the warmth from her body, leaving her frozen. Then his thin lips curled into a sneer so malevolent her grip faltered on the rapier.

After a year and a half of searching for the man who had killed her brother, she knew without question she was now face to face with him.

She couldn't move. She was mesmerized, her feet pasted to this spot. For a second, she even forgot to breathe, so caught in the strange, malicious magnetism of this bastard.

"I see you recognize me, though you did not expect to see me here. That was the plan—one your man followed perfectly, even if you couldn't. I sent my men out front to distract him, while I crept around the back for you." His voice was quiet, as equally unassuming as his features, yet somehow that made it more unsettling. If one did not know who he truly was, he was easily forgettable, the type of man who could slip easily through a crowd without anyone ever remembering he'd been there to begin with.

The type of man who could stomp out her brother's life without there being any witnesses to recall the violence.

That thought freed her from his thrall. She raised her rapier, thrusting out. Sauveterre dashed to the side, avoiding her blade. She stepped out of the doorway, further into the hall, expecting to follow Sauveterre. But he was still in the hall—he barreled into her, using his stocky weight to his advantage.

One minute she was standing on her own two feet, and in the next, the world spun around her. She was falling, falling. Her head crashed into the corner of the bedside table. Her hip slammed hard against the floorboard, sending a roar of pain through her.

Sprawled out on the ground, she gasped for air. Her head thrummed fiercely, and when she laid her hand to her forehead, slick, sticky blood coated her fingertips. Sauveterre was short, but he was far stronger than she'd anticipated and he knew how to leverage his bulky mass for optimum impact. And he was fast, so much faster than she was.

She heard the smack of Northley's feet against the floorboards. The maid came to defend her. Northley got in a good slash of her parasol, but then Sauveterre rounded on the elderly woman, his fist driving into Northley's nose with a revolting crack. As blood streamed from her nose, he punched her again and again, until she tumbled to the floor, no longer moving.

"No!" Vivian screamed. Her stomach roiled, bile rising in her mouth.

Quickly, Vivian sat straight up. Blood rushed to her head, and for a second she saw spots until her vision cleared. Northley's chest still moved. The maid was alive, but gore flooded her wrinkled face, disguising the liver spots with a horrific mask of crimson.

The sight of Northley's stricken form flooded Vivian with the desperate need to *stop* this butcher. No more people would be harmed by his hand. She found the strength to stand, though her knees were wobbly; though ache laced through her entire body from her fall; though fear for James, for her own life threatened to immobilize her.

She would fight, and fight again.

Sauveterre's sinister eyes observed her as she struggled and finally found her footing. "You are prettier than I expected, Miss Loren," he noted, with the same cool appreciation an entomologist had toward one of his mounted specimens.

"You'll address me as Her Grace, the Duchess of Abermont," Vivian sneered, jutting her chin outward, as regal as she could appear when claret trickled down from the open gash on her forehead.

"Ah yes, *that*. Who would have predicted Falcon was such a white knight?" A flash of irritation lit up Sauveterre's eyes, the first real rush of emotion she'd seen. He stalked toward her, crowding her, pushing her back against the bedside table. "Nowhere in my studies of the man did he seem gallant. He's a murderer, Vivian, worse than I am. Do you know how many French lives he's taken? My friend Nicodème, for instance."

James's broken speech as he admitted to taking the life of his sister's killer echoed in her ears. She couldn't fault him for what he'd done, or for other questionable acts he'd had to perform for this country—for her—to stay safe.

Out of the corner of her eye, she saw the metal rapier. It had tumbled from her hand when she'd fallen. Sauveterre must have kicked it away, for now it was across the room, by the desk. If she could just get there and grab it again, she'd stand a chance at him.

She stood stock still, keeping her eyes on him. She dared not look straight at the blade, for fear he'd sense her plan.

"James didn't kill my brother. *You* did." She flung the accusation at him, like the bullet she wished she could fire.

Sauveterre shrugged. "A necessary casualty. Your brother had some very important papers in his possession. I needed them. If he hadn't fought me, he'd still be alive. Now, Nicodème, his death achieved nothing."

To hear him talk about Evan with such cruel nonchalance sparked the rage within her she'd worked so hard to contain. She could not be calm. She launched herself at Sauveterre in a flurry of fists and kicks. She clapped his ears, and he winced, but he was not deterred. She jabbed her elbow in his stomach, and he responded with a punch to her shoulder. Pain resounded through her, but she kept going. She aimed for his eyes, jabbing her fingers in, but he grabbed hold of her before she could do much damage. He came at her again, the sheer speed of him terrifying her.

She remembered what Arden and James had taught her. Extending her hand upwards, she chopped him with the hard part of her wrist, hitting that carotid artery between his neck and collarbone.

He collapsed to the floor.

For a second, she remained stunned, staring at his downed body. When he did not move, she crossed to Northley, nudging her. "Come on, we have to go."

But Northley did not stir. Her breath flowed in and out, but her eyes were closed and she no longer remained consciousness.

So Vivian ran, ran, ran. She ran faster than she'd ever done before, her shoes slapping the floorboards, sprinting through the hall, past every closed door until she came to the main room.

It was not until she'd skidded to a stop at the front door that she heard Sauveterre's approach. Unlike her jagged, loud gasps for air, he sprinted with ease. Before she could put her hand on the handle, he was upon her, slamming her into the door. Her head smacked against the wood, fresh blood oozing from the existing cut on her forehead. Black spots swum before her eyes again, and for a second she feared her knees would give out entirely.

The rapier was still in the bedroom. She had no weapon, no way to get to a weapon, and her vision swam. Terror surged through her, white-hot and blinding. She was going to die. Killed by the same man who'd murdered her brother. Sauveterre wouldn't need to send James her teeth—he'd force James to view her mutilated corpse as she took her last breath.

To us, for we have survived when we wish we had not.

James's voice rang in her ears, powerful and reassuring. His love strengthened her. She had not survived the last year and a half to have her flame snuffed out so brutally. She wanted to live—not just for herself but for James. She'd just found him. They deserved a long life together.

She would not be taken from him so soon.

When Sauveterre stepped back from her, she straightened up, looking over her shoulder at him. She used the only ammunition she had on him: his dismay over the death of his friend. Her voice did not shake— no, she spoke decisively, even vehemently. "Nicodème deserved to die. He tortured and raped innocent women."

A dark shadow crossed Sauveterre's face. "That is one man's side of the story. Just because a man exhibited his basest passions around the so-called fairer sex does not mean his death is warranted. You should not speak of things you know nothing about."

"You disgust me," she hissed.

With one swift move, he spun her around so that she faced him, her back pressed up against the door. "And yet of the two of us, I'll be the one to leave here alive. I'll be the one to present Falcon, Songbird, and Nixon to the Talons. Me, Vivian. Let's see them mock my plans now. I have succeeded where they failed."

His appreciation of his own supposed genius repulsed her. She let him ramble, offering up no resistance, trying to lull him into a false sense of security. If she could get past him, she could use the fire poker as a makeshift épée.

"Abermont House was supposedly a fortress. Too well-guarded. They said no one could get in. They said I was fool to try." His lips perverted into a self-satisfied smirk. "So I thought outside of the box. I sent *you* in."

She took a small step forward, then to the left. Then another. If he'd keep reminiscing, she might make it to the poker.

But he had other ideas. He narrowed the distance between them, skimming his fingers underneath her chin, tilting her head up so that she peered directly into his black gaze. "What did Falcon see in you, Vivian?" Her Christian name from his tongue slithered down her skin, making her feel dirty. "Why couldn't you follow the plan? It was such a good plan. If you'd found the right information, I never would have had to threaten your life."

She tried to look away, but his hold on her chin tightened, affixing her.

"If you weren't going to help me, then I had to clean house," Sauveterre continued, his nasal voice disturbingly taciturn. "I couldn't run the risk that you'd be tracked to me, especially if I needed to send in a new operative to do what you could not. But I was good to you. I gave you one last chance, a little warning."

"You call sending me my brother's teeth being *good* to me?" Vivian ground out.

Sauveterre shrugged. "I could have sent you his balls. Would you have preferred that?"

She shuddered. "You're revolting."

"A pretty little governess is supposed to distract Falcon long enough so that she can get information. Our profession depends on the lure of sluts." His eyes left her face, trailing down her body. "But you, you must have a golden cunny to get a duke to *marry* your strumpet arse."

Vivian stiffened against his touch. "I am no man's whore, least of all yours."

He sniggered. "Your British law makes a woman her husband's slave. It is the aspect of your code that Bonaparte appreciates the most."

"Then Bonaparte is a sick bastard," she jeered.

He backhanded her across her mouth, the hit so hard she heard her own teeth rattle. "*Never* speak about the First Consul that way."

She spit out a mouthful of blood and saliva in his face. "If you wanted my loyalty, you shouldn't have killed my brother."

Fury spasmed across Sauveterre's face, altering his inconspicuous features in a petrifying manner. *This* was the man who'd stomped on her brother's face, who'd beat him until only his bloody coat could identify him.

He swiped a hand across his face, wiping off her spit. "Falcon should do better at training his bitches. Let's tell him that, shall we?"

As his voice became dangerously cold, she gave up any hope of subterfuge. She tried to run from him, but he rounded on her, wrapping his arms around her. He squeezed her so tight she could barely breathe. It was happening—the moment she'd worried about in training. He was taking to her another place, and she couldn't do a damn thing about it.

Sauveterre dragged her to the door, opening it. He shoved her out in front of him, hanging onto her arm in case she tried to escape. In one fluid movement he pulled a knife out from his sheath, bracing it against her throat.

She stood on the porch, the blade poised at the sensitive skin at her throat, and she surveyed the slaughter in the yard. Three men dead. Another two writhing in pain. Arden and Nixon stared at her, their faces mirror images of shock.

James, bruised but still standing, turned around. The color drained from his face.

"I love you," she gasped out, not daring to say anything more, for a trickle of blood seeped down her throat as Sauveterre dug in the tip of the knife.

CHAPTER 20

JAMES HAD THOUGHT he knew what fear was. The chill down his spine at a coming attack, or the dull ache of ominous precognition he could not shake. He had dared believe he was omnipotent when it came to fear, for in his twenty-eight years alive he had poured blood, sweat and agony into his country and gotten little in return.

He had been wrong.

He had never truly understood fear until this instant. *Real* fear was the pierce through his throat, as if Sauveterre held him too at knifepoint. It was the slow slide of crimson down Vivian's pale skin. The certainty that she would die at the hands of a madman because he had not saved her.

This was why spies did not fall in love.

Everything in his life turned to rot, and now she would pay for his sins with her life.

For a full minute, he could do nothing but stare at Vivian's face. He did not even register the spy behind her. The deadly silver glint of the blade at her throat stole his wits. He could not be the agent she needed. He could not breathe.

Arden recovered first. "This has nothing to do with her. If you want a hostage, take me. I guarantee you I will bring you more glory with Bonaparte than she ever would."

He heard Arden's voice on his left, but he dare not take his eyes from Vivian to verify her position. As if somehow, by the power of his thoughts alone, he could keep Sauveterre from cutting her.

Tenuously, he reconstructed his grip on reality. Arden's speech had centered him. Reminded him that he was not alone. He had two of the best agents in England on his side. His mind began to race, sifting through every possible combat maneuver he knew to free Vivian.

"I don't doubt that you'd be quite valuable, Songbird," Sauveterre said with a baleful smile, the knife still poised at Vivian's throat. "But I'll have you too soon. All in due time."

"How?" Nixon's gruff voice broke in. The jarvey was close enough on James's right that out of the corner of his eye, he saw Nixon gesture to the bloodshed behind them. "Three of your men are dead. The last three will die soon. You have *no one.*"

Sauveterre surveyed the copse scattered with dead bodies, as if seeing it for the first time. A spark of trepidation singed his dark gaze before it was promptly smothered. "I'll admit the circumstances are not ideal. I expected more from my fellow Talons. But life is a revolving set of disappointments, isn't it? The plan goes on. It evolves."

Recognition coursed through him in an unforeseen onslaught. Several years ago, he'd encountered another French assassin who spoke reverently of "plans." That man had been thinner; his hair was longer.

But his voice was the same. Throaty and nasal.

He was almost certain it was the same man. If he was right, then there was hope for Vivian.

"Bouchard," he called conversationally, walking

forward as though they were old friends. He did not need to look behind him to know that Arden and Nixon would back his play. Now, their expressions would be blank, revealing nothing to the enemy. Their bodies were poised to attack at a second's notice.

Like him, they constantly looked for the angle that would allow them to capture Sauveterre without harm to Vivian.

Sauveterre tensed, pricking the tip of the knife against Vivian's throat again. "Stay where you are."

A fresh spot of blood appeared underneath the point of the blade, sopping down. Vivian's body slackened. Her skin had become precariously white. He did not know how much longer she could stand on her own two feet.

Stay with me, love.

"Bouchard," he repeated, more insistently this time. Sauveterre's tautness reassured him he was correct in his identification. "I know it's you. Do not pretend you were not in Calais that March night four years ago."

While he addressed the man who had called himself Sauveterre, his eyes never left Vivian's face, silently willing her to believe the end had not yet arrived. He'd promised to protect her always, and he'd keep that promise with his last dying breath.

Sauveterre said nothing. But his left eye twitched and his nostrils flared, signs of indignation he could not contain under James's watchful gaze.

James had two options: either he could goad Sauveterre further in hopes that the man would become flustered and exhibit a weakness he could utilize, or he could back off and try to find another way to save Vivian.

God, what if he made the wrong choice? He risked her *life* on the chance that he was as good at reading people as he thought. He wished with all his will that he could turn back time, keeping her from this position.

She was so very still in Sauveterre's arms. Shoulders tight, knuckles white at her side. Her only movement was her rapidly blinking eyes as she stared straight ahead, her eyes appearing damp and excessively bright.

He could practically feel her terror, emanating off her in waves that threatened to drown him too. Though Sauveterre had ceased pressing the tip of the blade into her throat, the knife remained a threat. The wound on her forehead concerned him. She needed medical attention, not a continued stalemate.

None of them were close enough to rush Sauveterre—the bastard would slit Vivian's throat before they made it to the porch.

James sent up a silent prayer that the Lion was watching over them, guiding his actions to a fortuitous end. He lifted his gaze to Sauveterre, arching a brow at the Frenchman.

"You must remember," he urged, keeping his tone level while his mind plotted seventy different ways to kill the blackguard. "It was not the best time for you, was it? If I recall correctly, you'd just finished telling me *all* about where the Talon's latest cadre of weapons was located. Isn't that right, Bouchard?"

Sauveterre sucked his cheeks in, his brows lowering. "Don't call me Bouchard. That is not my name." The spy's grip appeared to slacken on the knife for a moment.

James's eyes widened in faux innocence. "My apologies. Is that not what they call you now? I distinctly remember LeGrand deeming you 'Big Mouth.'"

"Because of *you*," Sauveterre spat. "Because of you they refused to call me by my true alias."

Behind him, he heard a guffaw. Nixon, he was sure. Arden was too dignified.

Sauveterre flinched. The tiniest movement, barely

perceptible, but enough that his hand went limp again for a second. Vivian sucked in a hasty breath, her eyes shining with gratitude. She still could not risk speaking—not when the blade came back against her throat, tight again.

If he could get Sauveterre to loosen more...

"Your own people don't respect you," James said. "You're going to be the cautionary tale they tell new spies. 'Don't be like Big Mouth. He died in a draw match because he was too foolish to realize he was outmanned.'"

Sauveterre's craggy face reddened. "There may be three of you, but I'd say my odds are good. After all, I have your little whore here." With his right hand, he burrowed his fingers into the hollow above Vivian's hip.

She whimpered, her cry splintering her heart in two. There would not be pieces large enough to bury when he was done with Sauveterre.

"You see, I don't need a knife to inflict pain upon your lady love," Sauveterre said. "But I have waited a long, long time for this moment with you, Falcon. I will not wait longer. You took something from me—my friend, Nicodème. So I will take something from you."

Vivian's eyes bulged, her pupils becoming smaller, making her appear half-mad. The terror, combined with her blood loss, was becoming too much. At any minute, she might faint, risking the nick of the knife as she collapsed.

James let the full force of his wrath glide onto his features, his voice ice-cold. Sharp as the blade Sauveterre held. "You kill her and you sign your death warrant. Do you think there is a country you can flee to where I will not find you? I will hunt you to the ends of the Earth."

"I suggest you let her go," Arden commanded, her voice steely. "Or I will make damn certain you regret it."

"And I'll help," Nixon added.

"She isn't part of this." James took a step forward, emboldened by the cagy way Sauveterre's gaze flicked between him, Arden, and Nixon. "You want to fight with me, then fight *with me*. Not her. Or are you so little of a man that you must hide behind a woman?"

Arden—and Vivian, if he was lucky—would slap him later for that comment, but it had the desired effect on Sauveterre. He hesitated. His gaze drifted downward, head bowed. His fingers slid on the knife.

Vivian must have felt the blade relax, for the fear splashed upon her face tapered in accordance. Her lip no longer trembled. When Sauveterre looked toward Arden, James met Vivian's gaze, her blue eyes clear.

"I love you," he mouthed.

Her lips curled in a tiny smile, a bit of color coming back to her ashen cheeks.

"Little man, big mouth," James called, mocking Sauveterre. "Let's see if you can fight me without that albatross around your neck."

He looked directly at Vivian, praying she'd understand his hint.

She grabbed onto Sauveterre's knife arm to keep the blade steady as she flung her head back, her skull slamming into his chin with a sickening crack. Sauveterre fell back, the knife sliding ineffectively off her throat. She punched back, connecting with his groin, hitting him again and again, until finally he wilted, his knees giving out. Taking off at a gallop, she jumped off the porch and did not stop running until she was in James's arms again.

She'd saved herself when he could not save her.

He held her close to him as Arden and Nixon went for Sauveterre, crossing his hands and feet and then binding them. The bastard let out a pitiful groan, but James spared him no mind. This time, he would gladly leave his agents to dealing with the enemy—the most important person in their mission was already with him, snuggled up against his coat.

He pulled her closer to him, hunching over her to hide her eyes from the butchery around them. But instead, she lifted her head up from his coat, refusing to be shielded.

"You don't have to protect me anymore," she murmured. "You made sure I could protect myself."

"I will always—" He'd been about to tell her he'd always protect her. But he'd just watched her fight through hell and come out on the other side. He looked down at her, a proud smile on his lips. "I solemnly swear to never underestimate you again, my brave survivor."

"Your brave *spy*," she corrected.

He released her, his mouth agape. But before he could question her, she rose up on her tiptoes, kissing him. She drew him closer to her, anchoring her hand on his neck. He let her steer the kiss for a minute. Then he took over, claiming possession of her, plundering her mouth. He kissed her until every bit of her body was imprinted again upon his mind, until he slowly said goodbye to the guilt that had consumed him in this last year.

When they finally broke apart, it was because they could no longer spare their breath. Still she stayed in his arms, her head nestled against his chest. He knew that for the rest of his life, he'd want her by his side. She was a fierce minx. A damnably aggressive, impossible woman.

She was all his. Forever.

APPROXIMATELY AN HOUR later, Vivian sat on the settee in the main room of the cottage, a lukewarm cup of tea cradled between her hands. James had poured it for her, insisting that it would help her get her strength back, but she couldn't summon up the energy to lift the cup. She leaned her head back against the settee, shuddering.

Arden watched her from her perch across the room. She'd come to sit with Vivian after helping Northley into bed. The maid would mend from Sauveterre's blows, but she needed rest and relaxation to speed along the healing process.

"It will take some time to recover," Arden said, her quiet words a balm to Vivian's tired soul. Everything today had been too loud, too rough. "The first time you're taken hostage is always difficult."

"The *first?*" Vivian turned her head toward Arden, her brows arched. "How many times exactly have you been taken hostage?"

"Seven," Arden said, said after a moment of reflection. "But five of those times, it was a tactical move on my part to catch the enemy off-guard. The other two...well, I prefer to think of them as mistakes to learn from."

"I see," Vivian said, her head beginning to spin again. "I have much to learn about spycraft."

Arden smiled. "You have the best teacher in James."

Vivian looked toward the end of the hall, where James and Nixon had moved Sauveterre for a preliminary interrogation. She hadn't heard anything from that side of the house since they'd closed the door. Either the walls were thicker than she'd assumed, or they'd found a way to make the bastard talk without needing to inflict pain. Since all of his men were now dead, she suspected it was the latter—above all else, Sauveterre seemed to value his own life.

The door to the back room opened and James emerged. He started down the hall, his strides quick. Dirt and blood streaked his breeches. Stained his skin. His white shirt was ripped, and a pool of crimson stained his chest from where a knife must have nicked him. He came to a stop at the edge of the parlor, rubbing his hand against the back of his neck. His knuckles were raw and bloodied.

But he was alive.

And he loved *her*.

He crossed the room, coming to sit next to her. His baritone was the most welcome sound in the world. "We've finished with Sauveterre, at least for now."

"Good," Arden said.

"Did he tell you much?" Vivian asked.

"A few things." James did not expand on that thought further, and she did not ask. He would share what he could. "Arden, do you think you might give us a moment?"

Arden nodded. "I should go check on Northley anyhow." She stood, laying a hand on Vivian's shoulder as she passed by the settee.

Once she was gone, James turned to face her. "We have just barely started with Sauveterre. I believe that back in headquarters with our best people, we could obtain much more information from him."

"You mean you could torture it out of him," she supplied.

He blenched. "I was hoping for a more delicate phrasing, but yes."

"I no longer harbor any illusions about your work." Her smile was bittersweet. "It's bloody and distressing, but it keeps men like Sauveterre from harming innocent people."

"About what you said outside," James said. "Did you mean it? You want to be a spy?"

"Yes," she answered without hesitation. "I want to be a part of the Clocktower. I *need* to be a part of it."

"I was not expecting that response." He took her hand in his, the warmth of his palm steadying her rapid heart. Everything made more sense when he was around. "Though I am glad."

"But I want to do it on my terms," she said. "You

told me you'd assign my missions. After today, I know that there are some lines I'm not willing to cross."

James clasped her hand tighter. "I wanted to speak to you about that. With what he knows, we might be able to shut down the Talons permanently."

"That would be wonderful."

"It would be a huge blow to Bonaparte's government. Without his team of assassins, we stand a much better chance of unseating him." James pursed his lips. "But..."

She tilted her head toward him. "But what?"

James sighed, taking in a deep breath. Whatever he was about to say weighed heavily on him. "But with everything you went through to find this bastard, I can't take away your chance at revenge. Not after he hurt you like this."

"You're offering me the chance to kill Sauveterre?" She blinked, unsure she'd heard him right. "After everything you said before?"

"Perhaps I was wrong," James hedged. "Perhaps I had no right to tell you what you needed to grieve."

It was her turn to squeeze his hand now. "Or perhaps you were correct all along."

His jaw dropped.

"All this time, I have thought only of vengeance for Evan," she said. "As if that was the only way to ever make things right after his death. But I see now that I should have been looking for a way to honor the life he led."

Understanding crossed James's scratched face. "You did what you thought was needed."

"Perhaps it was Sauveterre's blasé justification of Evan's death." Her gaze drifted toward the back room. "He didn't care who he had to kill to achieve his goal. Evan. Me. Even Northley. I don't ever want to view human life as collateral damage."

"You could never be the horror that Sauveterre is," James assured her, his faith in her supporting her.

"Maybe not," she mused. "But I don't want to take that chance. When I looked into Sauveterre's eyes, I saw nothing but coldness. No feeling. If I take his life, then maybe that coldness settles in me too. I choose not to take that chance."

A wave of relief spread across James's face. His posture relaxed. Were it not for the dried blood clotting on his face, he would have looked truly *happy*.

In that moment, she knew she'd made the right decision. "If you can shut down the Talons, then Evan's death wasn't for naught."

The best way Vivian could think to carry on his legacy was to continue his work.

But she also never wanted to be a victim again. For too long, she'd put control of her life in the hands of other people. Going forward, *she* would control her destiny. James's instruction here had given her the preliminary resources, but it was not enough. The more she learned, the more she realized that this was where she was supposed to be: protecting people who couldn't help themselves. Who didn't even know that a threat was coming—and if they succeeded in keeping the nation safe, they never needed to know.

"Then I will tell Nixon to ready Sauveterre for transport. We're going back home." He released her hand, pushing himself up from the settee.

"One moment." She held up her hand, and he plopped back down. "Sauveterre isn't going anywhere. Could we just...sit here for a minute? You and me."

"Absolutely." He pulled her toward him, and she laid her head down on his shoulder.

They'd weathered the storm. They'd faced an assassin. The terrors of their past. And they'd come out stronger, better versions of themselves.

Together.

EPILOGUE

Three months later

"I'VE FOUND IT," Vivian whispered, waving for James to come over to her. As soon as he slid into place next to her, she shone her candle on the slip of paper, tapping her thumb on the postmark on the letter.

"Very good," James praised.

She'd expected that after three months of heavy training with the Clocktower, his commendations would begin to matter less to her. Yet with every new achievement, she still loved to hear him extol her success. He supported her, giving her enough free rein that she felt independent on missions, but he was still always there for her if she needed him.

"Now what do we do?" she asked, careful to keep her voice quiet.

They'd snuck off at a soirée hosted by a wealthy magnate, Mr. Samuel Rivers, who apparently owned half of Bristol. But more importantly, James had received a tip from one of his assets in France that Mr. Rivers had been seen last month with several key members of the First Consul's government.

James took the letter out of her hands, slipping it in his coat pocket. "We filch the letter and run like hell." He motioned toward the door.

She blew out the candle, dropping it in her reticule. Her new lady's maid, Kinsey, would decry the waxy residue, but desperate times called for desperate measures. She certainly couldn't leave the candle behind, nor could they risk anyone seeing the light. Moonlight already streamed in through the big windows, a spy's worst enemy.

But the risk was worth it. That piece of paper contained tangible evidence that Rivers conspired with one of Napoleon's top generals to provide him with several shipments of arms.

Besides, in the past three months, she'd grown accustomed to stalking about in the dark. Sometimes, she even preferred it now, for she no longer feared for her life when a shadow crossed her path. Sauveterre was heavily guarded in gaol, awaiting execution for his crimes. As James had predicted, he'd given them a list of all the people he'd personally known in the organization, including several names neither James nor the rest of his agents recognized.

She followed James, her slippers making no sound on the floor as she crept toward the entrance of the library. Every part of her body was on alert, ready to act.

Footsteps sounded outside the door, and James signaled for her to take cover. She ducked, scurrying behind the couch. She held her breath. The footsteps continued, past the library door and down the hall.

Vivian exhaled, her heart beat returning to normal. James stopped at the door, holding up five fingers. She should wait five minutes before exiting after him. He opened the door, glancing around to make sure no one was coming. Then he stepped out. He'd meet her in the music room, where some of the *ton*'s most eligible debutantes were performing a set of staid classical numbers, each one more boring than the last.

Yet the rest of the guests clapped eagerly, as though this night was the highlight of their lives. She couldn't help but pity them. They all turned up their noses when she entered a room, but she did not need their approval. She was the Duchess of Abermont. Their existences were sedate, a strict adherence to social strictures.

Her life was not summed up by the title, but in the thrilling missions of the Clocktower and the adoring embraces of her husband.

She knew real excitement, and she would never trade that.

The minutes passed. She peeked at the pocket watch she'd slipped into her reticule earlier in the evening. Five minutes were up. Time to meet James, and hopefully retire early from this dreadful party. Provided they weren't waylaid by any of his seemingly endless circle of acquaintances, they should have several hours to themselves at home before any of his sisters came home to the townhouse. Lord Thomas would already be asleep. Though she loved having his family near, she did cherish the alone time she spent with James.

She made her way back to the music room, cringing at the excruciating sounds coming from the pianoforte in the corner, as though the instrument was being beaten into submission by the raven-haired woman on the bench.

"I see we still need to work on hiding your emotions." James sidled up behind her, his breath hot on her neck. He stood with his back to the wall. He was far too close to her for society's standards, yet she certainly wouldn't tell him so.

"What can I say? I'm a work in progress," she murmured. "One success at a time."

His voice was so low that only she could hear him over the raucous tune. "I've handed off our bounty to

Archer." Deacon Drake attended the party, and he'd take the note to Wickham. Soon, they'd arrest Rivers for his treason.

"So that means we're free to take our leave?" She didn't bother to keep the hopefulness from her tone.

Because she stood directly in front of him, his hands were not visible to the greater crowd. He took advantage of this, squeezing her rear. "Precisely, Your Grace."

She felt his grin against her skin, and she spun around. "Good. Because I am quite ready to leave."

"Do you remember when I told you that there were things sweeter than revenge?" He placed his hand on her arm, leading her toward the exit. "I think I shall show them all to you tonight."

Thank You for Reading

Out of all the books you could choose, thank you for picking up *I Spy a Duke*. I hope you'll take a few minutes out of your day to review this book – your honest opinion is much appreciated. Reviews help introduce readers to new authors they wouldn't otherwise meet.

Covert Heiresses

I Spy a Duke is the first book in Covert Heiresses, which features four women that by day are the talk of the *ton*, and by night, England's top spies. Though each book is a standalone, it is best read in order for optimal character development.

To keep up to date on Covert Heiresses, sign up for Erica's newsletter and get exclusive excerpts, contests, and more
http://bit.ly/mlem4

Covert Heiresses:
I Spy A Duke – available now
A Spy Never Surrenders – Summer 2016
For Your Spy Only – Winter 2016
Spies Are Forever – Summer 2017

Read on for an excerpt from Erica Monroe's *Beauty and the Rake*

A Rookery Rogues Novel

Once she was beautiful…
Abigail Vautille dreamed of escaping the Whitechapel rookery and starting a new life, until one tragic night left her scarred and penniless. To save her family from debtor's prison, she strikes a deal with the rogue who owns her father's gambling vowels–if he excuses the debt, for two weeks, she'll give him her body, but not her heart.
Once he was charming…
Inspector Michael Strickland of the Metropolitan Police has always had a way with women. Success comes easily to him, and he glides through life on his good looks and family name. But Abigail lights a passion within him he never knew existed. He sees the beauty within her, not the beast she believes herself to be.
Together, their love is beyond a fairy tale.
After a dangerous figure from Abigail's past resurfaces vowing vengeance, things take a sinister turn. But Michael will stop at nothing to keep the woman he loves safe. When the stakes are high and the scars are more than skin deep, passion might be the key to a happily ever after.

Whitechapel, London
October 1832

RED WAS EVERYWHERE.

Abigail Vautille shouldn't have been surprised. Since that fateful day when her left hand was forcibly rammed into a working loom, the color red had haunted her. Deep red scars from the punch card of the jacquard crisscrossed her skin. Pockets of exposed flesh remained, mangled red bubbles now crusted black. The bones had been reset to give her a range of movement, but she couldn't feel the brace of a cold wind on her flesh or the touch of a man's fingers against her skin.

If only she could staunch her emotions so effectively.

But no, she was fated to face crimson. Scarlet was even the color of her once-friend Poppy Knight's hair. Poppy's investigation into their past employer had led to Abigail's torture.

Her stomach clenched at the shellacked ruby door of Cruikshank's gaming hell. A battered wreath hung in the center, the previously garnet holly berries shriveled and dead. No one bothered to use the carmine-rusted iron doorknocker. This was no longer a place that required a doorman.

Scoundrels came and went, invited by the new proprietor, Arthur Cruikshank. He was in league with Joaquin Mason, who ruled the rookeries from the back room of his main property in Shadwell, the King of Spades. With Mason's support, Cruikshank had turned this dank hole into a profitable gambling house.

Abigail knew the men here, their tells and their compulsions. Each battled a demon that only a hand of cards seemed to sate.

But familiarity didn't breed ease. The hollers of foxed men drifted from Cruikshank's, an unsettling cacophony. The building itself provided no comfort, constructed of crumbling gray stone, gray like her constant mood. Auburn brick made up the top floor, added after the original foundation.

Shivering in the frigid night air, Abigail drew her black cloak tighter around her to brace against the cold wind. With a glance upstairs, she brought the gloved fingers of her good hand to her lips to kiss for luck. She'd need all the help she could get in this godforsaken place.

After entering, she refused to give her cloak to the man who waited in the foyer. Cruikshank didn't employ him. When unsuspecting people presented him with their garments, he fled to sell them in the rag and bone shops. She couldn't help but admire his ingenuity.

Since she couldn't hold down honest employment any longer, she'd do best to follow his example.

Her eyes narrowed as she surveyed the crowd mingling in the lower rooms. Conversations drifted in and out, an indistinct hum. A sweet, pungent scent caught her attention from the open door to her right. Men reclined on dilapidated chaises in sleep or stupor, while two women blew into pipes, kindling the opium in their bowls until it glowed red.

"Mystery lady!" a man called, his unfixed gaze settling on her cloak. "Come back, mystery lady. Come play with me."

A lump formed in her throat. All these people drowning their sorrows. Little she could do for them now. The longer she stayed the greater chance she had of being a potential target for Cruikshank's less principled patrons.

She kept going, ignoring his summons, her skirts swishing against the dusty floor. Two staircases flanked the vast entrance hall. While the left staircase ended on a landing, the right staircase would take her up to the top floor where the faro and hazard tables were. The play was deep there.

She'd find her father at the back table. Inevitably, he'd be in the third chair, his hands shaking as he grasped his cards. There'd be a wrinkle where his thumb gripped too hard.

She reached down into the pocket in her cloak. No blunt. Not that she could pay the rest of her father's debts with a few coins. Settling the vowels for his last visit to Cruikshank's had taken the last of her savings. Years of hard shifts, aching knees and pricked fingers gone in an instant to the tables.

Now that she couldn't work in the factory, she had no way to earn back that money.

Three prostitutes lingered at the stairs, clothed in gaudy dresses with chemises peeking out of their stomachers. They roamed the halls in between their shifts in the cellar, which Cruikshank had converted into a whorehouse. He was always looking for willing lightskirts to fill the beds.

Abigail gulped as a flamboyant redhead with a gap-toothed grin caught her eye and waggled a brow.

Soon, she'd be one of them.

She mounted the stairs carefully, her uninjured hand grasping the railing for support. The hood of her cloak remained over her head, and she pretended it gave her a modicum of security. A shroud to hide behind, when it seemed everyone in Whitechapel knew her name and face.

People moved around her, passing her on the staircase and cursing her slowness. One foot in front of the other was never easy. Even before she'd lost the use of her hand, her unsteady gait had marked her as a cripple. As a child, she'd worked as a scavenger, sliding underneath the machinery to collect the broken bits of silk for reuse. The labor had distorted her body, and years of standing on her feet for fourteen hours, six days a week had worsened her knock-knees.

Each step higher made her joints scream for relief. Her lungs, weak from the poorly ventilated conditions in the factories, burned with the effort.

But she persevered, for life had given her no other choice. Everyone she used to consider a friend had abandoned her. The sole kindness she'd known in the last six months was the whisper of a stranger when she'd been in the hospital.

Finally, she arrived at the top floor. A throng of people waited outside the faro room. Falling in line, Abigail peeked inside. Candles shimmered throughout, casting a golden glow. At least it was warmer than outside.

She'd already pawned the last of her books to pay for coal so that her little sister, Bess, wouldn't freeze in their flat. Her heart panged at the memory. Those books had been more precious to her than any other possession, but Bess had to be her first priority.

Come tomorrow when the coal ran out again, there'd be nothing left to sell.

Nothing except for herself.

She couldn't think of that now. If she did, her knees would sway and her steps would falter. That would make her an easy mark. Already, she felt as though her movements were evaluated for signs of weakness. A chill skittered down her back. She shoved her battered hand into the pocket of her cloak and continued, trying to ignore the disconcerting sensation of being watched.

She was strong. She could survive anything.

The group behind her advanced, shoving her forward. She stumbled, but managed to right herself in time before colliding with the man in front of her. The herd dispersed at the door, ambling to the various gaming tables. Abigail made her way toward the far corner of the room, pausing for a moment to lean against a post and catch her breath.

She scanned the crowd for her father, expecting to find him flanked on either side by intent players. Tonight all the chairs were empty, except for three: the banker and two punters. A crowd of people watched the game proceed. The cards had split; the dealer took half of the bets on that rank. The onlookers let out a whoop of approval.

The mechanics of the game held little interest to her, for it'd always end the same: even if her father won, they'd still owe. Their debts were so high; they'd never dig out of this hole. She recognized her father: grizzly gray hair, the stoop of his shoulders, his threadbare green coat Bess had patched the week prior.

Across from him and facing her was a man Abigail did not recognize. As he purchased another check from the dealer, she swallowed back the dread that threatened to consume her. An unknown competitor meant her father might not receive leniency. Cruikshank had already told Papa that if he didn't start paying his vowels, he'd need to find a new place to gamble or he'd have to face Cyrus. Known as an unhinged pugilist with a taste for blood, Cyrus Mason could make the injuries she'd incurred from the loom seem like paper-cuts.

And so the cycle would begin again: another gaming hell and another night like this one. Before she'd been injured, she'd been able to make enough at the factory that the bills were paid. But now…it didn't matter to Papa that she'd cut her meals in half for the past few months to ensure Bess had enough to eat. Or that they were three months behind on rent, and if they didn't pay up soon, they'd all be out on the bloody street.

Nothing mattered to her father except the game.

Abigail slowly steered her way through the crowd, minding her steps until she'd made it to the back table.

"'Ey now," one man complained as she accidentally bumped him. He turned, catching her eye. Even in the cloak, he recognized her. So much for anonymity.

He motioned for a few of his friends to step to the

side to make room for her. "Move, mates."

Abigail nodded her gratitude, sliding into the vacated space. Her father hadn't noticed her arrival, so focused was he on the game layout.

"Come, Papa," she quietly bid. "Settle up your accounts and hope to God this man lets you by with incremental payments."

She hated having to say those words. She hated the humiliation of having to stand there, while all the men leered at her as if she was the choicest bit of flesh they'd get all night. But if she was going to be a harlot, she might as well start expecting this treatment.

The unknown punter across from her father coughed. A cough meant to distract, to clear the air. She looked up to see who would be so polite in this den of iniquity. She focused in on his features and her stomach did a flip. A purely physical reaction, for what woman wouldn't have felt a surge of fancy for the way his linen shirt stretched over his broad shoulders. His oval face was classically handsome, chiseled with an impossibly straight nose.

The man's blue eyes narrowed. "He owes me two hundred pounds. You can't expect me to excuse so large a debt."

Two hundred pounds.

His voice rang in her ears, like the steady drum that signals a firing squad. Two hundred pounds. Each breath was harder. Her throat closed. Two hundred pounds.

The mob erupted with cheers at the announcement, eager for a potential conflict. Their hoots barely registered when her heart pounded so hard she feared it might burst free of her chest. The world spun around her, and she prayed the floor might swallow her up.

Yet nothing changed.

Around her, the horde grew impatient for a response. Whatever leniency they'd shown in allowing her into their midst had disappeared. Now she was a part of the spectacle. Her pain on display for their enjoyment.

"'E don't got two hundred," one man jeered. "'E won't even pay me the two crowns 'e owes me."

"And 'e owes me twenty pounds!" another fellow added.

Oh, God. Her father had killed them all with the fifty-one cards of a faro game.

They were doomed. With vowels that large, surely her father would be sent to debtor's prison. Hell, maybe they'd all be sent to Marshalsea. The thought of her little sister living in such squalor made Abigail's heart tighten. How would Bess survive?

"I can't pay you," her father mumbled, as if he was just now realizing how much he'd lost. "Ain't got that."

"Then something will have to do be done," his opponent announced.

Thoughts sped through her mind. Bess couldn't go to Marshalsea. It'd ruin her in a way Abigail couldn't countenance. Sorrow had seeped deep into Abigail's life, ripping apart all her hopes and dreams, but Bess deserved better.

What could Abigail offer this man? Their coffers were as empty as their cabinets. The little blunt Bess brought in at the new textile factory already wasn't enough for the rent.

Abigail glanced down, taking in the plump curves of her breasts, her wide hips reputed to be perfect for grasping onto as a man tupped her hard. She was all the family had.

And if it were the last damn thing she did, she'd save Bess. This man knew Mason—perhaps a deal could be brokered to keep her father away from the hells too.

Abigail pushed back the hood to her cloak, revealing her blonde curls. Before her disfigurement, the factory boys had made it quite clear she stirred their attentions. But what was the price of her soul? Was she worth such an exorbitant sum?

"We can't pay you," she said, repeating her father's words. "But if you excuse my father's debts, I'll—"

The words wouldn't form. She gulped for air. A vision of Bess huddled in the corner of a filthy cell danced before her eyes. So this was how her degradation would begin, not in a brothel but in a hell. How could she actually go through with this? She'd be signing her soul away to the devil.

She couldn't think of another choice.

She needed to entice him. He wouldn't accept a single night for two hundred pounds—even as a virgin, she was not worth it. A man as good-looking as he was wouldn't pay that much for one lay with a working class girl.

One month with her. She dismissed that idea immediately. A month away from Bess was too much. Two weeks instead. She'd start there.

"I'll spend two weeks with you. My virtue in exchange for two hundred pounds."

READ MORE FROM ERICA MONROE

A DANGEROUS INVITATION

The Rookery Rogues – Book 1

She's given up on love, and wants only independence...

Torn from her life of privilege by her father's death, Kate Morgan survives in London's dark and depraved rookeries as a fence for stolen goods. The last man she ever expects, or wants, to be reunited with is her first love, who promised to cherish, honor and protect her, and instead fled amidst accusations of murder.

He's the reformed rake determined to win her back...

One drunken night cost Daniel O'Reilly the woman he loved and the life he'd worked so hard to create. If he ever wants to reclaim that life—and Kate—he'll not only have to prove he's innocent of murder, but convince the pistol-wielding spitfire that he's no longer the scoundrel he once was.

Together, they'll have to face a killer. Time is running out...

SECRETS IN SCARLET

The Rookery Rogues – Book 2

His business is discovering secrets…

When a girl is murdered at a factory in London, Sergeant Thaddeus Knight of the Metropolitan Police comes in to investigate. But it's not just the factory owners that Thaddeus wants information on–the devilishly intriguing Poppy O'Reilly is a puzzle he'd like nothing more than to solve.

Her life depends on keeping her past hidden….

All it took was one mistake for Poppy to lose her good reputation. Shunned by polite society, she's retreated to the one place no one from her old life would look for her: the rookeries. Protecting her young daughter is the most important thing to Poppy, and Thaddeus threatens the false identity she's carefully constructed. The last thing she should do is allow Thaddeus close to her family, yet she can't stay away from him.

With danger around the corner, will the secrets of a scarlet woman lead to their undoing?

ABOUT THE AUTHOR

Erica Monroe is a *USA Today* Bestselling Author of emotional, suspenseful historical romance. Her debut novel, *A Dangerous Invitation*, has been nominated in the published historical category for the prestigious 2014 Daphne du Maurier Award for Excellence in Romantic Suspense. When not writing, she is a chronic TV watcher, sci-fi junkie, comic book reader, pit bull lover, and slow runner. She lives in the suburbs of North Carolina with her husband, two dogs, and a cat.

Erica loves to hear from readers, so please feel free to contact her at the following places:
Daring Dames Reader Group:
https://www.facebook.com/groups/340385932818144/
E-mail: ericamonroewrites@gmail.com
Web: http://ericamonroe.com
Twitter: http://twitter.com/ericajmonroe
Friend her on Facebook:
http://facebook.com/ericamonroeauthor
Like her Facebook page:
http://facebook.com/ericamonroewrites
Pinterest: http://pinterest.com/regencyerica
Tumblr: http://ericamonroewrites.tumblr.com